UNITED STAR SYSTEMS MARINES

PROJECT CONTRIVANCE

HUNTER S. OPILLA

iUniverse, Inc.
Bloomington

United Star Systems Marines
Project Contrivance

iUniverse books may be ordered through booksellers or by contacting:

iUniverse
1663 Liberty Drive
Bloomington, IN 47403
www.iuniverse.com
1-800-Authors (1-800-288-4677)

ISBN: 978-1-4502-8630-5 (sc)
ISBN: 978-1-4502-8631-2 (ebk)

Printed in the United States of America

iUniverse rev. date: 03/04/2011

"I couldn't help but say to Mr. Gorbachev, just think how easy his task and mine might be in these meetings that we held if suddenly there was a threat to this world from another planet. We'd find out once and for all that we really are all human beings here on this Earth together."

-Ronald Reagan, 1985

PROLOGUE

In the year 2082, scientists at the European Center for Nuclear Research, unlocked the mystery of quantum particle physics. From the technology gathered using the Large Hadron Collider, European and American scientists propelled a solid object through a "wormhole" effectively warping space/time and instantly transporting the object to another location. This massive breakthrough in technology led to the development of spaceships that were able to travel to stars and planets close to Earth. Dr. Bjorn Faust, a German astrophysicist, developed the very first starship drive capable of faster-than- light speed- wormhole travel. Coined the "Faust Drive," this innovation would bombard a given mass of anti-matter with hydrogen protons at the speed of light, creating massive amounts of energy from the resulting reaction. The Faust drive would quickly change the course of history for the entire human race. Humans could now travel to the stars within the Milky Way galaxy unhampered by the vast distances that previously made it impossible.

Humanity quickly explored nearby stars using Faust drive ships, finding multiple worlds suitable for colonization within one-hundred light years from Earth. Within fifty years humans had established four large colonies on Earth-like, nitrogen-oxygen atmosphere planets and over a dozen colonies on less habitable planets and moons. An immense interstellar trading network was established between the colonies and soon piracy and looting became commonplace against trade shipments. The leading nations of Earth, the North American Union, European Union, and Asian Union, called for an interstellar system of government in order to regulate commerce between the colonies and protect merchant ships from the rampant piracy and the weaponization of space by rogue states.

In 2124, the leaders of Earth, Apollo, New Sydney, Talos, and Ares, (the four largest colonies) signed the United Star Systems Security and Partnership Act. This treaty between the colonies provided for an overarching system of limited government to provide security and cooperation between all colonies and Earth. It created a council of parliament with representatives from all planets. It also provided for an interstellar military force that was open to service from any citizen from any colony and whose mission was to keep the peace and secure trade routes. This all-volunteer military force would be called the United Star Systems Navy and Marines.

At first, the United Star Systems government was only a loose confederation of colonies and could not dictate policy of the individual nations of the different planets. Colonies were required however to pay a percentage tax based on the Gross Domestic Product of their respective planets in order to finance the USS Navy and Marine forces. Given the fact that a multitude of carbon-based life existed on the recently discovered garden-world colonies, the eventual contact with an intelligent extraterrestrial life form, capable of reasoning, was thought to be inevitable. Therefore, the USS parliament voted to slowly build up its defense forces in the event that a hostile, intelligent alien race was discovered in order that Earth and her colonies could be defended.

As the United Star Systems government slowly gained military and political power it began to overstep its bounds in regard to regulation and enforcement. It quickly grew in size and scope and established new departments of intelligence, commerce, transportation, and energy. New taxes and regulations put forth quickly caused a breaking point by 2165 when the major colony of Ares declared itself independent of the USS authority along with a half dozen smaller colonies in the outer rim of human explored space. The Prime Minister of the entire Ares colony declared that if any USS Naval ship interfered with their interstellar commerce operations they would be considered hostile and fired upon in self defense.

The government of Ares already had a reputation for being fiercely independent and harbored an extreme anti-Earth/isolationist political ideology. The people of Ares felt they were being over-taxed and regulated by the USS government due to their large production capacity of the strategic and extremely expensive antimatter particles, which were used as a fuel source for Faust starship drives. Antimatter was critical to the development of space-faring vessels and it was in very limited supply on Earth and the other major colonies. For the past twenty-five years, Ares had produced eighty-five percent of the refined antimatter for all of human space. With a booming economy, Ares was able to build up a substantial defense force for its colony in anticipation of USS aggression.

In the year 2166, the "Goshen Incident" sparked the first interstellar war between colonies. A USS patrol cruiser attempted to board and search a freighter shipping antimatter particles to the independent, small outer colony of Goshen. The freighter and its frigate escort opened fire with missiles on the USS cruiser as it closed in to board. The cruiser returned fire and destroyed both of the Ares vessels. The Prime Minister of Ares promptly declared war on the United Star Systems and boycotted trade to all of its allies. Several powerful mercenary groups seeking independence in the outer colonies also allied with the larger Ares colony, recognizing their need for antimatter resources and Faust drive starships.

The United Star Systems military was twice the size of the Ares Alliance forces and better trained but they would run short on resources for their Faust drive warships if the clash could not be resolved quickly. The conflict, called the Independence War by the Ares Alliance, or Conflict for Unification by the United Star Systems, has lasted on and off for two years now with no decisive winner or treaty passed. The war had become a stalemate with no large scale battles ever really taking place. The Ares Alliance currently remains on a defensive posture with heavy garrisons around their largest colonies while the USS military is continuously bogged down with politics and bureaucracy. With a dwindling supply of antimatter, the USS government is seeking a more diplomatic solution to the conflict. The mercenary groups from the outer edge colonies of the Ares Alliance began to exploit the restrictive rules of engagement practiced by the USS military and used the war as an excuse to raid fledgling USS- backed colonies for resources and slaves. The USS military did not have enough ships or resources to garrison its farthest-off colonies and these rogue mercenary states exploited the weakness at every step without any condemnation from the Ares Alliance government. The story now brings us to the current Earth-date of 2169 AD.

2169, Planet Hastati, farming colony, Tertias System, Septus Magnus Cluster

Kaleb Taylor leaned against the railing of his porch as he calmly watched the sun set into the Hastati horizon. Another day's work in the field done and another to come too soon tomorrow he thought to himself. At sixteen years of age he was full of energy and yearned for adventure that seemed so distant from his current occupation as a farm hand and brown rice harvester. Kaleb thought it more of a form of slavery than a job and he made sure to let his father, Waylon Taylor, know about it whenever he had the chance. He was nothing like his dad, and had no desire to be a farmer of any kind. His family had participated in the colonization of Hastati as part of the first flight of humans from Earth attempting to find their wealth in the rich topsoils of the planet. With a nitrogen-oxygen atmosphere and a temperate climate, Hastati was very similar to Earth in many ways. The real allure of the planet to the United Star Systems government was its thick layer of fertile topsoil, untapped and untainted by intelligent life. There was an abundance of carbon-based life forms such as mammals, reptiles, birds, and fish similar to Earth, which made it seem too good to be true for many citizens. It was like never leaving Earth in the first place for the people that chose to volunteer for its colonization. Hastati was the farthest garden-world colony from the USS controlled territory, being 127 light-years from Earth. The only problem was that it lay dangerously close to the rogue Ares Alliance colony of Shinwar, at just 6.2 light years away.

Kaleb was born one year after his family came to Hastati. His mother, father, and two older sisters came to the planet seventeen years ago when they participated in a mass colonization effort with over 2,000 other citizens from Earth. One thing that always intrigued him was the pure vastness of space, an endless frontier of adventure and discovery. He looked into the evening sky as stars began to show their positions. *Amazing*, he thought as he kicked the dark moist soil beneath his feet; that cursed soil which bound him to this boring, dead end planet.

"Hey, quit daydreaming and get off your ass and get that shipment of rice to the barn before dinner!" Kaleb's father barked. All day it was always about work, selling crops, planting crops, crop yield, harvest schedules, bushels of rice and the like. Kaleb hated it and he wanted out as soon as he was old enough.

He was very athletic for his age, being a starting linebacker on the local intermediate school arena football team. He had short, faded, dark brown hair and bright green eyes. He had the typical set of friends at school that he would hang out with. He cared little for the gossip and drama that went along with being in the popular group in school however. Kaleb preferred to go out on hunting or fishing trips into the local wilderness rather than getting drunk or high with his peers at some house party. It was the only real adventure he could find on the monotonous colony. It was like society had already laid out Kaleb's life- plan for him. He was supposed to graduate school, work on the family farm, marry a local colony girl and have a bunch of kids, and live right there in the settlement farming the rest of his life. That was the standard Hastati life progression for most; definitely not what Kaleb had envisioned for himself. *First chance I get, I'm getting off this god-forsaken rock,* he thought.

"Does it really matter if one more shipment gets to the barn, it'll be there tomorrow and there will be thousands of others after that one." Kaleb complained to his father. His dad was an honest and fair, but relentless when it came to the family farm and business. He was a large man, standing around 6'3" with long, dark brown hair and a full beard almost down to his chest. Always wearing a set of denim coveralls, he resembled more of a farmer from the 1800's back on Earth, rather than a high-tech, 22nd century interstellar colonist. He had risked everything volunteering for the colonization of Hastati. A steady job on Earth, kids in school, and a decent home. Earth had become congested and overcrowded however, not a safe or healthy place for children to grow up. Kaleb's father longed for open land, something he could call his own, instead of a cookie-cutter townhome development in the I-95 Metroplex. This was his dream, owning land in wide open, undeveloped space. So far it had been a very successful gamble, his farm being one of the top rice producing estates in the first Hastati colony. He only wished his son would take a liking to the family business as much as he did. He knew however that Kaleb had other plans and that he wouldn't be able to hold him back much longer.

"So I was thinking maybe the United Star Systems Space Merchant's Academy, if I could get in there I would be able to see a lot more of space. I would be able to stay in the farming business, just work on a ship that transports the crops to all the rest of the colonies, even Earth." Kaleb explained enthusiastically to his father, stalling his current chore.

"I would get a free education and there's a satellite school right here in the colony so I wouldn't be far from home. Then I would always be coming back and forth to visit as I pick up new loads to transport. Work my way up the ladder to Captain one day maybe." Kaleb was always coming up with new excuses as to how he could see the rest of space without leaving his family for months or years at a time.

Waylon hefted a burlap bag of rice onto a nearby shelf and then spoke, "So now you want to be a space trucker?" his father protested. "Son, you've got everything you need right here on the colony, that's why we came out here. Space travel is still dangerous and it's not something you need to get involved in. This whole planet is virtually undiscovered. Just stay here and find some land and set up your own business. It's too easy. You've got everything right at your doorstep."

Waylon already rejected his son's ideas to join the United Star Systems military years ago as his own father was killed in action while serving in the army during a meaningless proxy war with political motives back on Earth. Waylon was only ten years old when he lost his father and he vowed to not let his family get involved in corrupt governments and their use of soldiers to enforce their will. It was a perilous time on Earth back then with non-stop conflicts between nations which eventually brought about the unification of the larger unions on Earth and now a unified interstellar government, with the exception of the recent Ares Alliance secession of course.

"Well, I guess I'm destined to be just like everyone else in this place, a boring old farmer who all he has to talk about is the rise in the price of fertilizer," Kaleb spoke as he slowly drove off on a four-wheeler down a gravel road to the family's barn.

"You'll be thanking me in twenty years! You just don't know it yet! Dinner's in ten minutes!" Waylon yelled at his son as he drove off to the barn. He noticed a strange light beginning to appear in the evening sky but he thought nothing of it. Waylon walked into his pre-fabricated environment-sealed housing unit and kissed his wife on the cheek as she was setting the dinner table.

*   *   *   *

Several flashes followed by thunderous explosions broke the still quiet in the atmosphere above. "What the hell was that?!" inquired Waylon as he sat down in the dining room.

"Where's Kaleb?" his wife asked frantically.

"Still up at the barn I hope" answered Waylon. The bellow of Faust drive starships entering the atmosphere drowned out any further conversation. More explosions followed. The colonies' emergency alarm system began to sound all across the development of over 12,000 people. "Honey you and the girls get in the basement now, I've got to get to the barn and get Kaleb… and don't open the door to anyone unless you hear my voice understand?!!"

Waylon ran to his bedroom and grabbed his rifle out of the closet. His frantic hands fumbled the ammunition as he struggled to load the weapon. It was an old bolt-action hunting rifle from early 21st century design, good for hunting the local wildlife on Hastati, but ineffective against any type of armored target. Waylon desperately ran out of the house down to his ATV four-wheeler. The night sky was lit up with explosions from the center of the colony, two large starships of design he had never seen before hovered a few thousand feet above in the atmosphere. *What the hell is happening?* Waylon thought as he desperately struggled to start the small off-road vehicle.

Kaleb hid in the loft of the barn as he heard the explosions and witnessed a 6x6 armored rover approaching his location from the road 300 meters north of the barn. His heart pounding, he crawled over to the small open window on the north side of the loft and closely watched the vehicle. The vehicle's engine came to an idle as it stopped twenty meters from the entrance to the barn. Kaleb, confused and frightened, had no idea what was about to take place. A ramp lowered on the backside of the vehicle and three figures about six feet in height slowly trudged down it. The men were clad in a dark red and black type of high-tech body armor and carried large black assault rifles. *This can't be good,* Kaleb thought to himself as he spotted the menacing looking weapons in the clutches of the three dismounts. He heard several low-pitched grunts from the men and it appeared they had received orders to enter the barn. With his pulse skyrocketing, Kaleb scrambled to hide under some loose bales of hay before they heard him.

Suddenly a loud crack followed by an echo filled the night air. Kaleb froze in place; the sound of lead striking flesh followed. One of the men went limp and crumpled to the ground like a rag doll. A well-placed rifle round had penetrated the glass visor on his helmet, striking the man's forehead just above his right eye. The other men cried out in anger as they took cover behind their vehicle. *Someone shot him*! Kaleb thought, *someone's on the ridge over there with a gun*! Kaleb frantically leapt to the window to see what was about to transpire. The two other men remained behind the cover of the vehicle as it moved towards where the sniper had shot from on the small ridge on the western side of the barn. One man, who appeared to be the leader, shouted out curses and orders mixed together; frustration and anger dictated his vocabulary. Kaleb heard another shot from the ridge, then another, the .30-06 rifle rounds ricocheted off of the vehicle's steel armor. The nefarious men retaliated with automatic rifle fire. Between their salvos Kaleb heard an unmistakable voice yelling from the ridge. *It was his father, his father was the shooter!*

"Son, get out of there!! Run to the house!! Get your mom and sisters out of here now!!" More gun fire followed. Waylon sprinted back and forth between cover as the attackers closed in on his location. Kaleb jumped down from the loft and ran outside, he saw his father behind a boulder on the ridge attempting to reload his ancient hunting rifle. The men drew closer, now within fifty meters of Waylon. At this point they had zeroed in on his location behind the boulder. Kaleb wanted to yell back at his father but he knew it was pointless, it would give away his position and they would both be dead. Waylon waved hastily at Kaleb, motioning for him to get out from behind the barn and run to the house. Kaleb understood and he knew he had to get to his mother and sisters. One of the men provided cover fire upon the boulder Waylon was hiding behind as the remaining one moved to flank. Kaleb's father moved from behind his cover to get one last shot off at the leader. He raised his weapon and attempted to get a sight picture in his scope on the head of his assailant, knowing his weapon had no chance of penetrating any other area of the attacker's body armor.

"Come on you son of a bitch!" Waylon said as he gritted his teeth, trying to get a clear shot at the man running toward him. All of a sudden, he felt as though he had been hit by a dump truck on his left torso as three assault rifle rounds punctured his body. Waylon was immediately knocked to the ground, dropping his rifle in the process. His entire rib cage was shattered and he soon began to feel the taste of blood pouring into his mouth. His vision began to blur and fade into black as he exhaled his last breath of life. The leader walked up to Waylon's lifeless body and gave a sinister laugh as he took pleasure in shooting Waylon two more times in the head with his sidearm. Kaleb looked back as he sprinted into the rice fields that led up to the house. Witnessing the final blows to his father's motionless body, he forced his legs to move faster, the rice plant's rough leaves lacerated his skin as he ran; tears of hate and anger trickled down his left cheek.

*   *   *   *

USSN Raleigh- United Star Systems Navy Cruiser on presence patrol just outside the Helios system, Septus Magnus Cluster

"Sir I'm picking up a distress signal coming from the Hastati farming colony." The communications chief on duty transmitted over the ship's intercom.

"Very well, what are the details?" Captain Beck, the commander of the Raleigh inquired from his cabin.

"I only received about half of it, the rest got cut-off. It says they've been attacked by slavers, three or more frigate-sized ships of unknown origin. The local militia was unable to repel the attack. They've been taking all able-bodied civilians and loading them onto transports. That's all the info I've got at this time sir."

"Set course for Faust drive travel to the Tertias System immediately, engage battle readiness level three. Inform the rest of the task force of the situation. The training run is over, this is a real emergency. I'll be in the conn in five mikes," (minutes in military speak) Beck answered as he threw a wad of snuff tobacco in his bottom lip and walked out of his quarters.

Beck, a large man standing about six foot four with a blonde high and tight haircut and aging complexion, was a seasoned veteran of eighteen years in the USS Navy. He'd already seen several space Naval engagements during the Conflict for Unification. He was now the respected and revered commander of Task Force Saber which consisted of four of the new "Miami" class cruisers. They were prototypes of a faster, stealthier warship that packed more firepower than the standard service "Melbourne" class cruisers.

"So much for the shakedown run" mumbled Beck to himself as he walked through the narrow corridors of the ship to the command center or "conn." The task force had been on its first training run to test the full capabilities of their newly advanced fire control systems.

"Alright what's our ETA to Hastati XO?" Beck asked in his signature deep, raspy voice.

"We've got Faust drive engaged and should be on orbit around the dark side of the planet in approximately sixteen mikes sir," Lieutenant Commander Jorgennson, second in command of the Raleigh answered.

"I just hope that gets us there in time to catch those sons of bitches before they detect us as inbound," Beck declared. "Ready EMAs one and two, set targeting solutions for medium range engagement. Probably mercenaries from Shinwar, they could already have taken hostages on board their ships. We can't take the chance of blowing them to pieces. Radio to the Task Force, I want disabling shots put on their frigates, not kill shots."

"Roger sir" the communications chief replied.

"Officer of the Deck, get Lieutenant Horton on the internal. Tell him he's got fifteen minutes to have his Marines ready for a boarding operation to rescue any civilians," Beck ordered.

"Paging him now sir," the Lieutenant responded.

Planet Hastati, Tertias System, Septus Magnus Cluster

Kaleb banged on the basement door yelling, "Mom open the door it's me, we gotta get out of here now!" The door swung open instantaneously.

"What's going on? Where's dad?" his mother asked.

"They killed him mom! Its slavers or something, their coming right now we don't have any time, we have to get to the hills and hide!"

"They killed dad?" His oldest sister asked as tears formed in her eyes.

"Yes, now come on lets go there's no time! They saw me run from the barn they know we're here!" Kaleb screamed as he grabbed his sisters' arms and dragged them out of the basement. It was too late however; as the four of them ran out the back door another one of the slaver's rover vehicles was parked ten meters from the house. Three slavers appeared from behind the vehicle with weapons at the low-ready. A relatively short, about 5'6" man with short blonde hair spoke in what sounded like an Earth-born Australian accent.

"Now hold on a just a second there. Don't want to leave the party so soon do ya? We're just gettin started here. Yancey, put some cuffs on these little rebels." The man that spoke appeared to be the one in charge, as the other slaver, Yancey, moved in to place flexie cuffs on Kaleb and his family.

"This must be the family of that asshole with the hunting rifle Darius," Yancey said to the leader.

The slaver leader walked up to Kaleb's mom, "So, your man got off a lucky shot on one ah me boys eh? Well too bad he ain't here to save your sorry ass now!" he said as he slapped her across the face.

Kaleb's mom hit the ground, weeping; she struggled to speak, "Why are you doing this? What have we done to you people?"

Darius smiled, "It's not what you did *to* us, it's what you're going to do *for* us. See, we have a business going on here, and as you well know a business can't operate without a product to sell. So you see, you're the product, and we're due for a profit." Kaleb's mother jumped up suddenly and with a closed fist, hit the slaver in the face, breaking his nose in the process. Darius reeled back from the impact, stumbling over his own feet.

"You bitch!" Darius cursed as he held his face in pain. He reared back, throwing a punch that struck the woman's jaw, knocking her once more to the ground. Darius then reached for his pistol that rested in a holster on his right hip.

Kaleb, furious at this point, proceeded to run head on into his mother's attacker. Hands bound behind his back by the cuffs, he lowered his shoulder and plowed into the man's side, knocking him to the ground, causing Darius to drop his pistol in the process. Kaleb lost his balance from his own momentum and also fell face first into the topsoil.

"Dammit someone put some chains on these damn kids!" the leader exclaimed as he got up and dusted himself off. The assistant he called "Yancey" was a large man, standing at least 6'6" with a cleanly shaven head with tattoos covering half his face and neck. He placed heavy metal chains with collars around Kaleb and his sisters, binding the three together. The leader, Darius, gave a menacing stare at Kaleb as he stood in front of him, his face now three inches from Kaleb's, and his nose dripping blood.

"You've got a lot of energy young one, that's good, you're damn sure gonna need it when you get sold to those diamond miners on Shinwar. What'd you think Yancey, we could prolly get three thousands credits for this strapping young lad. Hell, if he puts on a show like this at the slave market we may get five thousand."

Yancey smiled and nodded in agreement, folding his arms across his chest as he stared at his captives. Darius wiped the blood from his nose and then re-chambered a round into the breach of his pistol.

"Ok, enough bullshit, lets get the kids to the transport and burn the pre-fab to the ground." Yancey nodded and grabbed the chains that bound the three teenagers together, leading them into the rover parked nearby. Darius looked back down at Kaleb's mother who was still lying on the ground a few feet in front of him. "As for you my lady…well, with that nasty bruise you've got on your face now, I just don't think you're worth my investment." He raised his pistol and took aim at her as she cowered below him. Darius squeezed the trigger, sending a round into her chest, killing her in a few short seconds.

"You motherfucker, I'm gonna kill you!" Kaleb did his best to hold back his tears as he witnessed the death of his mother, but Darius laughed at his empty threats.

"You little piece of shit. Do you have any idea who I am? You're just another number to me, credits in my account. So shut you your smart ass mouth before I staple your tongue to your chin, understand?"

"I understand that you're gonna die next time I get my han-", Kaleb fell to the ground before he could finish his sentence, unconscious from a crack on the head from the butt of Yancey's pistol who was standing behind him. The slavers picked him up and dragged him and his sisters into the rover. Kaleb's pre-fabricated housing unit erupted into flames as the slaver vehicle drove off towards the transport ships.

According to the Ares Alliance government, slavery was not an outlawed practice and could be used by its mercenary allies in the outer colonies so long as cruel punishment was not used. The United Star Systems government however, considered any colony that practiced slavery to be a rogue state and would not be recognized as an official member of the interstellar community. Raids by slavers from the rogue colony of Shinwar had become common during the Conflict for Unification as the USS Navy had failed to properly garrison its outer edge colonies.

*   *   *   *

"Alright lets get a move on here, move with a goddamn sense of purpose for once in your life!" Darius complained. "Get those damned slaves onto the transport! I swear to god you people move slower than my 400-pound mother in a marathon race!" The slavers ruthlessly beat and cursed at the former colonists of Hastati as they led them into three different transport vessels that would take them up to the slaver's Faust drive ships hovering just above planet's atmosphere. Smoke, dust, and flames rose from the center of the colony, the by-product of Darius's slaving operation. *This is a routine operation for a seasoned mercenary such as myself* he thought. *I've been raiding colonies and profiting at the expense of others for eight years now without even coming close to being caught. It may be a dirty trade, but it's necessary. Someone has to do it. Slaves are a major source of profit and labor within the Ares Alliance,* he continued to justify to himself….. Yancey hastily approached Darius with an apprehensive look about him.

"Darius, we've got trouble. I just got off the net with our ships up top, they're picking up four USS cruisers inbound to our vector.

In fifteen minutes they'll be all over us." Darius paused for a few seconds with a puzzled look about him.

"Bloody hell! Close up the transports, now! Get them in the air and lets get the hell out of here!" he screamed. The slavers ran about in total chaos in the knowledge that it would be nearly impossible to get the transports loaded into the ships before being intercepted by USS Cruisers. Two of the transports immediately took off leaving several of their own crew behind, the small ship's rocket-boosted engines vaporized the captured slaves and slavers on the outside that were attempting to enter the ramp to the interior of the vessel. Darius ran into the cockpit of the final transport, the one holding Kaleb.

"Goddammit get this thing in the air now!!!" he yelled. The transport's engines grumbled as they struggled to warm up to operating temperature. The sudden G-force of the rapid take-off in Hastati's thick atmosphere woke Kaleb from his unconsciousness. He tumbled to the rear of the transport as the vessel undertook a ninety-degree climb out of the atmosphere. The captured colonists had not been secured inside the ship and fell on top of each other from the sheer force of the rapid takeoff. The unlucky colonists who boarded the transport last were stuck on the bottom of the pile of bodies, many of whom screamed as they were crushed to death from the weight of the others on top of them. Kaleb was one of the lucky few who was placed on the transport first and was near the top of the pile. After ten minutes of agony, they broke free of the planet's orbit into the zero gravity of space. Out of the fifty colonists on board the transport's cargo hold, over half had been either crushed to death or suffered blunt trauma from banging into the walls of the ship. Bodies began to float inside the cargo hold from the lack of gravity. The gruesome scene in front of Kaleb caused him to throw up what food was left inside his stomach. The liquid/solid excrement hovered in front of his face, simply adding to the horrible panorama going on around him. A pressure release sounded as the artificial gravity system within the cargo hold engaged. Everything dropped suddenly to the deck, including Kaleb's vomit, right into his lap.

*   *   *   *

"Sir we're too late, they have engaged their Faust drives, unknown trajectory; I've lost their signature on scope." The Raleigh's sensors officer explained to Captain Beck.

When a starship makes the transition from normal, real-time power to its antimatter-powered Faust drive, it essentially makes a jump through space and time. When this occurs, the vessel is transported at speeds exceeding hundreds of times the speed of light to a pre-determined location in the galaxy. The speed of the ship depends on the size and efficiency of the Faust drive. There is not yet a known method for one starship to track another while it is traveling through space at Faust drive speeds. Therefore, when the slavers engaged their Faust drive, it was an effective tactic and allowed them to safely escape their pursuers.

"Wait, I'm picking up a small heat signature on the light side of the planet just above the initial atmospheric level…. switching to thermal image enhancement. I'll put it up on the view screen sir," the sensors officer explained.

Captain Beck adjusted his position to view the large flat screen image in the center of the ship's conn. "They left one of their transports behind. Maneuvering, bring us right on top of those sons of bitches" Beck said with a sense of renewed hope. The Raleigh's drive engines roared as the ship accelerated to full speed, circumnavigating to the light side of Hastati. The slaver's transport came into the ship's line of sight within a few minutes. "Inform me when we are within missile range chief, set your targeting solution for a precision disabling strike on the transport's engine compartment," Beck said to his weapons chief, maintaining total composure. Captain Beck was known across the USS Navy for his raspy, monotone voice and extremely calm and controlled demeanor during even the most intense starship battles.

"Aye sir, ETA on targeting solution two minutes, striker missile armed and ready sir," the weapons chief quickly responded.

Captain Beck turned to the young Marine officer standing a few feet behind him. "Lieutenant Horton, get your platoon of Marines into the Raptor, we'll send a route to your nav computer to land you right on top of the upper escape hatch of that transport. There's got to be some colonists left in there Lieutenant and I want them safely returned to my ship." Beck commanded.

"Roger sir, we'll get it done," the Marine answered.

"LT, I've got the layout of the ship on screen now. It's a medium weight class freighter, sending it to your data pad now," the sensors officer said with a sense of accomplishment.

"Got it on file, we'll be ready to roll in five mikes Captain," Horton nodded to Beck.

"Make sure you give those slaving bastards a warm welcome Lieutenant, courtesy of Task Force Saber," Beck slapped the young officer on the back with his large, firm hand.

3

Hastati orbit, 800 miles above the surface of the planet

"Dammit doesn't this thing go any faster! I can't believe those worthless pirates! They dare leave me behind to be slaughtered by the USS Navy!? You tell your friend, that sorry excuse for a frigate Captain, that I'm gonna dig his eyeballs out of his bloody skull with my pocket knife next time I see him!" Darius yelled at the mercenary transport pilot.

About three hundred miles to the transport's six o'clock, the Raleigh opened one of its sixteen striker missile bay doors, there was a bright blue flash as the missile launched from the hull of the ship. Traveling at over 30,000 miles per hour through space, its control fins adjusted its course as it acquired its slow, lumbering target.

Naval engagements in space are conducted over vast distances due to the lack of an atmosphere and gravity that would normally hinder a ship's speed and maneuverability. In inter-system engagements, cruisers and frigates are able to travel through space at speeds exceeding well over 20,000 miles per hour, and weapons range becomes virtually unlimited. It is not irregular for a cruiser to open fire on an enemy ship with its electromagnetic accelerator (EMA) at distances exceeding thousands of miles. Electromagnetic accelerators (a.k.a. EMAs or 'rail guns') changed the face of space combat. A space-based ship with an up to date targeting computer could fire on another vessel at extreme distances of thousands of miles with startling precision. An EMA would accelerate a solid mass projectile, (usually steel or tungsten) to speeds of up to 3,000 miles per second in space. This projectile would impact with enormous energy causing massive damage on the scale of an atomic weapon. Inter-system missiles were also developed for close range engagements with pirate vessels. Some of these missiles could be thermonuclear-tipped if needed.

The firing solutions for attacks at such an extreme range are too complex to be calculated by a human mind. Therefore, each USS warship is equipped with a highly advanced and precise targeting computer that borders on being an artificial intelligence. This supercomputer also manages all the ship's systems from the Faust drive to weapons and heat management. Self-guiding missiles are utilized in short range space engagements because of their maneuverability. Once an electromagnetic accelerator round is fired it does not have the ability to guide itself onto a target like a missile does, hence the need for a near perfect firing solution at long ranges when using an EMA weapon system.

$$*\qquad*\qquad*\qquad*$$

Kaleb did his best to compose himself inside the dark compartment where he and the colonists were being held. He heard people yelling in pain and a girl crying but could not tell from who or where exactly it was coming from. With bodies strewn about the deck and the absence of light in the holding cell, he began to crawl towards the sounds. Kaleb's mind was in shock at this point and was operating strictly on reflexes and natural instinct. He came across a middle-aged man who had apparently been shot in the arm by the slavers before he was boarded onto the transport. The man was crying and babbling on in gibberish about his wife and home. Kaleb looked at the bleeding wound and thought for a split second. He took off the jacket he had been wearing and tied it around the man's arm in a futile attempt to stop the bleeding. The man looked Kaleb in the eyes and gave in a small nod as if to say "thank you" and then continued sobbing as before. Kaleb still heard what sounded like a small girl crying coming from over in the corner of the holding area by a large bay door. He again crawled through the darkness towards the sound of the girl.

The freighter's pilot attempted a well-intentioned evasive maneuver but to no avail, the striker missile was designed to intercept much smaller, faster, and more maneuverable fighters launched from an enemy carrier. The modular freighter transport was an easy a target for the missile's advanced tracking system. The striker honed in on one of the transport's two thruster ports.

"Five seconds to impact sir, striker tracking hot and normal," the weapons chief reported to Captain Beck.

A loud crash sounded as the freighter shuddered from the detonation of the striker missile's high-explosive warhead. The ship began to list to the right as its engines started to lose power.

"Bloody hell, they're all over us!" Darius screamed frantically.

"We're … losing… power, engine failure," the mercenary pilot grunted, struggling to keep control of the vessel.

"Of course we are you idiot, they're trying to disable us and rescue those pathetic colonists. I suggest you find a way off this ship before we get boarded by Marines. No way in hell are they taking me alive," protested Darius. "Guess I'll see you in hell eh brother?!" Darius punched the distracted pilot square in the face with his pistol, knocking him unconscious. He unbuckled himself from the co-pilot seat and opened the cockpit hatch to the rest of the interior of the ship. The transport's collision alarm began to sound as red warning lights flashed throughout the storage compartment. He recklessly ran about the deck looking for an escape pod. "Ha-ha! Got it," Darius said excitedly to himself as he pulled a large red lever exposing the hatch entry to the ship's sole escape pod.

The USS Marine Assault Transport, aka "Raptor," is a small troop carrier used for boarding operations and planetary assaults. Each USS cruiser was usually standard equipped with one Raptor and one platoon of Marines on board. Larger ships like carriers and heavy assault battleships can carry up to sixteen Raptors and up to a battalion of Marines. The Raptor is about the size of three fighters and is able to hold up to forty-two Marines. It is specially designed with heat-resistant steel/titanium plating in order to protect the craft from burning up during high-speed atmospheric entry during a rapid planetary assault. Equipped with a pressurized extendable entry hatch, it can latch on to another ship and allow personnel to enter it through the hatch in an artificial gravity state. It also boasts an armament consisting of a 30mm chain gun below the nose of the craft, as well as two air-to-ground missile pods under each wing.

The Raptor steered toward its target and slowed so as to not overshoot the transport. At this point the freighter was essentially drifting through space with its engines inoperable. The Marines inside the transport performed final checks of their weapons and body armor systems.

The standard USS Marine was equipped with a 6.8mm assault rifle and .45 caliber pistol. With the replacement of gunpowder with tri-foam in 2112, projectile velocities increased significantly in small arms weaponry. The Marine standard issue MR-6 assault rifle could fire its 6.8mm center-fire, tungsten, armor-piercing round at a speed of 4,120 feet per second in normal Earth atmosphere and gravity, causing devastating impact force.

The Advanced Body Armor System (ABAS) that Marines wear is made of a light ceramic outer layer of armor able to stop several small arms projectiles up to 8mm rifle size before failing. The under layer is made of a thick, environmentally sealed Kevlar-canvas material to provide padding and protection from extreme conditions. An internal cooling system is standard as well as the ability to engage toxic and atmospheric sealing in order to allow the Marine to survive in the harshest environments. Black is the standard armor color for Marines stationed on USS warships; however special operations forces and Recon Marines usually wear a digital camouflage pattern, depending on the environment they are operating in. The helmet system provides the Marine with a heads up display, motion sensor, navigation interface, and also can be programmed to provide a sight picture for wherever the Marine points his rifle.

"Alright listen up!" Lieutenant Horton sounded inside the cabin of the Raptor. "1st squad will conduct the initial breach and entry of the upper escape hatch. According to the layout we should be dropping down into an open cargo hold. The civilians will likely be held in these two compartments within the hold. 1st squad will enter and clear the cargo hold and maintain security on the hatches to the engine room and the cockpit. 2nd squad will then enter and stack on those two hatches to prepare for entry. 3rd squad will enter last and establish a CCP (Casualty Collection Point) in the center of the cargo hold and help the captured colonists up into our Raptor for extraction. 2nd squad will then breach and clear the engine room and the cockpit. Do not fire unless fired upon, we have clear orders to take prisoners if they surrender. I don't want anyone taking any chances though. If one of those slavers so much as turns his head in your direction with a weapon in his hand, take his ass out. Once the transport is cleared of enemy personnel and we have loaded all civilians into the carrier, 3rd squad will remain behind in the cargo hold while intelligence personnel come in and hack into the ship's navigation logs. Everyone clear on the mission?" In unison the Marines on board yelled "Roger sir!"

*   *   *   *

Kaleb struggled to give what little first aid he knew to the small girl he found in the corner that had broken both of her legs during the takeoff of the transport. She was sobbing and wanted to see her "mommy."

"Don't worry" Kaleb assured her, "you'll see her soon. She was probably put on one of the other ships, but someone is coming to rescue us any second now. They'll get rid of all these bad people and bring your mom back."

Through all the crying and screaming of the captured colonists grieving over their current plight, Kaleb somehow knew they were going to be rescued. He could no longer hear the constant hum of the engines. That loud crash must have had something to do with it. Maybe the engines just broke down, or maybe it was space debris that hit the ship he thought. *No*, he assured himself, *it was USS Navy, and they surely wouldn't let these people get away with what they had just done. Not against one of its most successful colonies, there had to be a patrol out there somewhere protecting Hastati.* He watched as several mercenaries nervously marched about the cargo hold with weapons at the ready, something was up he thought. *Why else would they be so on guard?*

The ship shuddered as metal to metal contact sounded on the outside of the cargo hold's walls. Kaleb heard the mercenaries yelling frantically as some hid behind the cover of boxes or crates. A bright flash caught Kaleb's eye as brilliant orange sparks poured out from a hatch just above a ladder in the center of the cargo hold.

"Someone's boarding us! I knew it!" Kaleb exclaimed with little reaction from the rest of the captives. Kaleb got up and walked over several wounded colonists to get a view out of the window in the large bay doors that kept him locked into the compartment. A man with a bloodied face grabbed Kaleb's leg as he stepped over him.

"..Help….me, they will… kill… you… please…" Kaleb jerked his leg free of the disoriented man and continued up to the small window. There were no more sparks flying out of the hatch seal and the slavers all stood behind cover, weapons pointed up at the hatch, waiting for something to kill. *Oh no! They're gonna get slaughtered*, Kaleb thought as he saw the slavers armed to the teeth poised and ready to bring death to whatever came down the hatch.

"Charges set LT, on your order," one of the Marines said as he crawled up out of the boarding hatch back inside the Raptor. Each platoon of Marines was assigned a demolitions specialist for operations such as this. He had placed several imploding charges around the hatch that would cause it to implode inside the transport without damaging the hatch to the Raptor.

"1st squad in position ready for entry sir," the squad leader updated the Lieutenant.

"Alright…. Blast it!" Horton yelled. A deafening boom echoed throughout the transport as the top escape hatch crumbled and fell to the deck, leaving a clean opening for the Marines to fast-rope down into the cargo hold. Assault rifle fire filled the air with the rapid panging sound of tungsten rounds being shot out weapon barrels at blinding speed. The gun fire ricocheted off the walls around the upper hatch which was now just an opening in the ceiling of the transport. The slavers yelled out obscenities as they haphazardly fired their weapons at no apparent target. Kaleb observed two small, cylinder-shaped objects drop down from the opening and bounce a few times on the deck of the transport. His heart was pounding as he witnessed all of the action taking place. He wondered what the two objects were that fell, and if anyone was ever going come down through the opening. All of a sudden, an intense white flash blinded his eyesight, followed by an earsplitting explosion which caused a high-pitched ringing in his ears.

"Flash bangs out! go go go!" a Marine yelled from inside the

Raptor. The first squad of Marines fast-roped down into the cargo holds with deadly efficiency and speed. The flashbang charges disoriented the slavers who, at first, appeared to have the upper hand from their covered and concealed positions inside the cargo bay. The men that were within the blast radius held their heads and struggled to see or hear what was going on. One slaver screamed and blindly opened fire with his weapon, sweeping the cargo hold with bullets, several of them hitting one of his fellow mercenaries in the chest, knocking him to the ground. The Marine squad quickly and methodically swept through the cargo hold, checking behind cover and clearing the corners. Short, controlled bursts from their MR-6 assault rifles brought down the slavers, one by one. After a few seconds, Kaleb began to regain his eyesight and hearing. He saw two Marines through the window of the bay door with their weapons drawn down on a slaver.

"Put the fucking weapon down now!!" one of the Marines shouted. The slaver attempted to quickly raise his weapon and get off a shot at the Marines but it would be the last mistake he would make in his lifetime. A quick burst of fire from the Marine's assault rifle ripped through the slaver's body armor, throwing his lifeless body to the deck.

As Darius crawled into the escape pod a hired ship guard ran toward him screaming hysterically, "Marines.. they've.. entered... the ship! Let me in the pod! We're all screwed!" Small arms fire began to echo through to decks of the ship as the mercenary guard ran desperately attempting to dive into the pod.

"No you ugly son of a bitch! Get the hell out of my escape pod!" Darius screamed as he met the man's large forehead with the heel of his boot, kicking him out of the hatch. Darius flipped a bright red switch, pressurizing the escape pod and releasing it from the transport. A rocket booster initiated and the pod blasted towards Hastati's atmosphere. Darius breathed a sigh of relief as the planet grew bigger and bigger in his viewport. "Hah, bloody Marines still aren't fast enough to catch me eh?" he smirked to himself.

Blood was splattered all over the walls as Kaleb saw the remnants of what he once thought was a formidable group of mercenaries, poised for attack. All that remained of the slavers in the cargo hold were eight motionless bodies that littered the transport's deck. The second squad of Marines fast-roped down into the cargo hold along with Lieutenant Horton.

"Sir, cargo hold secured, ready for colonists' extraction," reported the 1st squad leader.

"2nd squad stack and clear engine compartment and cockpit," ordered the LT. The second squad leader motioned with hand and arm signals for his teams to move to their respective objectives. 3rd squad entered the cargo hold and began to hack into the locked bay doors that held the colonists. Kaleb watched the Marines intently as they went through their battle drills. He was amazed at how quick and efficient they were. They moved like a well-oiled machine, precise and accurate. He heard the steel locks on the bay door he was leaning against release the air pressure holding them in place. Kaleb stepped back as the large door rose up, revealing a squad of Marines in black armor and the rest of the cargo bay.

"Holy shit," one of the Marines slowly expressed his sense of astonishment at the sight of the bay that held the colonists. Half of the colonists lay dead, crushed from the rapid takeoff. Blood riddled the walls and floor, as sounds of moans and weeping from the injured caught the 3rd squad leader's attention.

"Sir…. you're gonna want to come take a look at this," the Non-Commissioned Officer said to his platoon leader over their internal communications net.

"What is it?" Horton answered.

"The colonists' sir….. We've got a lot of dead and wounded here.

We're going to need medical and extraction equipment… its bad sir," the squad leader said in a shaken voice.

"Roger, I'll radio back to the Raleigh to send medevac and mass casualty personnel ASAP," said Horton. "Raleigh Mike this is Bandit 6, sitrep as follows, break… Transport cleared of all opposition, eight enemy KIA break…. I have over half the colonists dead upon discovery, the rest wounded or unconscious break… request immediate medevac and mass casualty support to my location over."

"Roger Bandit 6, support is on the way, ETA fifteen mikes, Captain Beck is coming aboard with them to assess the situation personally, over," the Raleigh communications chief answered.

4

Hastati Orbit

One of the Marines walked up to Kaleb and put his hand on his shoulder. "Man, looks like you're the only one to make it without a scratch... oh wait looks like you got a nasty bruise on the side of your head there, we'll get the medic to fix that up for you." Kaleb looked up at the Marine with a despondent glare and answered.

"They killed my family.... took my sisters.... their leader hit me with his pistol after I tried to tackle him. Did you guys get him?... His name was Darius I think."

"I'm sorry bud... we think he made it out in the escape pod before we could get to him... we made the rest of them pay though, and we'll get the guy you're talking about too once we track where that pod landed. I'm sorry for your loss, you were brave you know that? No one should have to go through something like this," the Marine attempted to comfort Kaleb. "Come on, let's get you up to our ship to get looked at by the doc and get you some food and water." The Marine led Kaleb over to the escape hatch where the Marines had entered the transport during their attack. Kaleb began to climb up the ladder to the Raptor when a large boot came into view and almost hit him in the head.

"Excuse me son," said a deep, rough voice. Captain Beck planted his feet on the deck of the transport and scanned the compartment.

"Attention on deck!" one of the Marine squad leaders sounded.

"Nice work LT, too bad we didn't catch the bastard that got out in that escape pod, how many civilian casualties?" Beck inquired.

"Numbers confirmed at thirty-two dead, seventeen wounded sir," the LT reported.

"Damn," Beck said with a sense of lost hope.

"Only one to get out without a major injury was this guy right here," the LT firmly patted Kaleb on the back. Beck looked down upon Kaleb and placed one of his large hands on his shoulder. He paused for a few seconds, as if analyzing him.

With a nod, Beck spoke, "Son, what happened here was a horrible thing and you won't ever be able to put it past you. The only thing you can do is drive on with your life and hope that one day we can put a stop to these evil men. I will do everything in my power…. and be assured you can trust me on this one… I will do everything possible to make these heartless cowards pay for everything they did. For you, your family, and the rest of these people that suffered this tragedy today." Kaleb sensed sincerity and earnestness in Captain Beck's voice that he had never before experienced. Something about Beck's presence convinced Kaleb that this man would follow through on his promise, and it comforted him to a small degree.

Kaleb nodded and acknowledged the Captain's remarks with a quiet, "Thank you sir." He climbed up the ladder into the Raptor to be brought to the Raleigh's medical bay.

Beck stepped away from Kaleb and continued to scan the transport. With a sigh he continued on, "What a damn mess Lieutenant." Marines were placing the dead in black body bags and hauling them up to the cruiser for funeral and disposal. Blood stains were painted on the walls of the freighter.

"Right about that sir….. uh, Sir? What are we supposed to do with the survivors that lost their families and homes? I mean, it's not like they can just go back to their colony on Hastati, it's been burned to the ground."

"I know Lieutenant, I know… I'm still trying to figure that one out." Beck pondered, and then changed subjects. "What's the status Marines? Found any possible leads as to where these slavers came from?"

The intelligence NCO turned and saluted, "Sir, nothing real concrete yet… they've been all over the Horus cluster…I've got one possibility though. This transport made weekly stops in the Fahkar System; nothing pinpointed however, could be a possible resupply point for the slavers."

"You're damn right it is, download all those files. I want any possible location in that system investigated. I'm done playing soft with these people," Beck commanded.

* * * *

Kaleb woke up in cold sweat. He had been dreaming. Disoriented, he couldn't figure out where he was. The room was dimly lit and his vision was blurred. A piercing headache caused him to wince in pain. He was dreaming about his family back on the farm on Hastati. Then, reality struck in, he realized what he just went though was not a dream at all. He was in the medical bay of USS Naval cruiser. His parents were dead, sisters lost, probably dead, and his home destroyed. A feeling of emptiness came over Kaleb. *What am I supposed to do now?* He thought to himself. Feelings of hate swelled within him, hate for the slavers, Darius, the Ares Alliance, and his circumstances. *Why did this have to happen to me?* He thought. *What did I do to deserve this?* Kaleb observed the room he was in. The survivors of the Hastati attack were all within the bay receiving medical treatment for their injuries. He saw the little girl with the broken legs he tried to help on the transport. She peacefully lay sleeping in a hospital bed a few rows over. Kaleb wondered if she had lost her family too. He began to re-create the events of his family's capture on the farm in his head. *What could I have done to prevent this? I could've saved my family maybe if he hadn't hid in the barn. I should've tried to kill the slavers, they probably would've killed me, but at least I would've died with my family.*

Now it was just him, alone in the world to fend for himself. His father wouldn't be there to give him guidance, teach him, his mother could no longer comfort him, cook his meals, and make sure he did his schoolwork. He knew he had to become a man on his own and avenge his family, one way or another. Kaleb had always been an independent person, always seeking adventure as a child; rebelling from his parents at every chance he was given. He loved his parents though, and they were a huge part of his life. Going on without them would mean a void would exist that would have to be filled. He did not know how to fill that void. He once again fought off tears…. No, he thought, *I won't cry, men don't cry, it won't help anything.*

The lights in the med bay brightened. What appeared to be two United Star Systems Naval officers entered the bay. They quietly spoke to the nurse and she then turned to the surviving colonists receiving rest and medical care.

"Attention everyone, I know you have all been through a lot and you would like to rest and heal, but the Ship's Captain will be coming down in five minutes to address all of you and your concerns on where you will be staying and how we can re-unite you with your families." Kaleb sat up on his bed and attempted to appear alert and healthy.

"Attention on deck," one of the officers said as Captain Beck entered.

"Carry on, carry on, this is an informal session Lieutenant,"

Beck calmly stated. The colonists in the room that were able gave their undivided attention to the Captain. "Good morning, to all of you, I'm Captain Beck, commander of the USSN Raleigh, the ship that you're currently on. All of you have suffered a great tragedy, many of you have experienced loss and suffering on a level with which others will never understand. I can assure you however that the people that did this to your colony will be brought to justice, whether it is by our judicial system or on the battlefield, I will find these slavers, and end their existence. In the meantime, we all must look forward to a new beginning, a fresh start to your lives. My crew will do their utmost to re-unite you with your families when we arrive at our destination, Talos station. Those of you that have suffered the loss of family, there are personnel services available at the station that can give you temporary housing and travel to other systems. For you children that have lost your families, for the time being, you will be placed under a foster family program there."

Kaleb rolled his eyes and shook his head. The last thing he wanted was to be forced into some stranger's apartment with a bunch of other orphans on a space station. He would rather just try to make it on his own, *maybe I can reach my uncle back on Earth and live with him. Fat chance of that happening though. Last I heard of uncle Larry was that he was doing hard time for multiple drug offenses and fraud. Probably not a good idea.*

"Are there any questions?" No one raised their hand or spoke; just puzzled faces looked at Beck in confusion and remorse. "Very well, Lieutenant Li here will go over each of your issues personally and help you decide on a course of action to take when we arrive on station. We'll be arriving at Talos in approximately fourteen hours. From there you will depart the ship and be taken to the United Star Systems Personnel Command to sort out any other issues you may have. I pray that all of you get well and are able to put all of this behind you, thank you for your time." Beck turned to walk out of the med bay but not before looking at Kaleb and giving him a nod of approval. "Don't worry son, we'll get you taken care of," the Captain's words now seemed empty and hopeless to Kaleb.

Lieutenant Li made her rounds to each of the colonist's beds. Everyone had some kind of issue of family, their home, where would they live and she copiously took down notes for each person's concerns. She made her way over to where Kaleb was sitting up in his bed.

"Hello I'm Lieutenant Li and I'll be helping to assign you new place to live once we get to Talos station. The Captain informed me of your situation. No surviving grandparents, your only uncle apparently is serving time in prison back on Earth for drug smuggling, no designated legal guardians. You must be very upset; I can't even imagine what you've had to go through."

Kaleb glared at the young officer, "You're not putting me up in some foster care orphanage. I don't care what you say. I'll be just fine on my own."

The LT countered, "You have to be able to stay somewhere Kaleb Taylor. You're only sixteen, where are you going to work? Where will you get food? A place to sleep? You're not old enough to buy an apartment on the station let alone make enough money to pay for it. Foster care is your only option right now. I know it's not what you want but it's the only way."

"I'm not doing it," Kaleb looked away as he stated firmly.

"Alright…there is one other option I could throw out there if you'd let me," Li offered.

Kaleb skeptically looked back at the LT, "And what is that?"

"Until you turn eighteen and are considered an adult, I can have you sign on as an apprentice to the Talos station armament shop. My father is a civilian contractor that works there and pretty much runs the place. He has been looking for more help and he happens to have an extra apartment next to his on the station you could live in. You'll be able to live and work on the station and learn the gunsmith trade from my father. There is a small school on the station for military families where you can finish out your classes and graduate. My father will treat you well and see you're taken care of, besides, you look harmless, and he could use the company… and the help in the shop. He's been complaining about being bored since I left for the fleet. Your rent to my father for the apartment will be your work in the shop. Live there till you're eighteen then you're free to do whatever you want….or you can live in the alleyways with the homeless scrounging for food all day, what will it be?"

Kaleb's facial expression didn't show much excitement. "Doesn't seem like I really have much choice right now. No way am I living in foster care, I'd be better off on my own. As long as your dad's not a lunatic or something I think I'll be alright."

"Cute," Li sarcastically smiled. "Very well, I'll get started on your paperwork. Just bring these forms with you to the personnel processing office and they will set everything up for you. I'll introduce you to my father once we disembark the ship; he's waiting to see me at docking bay. Just look for the old short guy with gray hair. I'm happy I could help your situation a little bit. Is there anything else you need?" Li asked.

Kaleb's expression turned to sorrow once more. "What about my sisters? They were taken on one of the other ships, will they find them? How will I know if they do? They could still be alive."

Li pondered the question for a moment, "I'll forward your sisters' names to the Intelligence Office on station as missing USS citizens. They'll be put in a database with other missing personnel and whenever someone is rescued or found it will be updated. While you're on Talos station, check in weekly with their office, I'll list you as the point of contact for when they are found. We have several leads as to where those other slaver's ships fled to and the fleet will be searching these areas for them, it's all we can do at this point. Don't worry, if they are still alive, we'll find them."

Disappointment was evident in Kaleb's demeanor upon hearing this, "They could be anywhere in the galaxy, I hope you're right."

"Just don't ever give up hope. I know it might not seem like it right now, but there is a plan for everyone in the universe, and all these things happen for a reason. God has a plan for all of us and you will be part of it too," Li attempted to comfort Kaleb.

"Yeah right, God doesn't exist right now as far as I'm concerned," Kaleb mumbled as he looked down at the floor.

"I guess I can respect that opinion given your current situation…. It was a pleasure meeting you and I think you are a very strong-willed person for your age. Maybe I'll see you in the fleet someday Kaleb." Li shook Kaleb's hand and wished him luck as he started his new life. A life that he once had mapped out so clear, was now just a blur, he had no idea what the future would bring him as he faced the galaxy on his own.

2169 Talos Space Station, United Star Systems Naval headquarters, Pylos Cluster, Cutler System

Talos Station was the largest space station to be built by humans to date. It was slightly larger than the International Space Station (ISS) that orbited Earth, which was a massive multinational station where the first colonial missions embarked on their journeys through unknown space. Talos station was aptly named after the planet that it orbits; Talos. Talos was the third major garden world colony founded by humans after Apollo and New Sydney. The station was at first built as a massive starship construction facility by Raytheon-Lerhter. The United Star Systems Navy eventually bought the station from Raytheon-Lerhter and transformed it into its Naval headquarters. Talos had a very conservative-minded populace and was a loyal colony to the USS government; it therefore was chosen to be the main operating base for the USS military. With a fast-growing population of over 350 million citizens coupled with abundant heavy-metal resources, the colony of Talos was the hub of USS defense-oriented production. Armored rovers, body armor, small arms, and battle cruisers were all designed and built on Talos.

The station was of the Stanford-Torus design, essentially a huge, hollow ring over fifteen kilometers in diameter that spun around itself as it orbited Talos, creating its own artificial gravity on the interior of the station. USSN ships docked around the interior of the ring and everything from living quarters, to training areas, shopping malls, and entertainment venues existed within the ring. Consisting of forty-two starships, "Talos Fleet" was the USS Navy's largest and was nicknamed "The Sentinel of Humanity." The massive USS controlled station was built to ensure quality, control, and sensibility to the colonizing of new worlds while providing a deterrent against piracy and mercenaries.

The helmsman of the USSN Raleigh steadied the cruiser as it approached the Cutler Star System. The sleek, maneuverable ship glided through space towards the station. Two Jupiter-class heavy assault battleships passed above the Raleigh. Battleships were the hammer of USSN fleets and the most deadly of all warships. They measured over 1,200 meters in length and contained two massive electro-magnetic accelerators. The fifty-two pound projectile that was propelled through space out of a battleship's EMA traveled at speeds that gave it as much impact force as a twelve kilo-ton nuclear warhead, minus the radiation. The USS Navy only had three in service with two more under construction. These multi-trillion credit starships were another reason for the secession of the Ares Alliance as they viewed the ships as unnecessary and an extreme waste of their tax dollars.

"Man, I still can't believe the size of those things," the helmsman said as he stared at the ships through his viewport.

The Raleigh's XO, Lieutenant Commander Jorgennson swiftly answered, "Don't be so quick to fall in love with those slow-moving pieces of scrap-metal chief. I'd much rather be on a high-tech fast mover like what we got here. We're where the real action is, up close and personal engagements, maneuverability, and speed. You can't get all that on a Jupiter-class. Besides, how hard can it be to sit back behind the front line of the fleet and shoot at a ship tens of thousands of miles away?"

"You know I'd never leave you and the Captain sir. You two wouldn't know what to do without the best pilot in the fleet," the chief replied with a laugh.

A voice came over the ship's net, "Raleigh, this is Talos Station Main, approach vector approved, docking bay two-four, immediate priority for ship re-generation and unloading of civilian personnel."

"Roger Main, tango mike," the helmsman said into his headset. The Raleigh circled the station and gracefully slid into its assigned docking bay. Locking arms attached to the ship's hull, grounding it in place. The ship's drive engine lowered to idle operation level and a pressurized bridge extending from the station sealed itself with the Raleigh's main exit hatch. Kaleb was guided out of the ship by several NCO's. Captain Beck stood at the end of the gangway that led from the ship to the interior of the station. He looked down at Kaleb as he approached and smiled. He gave him a firm handshake and slapped his right shoulder with his other gargantuan hand.

"Alright son, I wish you the best of luck in the armament shop. I'm glad we were able to work something out for you. Don't worry about a thing, the USS military is going to take good care of you from here on out on Talos station. As for your family, I've already got leads on where your sisters could have been taken, so don't worry we'll find some closure for you as soon as we can. For your parents, their memory can only live on through you and what you make of the rest of your future. Make them proud by driving on and overcoming their loss…." Beck gave a stern look directly into Kaleb's eyes. "I can see you shouldn't have any trouble doing that. Maybe one day you'll come back and see me and we can make you into a Marine."

Kaleb nodded despondently. He didn't need this man's

sympathy. Beck had no idea what Kaleb had been through. He replied, ensuring to show a lack of enthusiasm for Beck's failed words of encouragement. "Thank you for your help sir. Guess I'll try to make it on my own here." Kaleb looked out with despair upon the cavernous main hall of the station. It was an entirely foreign land for him with no one to ask for help besides some strange foster dad named Li.

Nine months later, Talos Station 2170

Lieutenant Li's father had taken Kaleb under his wing from the start at the armament shop and for the first few months Kaleb Taylor was able to somewhat happily go on with his life. He grew to like and respect Mr. Li and was grateful to him for providing a place to stay and work when he had nowhere else to go. Kaleb quickly became proficient in all forms USS Marine small arms weaponry in their operation and repair during his apprenticeship to Mr. Li. He would hang out with the Marines on station and talk to them about life in the military, what schools to go to, what basic training was like etc. Mr. Li would let Kaleb shoot at the indoor range at the shop during his down time. He enrolled Kaleb in the Talos intermediate school on station where he would be able to finish out the rest of his classes and attain his diploma. Kaleb admired the Marines and Naval servicemen on the station that he constantly interacted with. In the back of his mind he thought it could be something he could maybe do. Enlisting in the Marines would give him a chance to get even with the mercenaries and slavers of the Ares Alliance. It would also be a means to get off of Talos station and start a new life for himself. The USS military would give him a paycheck, free place to stay, and three free meals a day. Not bad for a kid who had no family and no future ahead of him.

Everything seemed to be going fine until about four months

into the apprenticeship when the loss of his family finally began to hit home. He fell into the wrong crowd of teenagers on the station and took up their habits of drugs and alcohol. Kaleb felt empty inside, as if something was missing from his soul. The United Star Systems military never sent word of finding his sisters or of having any possible leads. He knew that they were most likely dead and he eventually gave up all hope. To replace this emptiness he used alcohol and drugs, rebelling against Mr. Li whenever he had the chance. Kaleb began to show up late for work at the shop, sometimes not at all. He was barely passing his classes at the station's school. He lost his will and motivation for life. Here he was, stuck on this deep space station, with no family, he'd never find his sisters, had no real friends and no place to call home anymore. He also no longer cared to enlist in the USS Marines. *What was the point?* He thought. *Why bother? They didn't have enough decency to let me know the fate of my sisters, let alone bring the slavers to justice that had devastated my life.* Kaleb longed for things to be normal again. Back with his family, working on the farm on Hastati. Life was so much simpler and easier then.

He found it hard to make friends at the station as his peers were constantly coming and going as military families moved from one station to the next. He couldn't identify with the other classmates; they didn't have to go through what he did. They all had families, some one that loved them, a nice place to go home to everyday. He missed the lush green fields, mountains, and forests of Hastati, the small creek that ran through the middle of the pasture at his home. He missed the little things like working in the field, planting crops, going to into town to meet with his friends, his mother's cooking and his father's constant voice of guidance. Things that he took for granted before. Kaleb realized how great his life had been, how lucky he used to be. Now all he had was the dust-filled armament shop and Mr. Li. He gradually sank into loneliness and drunkenness. The slavers that attacked his family were long gone, he'd never find them. Mr. Li became concerned with Kaleb's condition and would ask him how he was doing and if he needed some professional help. Kaleb would only answer with curses and deny that there was anything wrong with him and to be left alone.

Kaleb, now seventeen, was just drifting along at this point, not really caring what the future held for him. In two weeks he was to graduate the Talos Station intermediate school and would be forced to get a real job somewhere on the station until he saved up enough money to move out of Mr. Li's extra apartment. Mr. Li did not make near enough money to send Kaleb to a university or technical school off of the station. Kaleb would have to pay his own way if he wanted to do that and it would take several years of full-time work at the station before he would have enough money to book a space flight to Earth or one of the colonies. Deep down inside, Kaleb still knew that the quickest way for him to get off of the station was by enlisting in the USS military.

*   *   *   *

The bell rang signaling the end of classes for the day at the Talos intermediate school for military families. Relieved that the monotony of galactic history class was finally over, Kaleb immediately picked up his bag and walked out of the classroom, not caring to socialize or gossip after class in the hallways like the rest of his peers.

He walked down a long corridor towards an elevator that would take him down to the entertainment level of the station. Kaleb usually spent his time there after class using the internet terminals, attempting to get into bars or gentlemen's clubs, or the occasional attempt to score some liquor or weed off one of the station locals. Today, Kaleb was feeling especially sober, something that he needed to remedy quickly after a long day in class.

He pulled out a fifth of liquor from his back pack and put it inside a brown paper bag to conceal it for purposes of drinking in public. Unscrewing the top, he took a quick sip of the Earth-distilled bourbon and winced as the taste hit his tongue. *Refreshing,* he thought to himself. The elevator door opened, revealing the large entertainment venue of Talos Station. Life could get boring on a space station, especially when the majority of the 30,000 plus population was enlisted USS military. Bars, restaurants, nightclubs, and a shopping mall packed the third level of the station as a method to keep the Marines and Naval servicemen occupied during their off-hours. By law, the drinking age on the station was eighteen, however Kaleb looked a little older than he was and had never been stopped by the military police that patrolled the district. He took some more sips from the liquor bottle and observed his surroundings. His eyes focused on the local bar called "The Brown Dwarf," where he knew the owner and was sure to be able to drink underage for the remainder of the night. His favorite pastime was to try and pick up older women at the bar. He especially liked to hit on the female Naval officers that frequented the place. Once they figured out how old he was it usually was a bust however.

Kaleb carelessly strolled across a bridge where an artificial creek ran through the entertainment district. There were green trees and plants sporadically placed about the entertainment level in order to give the station residents the feel of being back on Earth, a place Kaleb knew nothing about and cared little for at this point in his life.

As he slowly made his way towards the bar he couldn't help but overhear some shouting coming from about fifty meters down a poorly lit corridor that led to another elevator to the lower levels of the station. He looked over his shoulder to see where the noise was coming from when he noticed several guys and a girl from his school in a heated argument. Curiosity got the better of Kaleb and he turned to walk over and investigate the ongoing altercation, hoping to perhaps witness a fight, something of which would bring some excitement to his boring day.

As he got closer to the group of fellow students, he recognized them from some of his classes. Two of the bigger guys were shoving and shouting at the smaller one, with the girl crying, pleading for them to stop. The two aggressors were Bryson Jennings and Cory Davies, both military brats of high ranking Naval officers on the station. They were of the popular group in school, always walking around as if they were better than everyone else. Being on the basketball team, they set the standard for what was "cool" and always had the hottest girls around them. The other smaller kid which appeared to be their victim was Larry Pewter, somewhat of a loner and an internet-gaming junkie, he was supposedly one of the smartest kids in the school and Kaleb enjoyed talking with him from time to time as they had a little bit in common. His father worked for a defense contractor on some backwater colony. He had left Larry and his mother when Larry was only six years old. His mother took a job on the station shortly thereafter and he'd been on Talos ever since. His girlfriend, Analise, was there with him crying and trying to get the two aggressors to leave them alone.

Kaleb took another swig from his liquor bottle and approached the fracas apathetically.

"Just leave him alone you assholes! He didn't do anything to you!" Analise cried out as she wept.

Bryson, a fairly large individual, standing at about 6'4", ignored her and slammed Larry up against the wall, digging his elbow into Larry's scrawny neck. "Come on Larry, I know you've got those online finance mods, just give me the access codes and we'll be on our way!"

"Screw you man; even if I did have the codes to the finance center, I wouldn't give them to you," Larry bravely protested.

"Don't lie to me Larry, I know you've been skimming credits off the station's bank files for the past three months, now give me the damn access codes," Bryson countered, digging his forearm further into Larry's throat, choking him.

"Not… a…chance…dick…head," Larry struggled to say with the pressure on his neck.

Bryson released his forearm from Larry's neck, causing him to fall to the ground. "Alright smart ass, guess you leave me no choice…" he smiled and reared his leg back, kicking Larry in the face and knocking him on his back against the wall. Analise let out a scream as Bryson grabbed Larry's throat and pulled back his fist. "I guess I'm gonna have to beat it out of you, is that what you want?"

Kaleb moved in closer and spoke up confidently, although somewhat buzzed from the whiskey. "Hey douche bags, let him go."

Bryson and Cory glanced over at Kaleb with a confused look on their faces.

"That's right assholes I'm talking to you," Kaleb answered.

"Get out of here Taylor this has got nothing to do with you," Cory said.

"Yeah why don't you do us all a favor and go drink yourself to death or something you homeless bastard," Bryson sneered.

At an athletic 5'11" and 185 lbs, Kaleb was still smaller than both of the attackers. He knew he'd have to get lucky if something went down between them. At this point in his life he really didn't care whether he got his ass kicked or not. *Eh, what the hell?* Kaleb quickly thought to himself as he pondered the idea of trying to be a hero and fight the two of them. Bryson's homeless bastard comment had particularly irritated Kaleb as well. He stepped up about two feet from Bryson and looked up at him.

"Drink myself to death? Hmmm. Not a bad idea, but I don't do requests…..There is something this homeless bastard *can* do for you though." Kaleb said in a smart ass tone.

"Hah, and just what is tha-?" Bryson was interrupted by Kaleb's whiskey bottle smashing against the side of his head, knocking him to the ground unconscious. Shards of glass from the bottle flew everywhere. Cory Davies's eyes widened and focused on Kaleb. He reared back with his right arm and threw an exaggerated right hook towards Kaleb's face. He saw the incoming fist out of the corner of his eye and instantaneously ducked down; avoiding what would've been a knockout punch. Cory fell forward from his own momentum and struggled to stay balanced. Kaleb capitalized on this mistake and put Cory in a bear hug from behind; wrapping his leg around the front of his victim, he forced Cory to fall to the floor with Kaleb on top of his back. Kaleb wrapped his left arm around Cory's throat and got him in a rear choke hold. He squeezed as hard as he could as Cory's arms flailed around aimlessly, struggling to break out of Kaleb's grasp. Kaleb furiously threw punches at his face with his free arm, drawing blood from Cory's nose and mouth. In a strange way it felt good beating the hell out of somebody. It was a release from all of his built up frustration since the attack on Hastati.

"Kaleb, chill out, you're gonna kill him!" Larry Pewter yelled while he struggled to pull him off of Cory.

Kaleb continued to strike Cory's face repeatedly until he himself was struck in the back of the head by a solid object. He fell over disoriented and in a daze. Through his blurred vision he saw what appeared to be a military policeman with a baton in his right hand. The MP rolled Kaleb over and immediately placed handcuffs on him.

"Don't move a muscle if you know what's good for you buddy!" The MP shouted, pulling Kaleb up off the ground. He called in on his radio ear-piece for back up and for a medic to check Bryson and Cory for injuries while he checked Kaleb's ID.

"Kaleb Taylor, seventeen years old, no legal guardians, address… Talos Naval armament shop? So… You want to tell me just what the hell you think you're doing?!" the MP asked after reading off the Talos station ID card.

"I was just trying to help these two out sir, they were attacked by these guys," Kaleb answered as he looked for Larry and Analise but was unable to locate them. Apparently, they ran off when they saw the MP coming, afraid they would get into trouble.

"Attacked by who? What the hell are you talking about?" the MP gave an agitated reply.

Bryson eventually came back to his senses and sat up from the floor, rubbing the side of his head.

"Are you alright kid? I've got paramedics on the way. What happened here?" the MP asked.

"Uh… I'm not sure officer, I was just… walking down the hall when this guy came up behind me… and…smashed me on the head with a bottle." Bryson lied to the MP.

"He's lying sir, they were ganging up on a kid from school, trying to steal something from him; when they started hitting him I stepped in to stop them." Kaleb explained.

"Wait a minute, aren't you Admiral Jennings son?" the MP asked curiously to Bryson.

"Yes sir, I was actually just going to see my father in his office when I got attacked by this guy," Bryson again avoided the truth hoping that his father's status would sway the MP's opinions. The paramedics had arrived and began to patch up the two injured teenagers.

"So you're saying this kid just attacked you guys for no apparent reason?" Cory and Bryson nodded, trying to look as innocent as possible. The MP sniffed the air near Kaleb who had been standing next to him. "Is that alcohol I smell on you? Are you aware of the legal drinking age here on the station?"

"Yeah but I guess I figured the law didn't apply to me since it apparently doesn't apply to these two assholes if they can run around bullying people and not get in trouble," Kaleb protested.

"Oh, ok, smart ass huh. That's fine. I figure a few days locked up at the MP station can fix that. Corporal, take his sorry ass back and write him up for hmmm, let's see… assault and battery as well as underage public intoxication and possession of alcohol." The MP Sergeant's assistant nodded and pulled Kaleb away by his hand cuffs up towards the military police station.

Kaleb shook his head as he was pulled away from the Sergeant. "Great job officer, way to see that justice was properly served….. *asshole,"* Kaleb said under his breath as he was carried off.

✳   ✳   ✳   ✳

Three hours later, Talos station

"Wake up boy!" Mr. Li yelled through the bars of the holding cell at the MP station. Mr. Li was a small man in his late sixties, originally from the Asian Union back on Earth. He was not the least bit happy about having to come and bail Kaleb out of jail during his shift at the armament shop.

"Mr. Li? Hey, what's going on?" Kaleb said lightheartedly as he rose up from the cot in the holding cell.

"What's going on? Maybe you'd like to tell me what's going on. You're the one that has me down here paying two-hundred credits to bail you out of jail for getting into some drunken brawl with the station commander's son!" Li countered.

"Aw man, don't worry about paying the bail Mr. Li, I can just stay here until my hearing next week. It's not too bad, I get three free meals a day, plus I'd get to skip my classes." Kaleb joked.

"This is not a laughing matter Kaleb!" Li protested heatedly. Now get your stuff and let's get out of here. We just received a shipment of one-hundred and four MR-6 rifles that need to be serviced in the next two days. I've got plenty of work for you to do."

*   *   *   *

Kaleb cleaned and polished his last weapon of the day and let out a sigh. Mr. Li had put him on a six hour cleaning detail everyday for the past week at the shop as punishment for getting arrested. That, on top of the forty hours of community service that he was ordered to perform by the station Judge Advocate Office gave Kaleb plenty of time to think about what he'd let his life come to. *Man, I bet your parents would be proud of you now huh?* Kaleb thought and shook his head as he wiped down his work station. He had just graduated from the station intermediate school a few days ago, skimming just above the pass rate on most of his classes. Kaleb now had a criminal record working against him, no future plans, and hardly any credits in his account after paying Mr. Li back his bail money. As far as he knew he was stuck working for Mr. Li for the rest of his life, something he was deathly opposed to. This made him once again give serious thought to joining the Marines. He looked across the work table at Mr. Li and smiled. He had made up his mind.

"Mr. Li, I've been thinking about some things lately," Kaleb began.

"Oh no, no think, just work. Keeps your mind focused. Keeps you out of trouble," Li said, shaking his head and continuing to work on a weapon.

Kaleb laughed, "Come on Mr. Li, I'm trying to be serious here."

"Ok boy, go ahead, speak, if you please," Li grumbled.

"Like I was saying, before I was rudely interrupted. I've been thinking lately. I've made up my mind. I'm going to enlist in the USS Marines."

Li stopped what he was doing and looked up at Kaleb with curiosity.

"You know, I mean, I can't just stick around here my whole life bothering you and getting into trouble. Don't get me wrong Mr.

Li, you've been great to me. You gave me a place to stay, a job, food to eat, and got me to finish school. But I was thinking that if my family was still here, what would they think about what I'm doing right now? They'd be pissed off at me I'm sure. I've got to try to make something of myself, not just sit around this station like a bum my whole life. So tomorrow I was going to go down to the recruiting office and talk to the Marines there and see what my options are. If I like what I hear I think I'll go ahead and do it. I think it's the quickest way for me to get out of here and get my mind off of my family…"

Li smiled at Kaleb's assessment, "I think there may still be a smart kid inside that head of yours. Maybe you don't act like it on the outside, but on the inside you show wise judgment. It is your decision, but I have a feeling you will be successful in all that you do in life. I will accompany you to this recruiting office tomorrow and support whatever decision you make."

"I appreciate the help Mr. Li. You know, you're a pretty cool guy for being so old," Kaleb said gratefully as he laughed.

Li gave a sarcastic response, "Old yes, but at least I am happy. Hah, at least now with you joining the Marines I can rent out my extra apartment to someone that actually pays me for it."

"Very funny Mr. Li….come on, you know you'll miss me," Kaleb replied.

6

Two months later, Earth, USS Marines Proving Grounds, Amazon region, South America.

All United Star Systems Marines started their journey at the Proving Grounds. It was basic training, ten weeks of military indoctrination consisting of hazing, running, obstacle courses, marksmanship, battle drills, and discipline. A 40,000 acre complex set in the jungles of the Amazon, the Proving Grounds was meant to be a harsh place. The high temperatures and humidity alone caused many recruits to fail or drop out from heat injuries. It was imperative that all USS Marines were able to fight not only on the ground, but in space and on other planets with harsh environments. With the advent of interstellar travel, the Marines began to overshadow the army and became a much more important force for a nation's military. Marines were able to fight from ships and conduct assaults from orbit, boarding operations in space, and operate out of space stations. The Army became more of a national guard, a militia maintained by each colonies' or nation's government. The Marines worked for the United Star Systems government and protected all human worlds and surrounding space. Therefore, out of all the services, Army, Navy, and Marines, it was toughest to become a Marine and more pride came along with it.

A large Navy transport ship touched down on a landing pad surrounded by jungle. Kaleb glanced at the young recruits that were crammed inside the ship with him. Most of them were probably only seventeen to nineteen years old. Many of them looked nervous or scared. Bright sunlight poured into the compartment as the cargo ramp lowered, exposing the human home world of Earth for the first time to many of the recruits on board.

The USS military used Earth for all of its initial entry training because they felt it inspired a sense of pride among its recruits. The USS government wanted to make sure its Marines knew what they were fighting for, where they came from, and their history. Kaleb had never been to Earth before. His first glimpse of the planet was enlightening as his view was flooded with verdant green plants and trees, denser than he had ever seen before. He heard a symphony of birds and insects coming from within the jungle that surrounded the military base. Hastati was not so similar after all; it didn't have nearly this much vegetation and was much cooler in temperature and more arid. The humidity hit Kaleb as the ramp hit the concrete tarmac and fresh air flowed into the transport. He immediately began to sweat profusely and struggled to breathe the heavy, moisture filled air.

He saw a large figure dressed in green/brown digital pattern fatigues quickly approaching the transport ramp. One of the recruits sitting across from Kaleb said under his breath; "Now the shit really hits the fan." Kaleb was surprised with the comment and looked back at the man in fatigues who started up the ramp. He saw three small pointed stripes on the right sleeve of his uniform, *must be a Sergeant*, Kaleb thought to himself just before his ears trembled at the sound of screaming just above his head.

"Alright you cocksuckers get the hell off of my ship now! This ain't no bullshit charter flight, get your gear and double time down to that parade field, you're in the USS Marines now!" Kaleb was taken aback by the Sergeant's abrasiveness and immediately began to think that enlisting may have been a bad idea. He anxiously picked up his backpack and ran out of the transport, joining in the stampede of other recruits. Several of the recruits fell amongst the chaos and were trampled by their peers. The Sergeant was quick to jump on top of the fallen recruits, screaming in their ears as they struggled to get up.

"Get up you weak son of a bitch!" The Sergeant grabbed a recruit running past one of the ones that had fallen down. "What the hell are you doing? Are you just gonna leave your battle buddy behind to get trampled on and die? Get his ass up and help him you selfish piece of shit!" Kaleb fell into line with the other recruits on the parade field and nervously stood as still as possible so as to not draw any attention of the Sergeant to him. The eighty-four new recruits stood in four crooked rows, confused and disoriented as to the immediate harshness they had been greeted with. Kaleb was not enjoying his first five minutes of being in the Marines whatsoever.

The Sergeant slowly walked up to the front of the gaggle of recruits. He looked fairly young, probably in his early twenties Kaleb thought as he watched him walk by. The Sergeant was short and stocky, but not over-weight, he had a solid look to him. His Caucasian face was full of energy. He stared each recruit in the eyes as he walked past, surveying his fresh shipment of Privates. No one spoke a word. They waited for the next verbal thrashing from the stranger that so roughly introduced them to military life. Kaleb's heart sped up as he heard the Sergeant yelling once again.

"Oh my God! You call this a formation! Holy shit, I have never seen such a rag tag bunch of worthless cocksuckers in my life! You people want to be Marines? You've got to be fucking kidding me. I can see I've got my work cut out for me this time." It almost sounded like the Sergeant was barking when he yelled. Kaleb wondered if he wanted to sound like that on purpose or if there was something wrong with his voice.

`"Listen up retards, in a few seconds you will be introduced to your Senior Drill Sergeant. You *will* show him the utmost respect at all times understood?!" The recruits said nothing. "Oh I'm sorry… What?... Am I talking to myself?! Listen up! From here on out in your pathetic military careers, *every time* you are asked a question you will answer with a loud and thunderous yes or no Sergeant! Now, do you understand?!!"

The eighty-four recruits mumbled, "Yes Sergeant."

"Do you understand?!!"

"Yes Sergeant."

"Holy shit, you people sound like a fucking wet rag. Get some goddamn enthusiasm for life! You all should be excited to be here, this is the Marines for god sakes! Now sound off when I ask you a damn question! Do you understand?!"

"YES SERGEANT!"

"Good! You dumb sons of bitches finally learned your first essential task of being a Marine. When asked a question you will always sound off loud and confident with a direct answer, do you understand?!"

"YES SERGEANT," in chorus the eighty-four Marine recruits screamed at the top of their lungs.

Another figure in combat fatigues and a black baseball-type cap that showed his rank walked up. This one was taller, about 6'1", but leaner as well. He had three stripes on his uniform as well but also one curved one below the three. His dark hair and mustache was in contrast to the younger Sergeant that first introduced him. He wore dark sunglasses so no one could tell where he was looking. The stocky Sergeant stood in front of them and saluted to the taller one.

"Platoon formed and ready Staff Sergeant Hollis," the younger one reported in a much calmer and controlled voice.

"Roger Sarn't," the senior Sergeant answered calmly as he returned the salute. He slowly looked up at the rabble of recruits and surveyed his next challenge. He spoke loudly and clearly but without screaming like the previous Sergeant; "I am Staff Sergeant Hollis your senior drill instructor for the next ten weeks of your worthless lives. Each and every one of you will get to know myself and Sergeant Randal over here very well during that time period. We will teach you every step of the way, and although you may not like our teaching methods… you *will* learn, and those of you that are tough enough, *will* become Marines." Hollis paced back and forth in front of the recruits as he continued.

"You all have made a choice… volunteered for a higher calling. From this moment on, you cease to be civilians, individuals… selfish and ungrateful to the security that the United Star Systems military provides to them. *You* will now be the ones that provide that security. You are now part of a team, a family… there is no more me or I. It is only we and us. Your Marine battle buddy will be your lifeline, your family, your brothers and sisters and you are all part of my Marine family. So, drop your personal effects and attitudes here. From here on out you will be uniform and equal to your fellow Marine. You will learn what is to live with honor, courage, and commitment; to be able to rise above hardship and folly. To learn to improvise, overcome and adapt to be successful no matter what the circumstances. If any of you cannot handle living by these principles, now is your chance to pick up your shit and go back to whatever cesspool you came from. That transport leaves out of here in five minutes; I suggest you get on it if you think you can't hack it. We will wait…"

Thoughts of quitting already entered Kaleb's thoughts. *All you gotta do is pick up your stuff and get back on that transport and you won't have to do this crap.* He looked amongst the formation; two males dropped back and ran back to the ship that was revving up its engines.

"Whoa! There we go, we got two quitters already Staff Sergeant!" the shorter, stocky Sergeant Randal boyishly blurted out.

"Anyone else? Anyone else make a big mistake?" Hollis said. No one budged from the gaggle. Kaleb stood his ground. *No, I'm going to do this, I know I can do this… no way can I go back to Talos station* he reassured to himself. Kaleb watched as the transport lifted off the ground and rocketed out of the atmosphere, the sound was deafening. The ship got smaller and smaller as it gained altitude and eventually disappeared. Staff Sergeant Hollis spoke up once again and excitedly clapped his hands together once.

"Alright, now we can get started! Sergeant Randal!"

"Yes Staff Sergeant Hollis!" Randal excitedly answered.

"Get these jerk-offs out of my face and get them to the barracks… we got a long day of training coming up." Hollis smiled as Randal ran up to formation screaming.

7

Nine weeks later- Aboard USSN Vancouver; USS Navy training cruiser, Sol System

Kaleb fidgeted in his Advanced Body Armor System (ABAS), trying to get comfortable inside the extra eighty pounds of armor he had been training in for the past three weeks. He sat in the troop ready room of the Vancouver, a training cruiser used in the culmination exercise for all USS Marines. They were just outside orbit of the planet Mars, where Kaleb and his platoon of now fifty-eight remaining Marine recruits were about to conduct their final training exercise in order to meet the requirements for graduation; a planetary assault from orbit on a groundside objective. Almost one third of the initial recruits dropped out due to physical injuries, failing land navigation, marksmanship, physical training, or just plain quitting. Kaleb performed extremely well throughout basic training and was currently at the top-five of his class on the platoon's order of merit list. He had excelled in all areas, especially marksmanship with all weaponry due to his gifted 20/10 eyesight and all of his time spent around Marine weapons at the armament shop. Kaleb remained quiet and avoided direct "ass chewings" from the drill Sergeants. He found it easy to be a Marine, just do what you're told by your

Sergeant and you won't get yelled at. It was so simple and Kaleb was starting to actually enjoy it. He had a new family now, his fellow Marines took care of him like brothers and sisters, his Sergeants were like parents, a little harsh and abrasive at times, but they provided for him and made sure he was prepared for whatever he faced. Most of all, it helped to keep his mind off of his family. The other Privates began to look up to Kaleb to set the example and provide leadership for them. Staff Sergeant Hollis took notice of Kaleb's abilities as well. He had become a quiet professional and respectable leader amongst his peers.

The recruits were all busy conducting their final checks of oxygen tanks, combat suit seals, and weapons; ensuring everything was mission ready for their first orbital assault. Many of them appeared nervous and unsure of the risks involved in descending two-hundred miles in a Raptor transport through Mars' atmosphere to the planet's surface in less than twenty minutes.

Appointed by Staff Sergeant Hollis as the recruit 1st squad leader, Kaleb went to each of his fifteen Privates he was in charge of and checked their equipment to ensure its readiness. During the last three weeks of basic training, the Drill Sergeants designated several of the top recruits in the platoon to serve in "leadership positions." There was a recruit platoon Sergeant, 1st, 2nd, and 3rd squad leaders, and two team leaders per squad. This gave the recruits leadership experience and also took some of the pressure off of the Drill Sergeants having to execute all training and Pre Combat Checks. The platoon of recruits was now at a point in their training where the Drill Sergeants would issue out orders to the recruit leadership and they would be expected to execute. If the leadership failed to execute the mission given, they would be fired and replaced by another recruit. Kaleb had managed to keep his slot as 1st squad leader for the entire three weeks and was not about to get fired on the culmination exercise about to take place.

"Platoon, At Ease!" a recruit sounded as Staff Sergeant Hollis and Sergeant Randal walked into the ready room.

"Alright Marines, are we ready to get hot?!" Sergeant Randal appeared more revved up than usual. He was naturally a hyper individual, a quality well-suited for a drill Sergeant but not always liked by the recruits. He must have downed a few energy drinks recently, a habit he was known for by the recruits.

"YES SERGEANT!" the platoon sounded off in unison. The recruits had gone from a bunch of rag-tag civilians to a well-trained and disciplined team in just nine short weeks. Hollis turned on a projector screen in the room that showed a 3-D terrain map of their objective. There were grid coordinates highlighted in bright red and navigation routes in green, the objective, a small warehouse, was lit up with possible enemy defensive positions.

"Alright Marines get your shit on and give me a horseshoe formation around the briefing map…Private Sanchez!" Hollis said.

"Yes Sergeant!" a female voice yelled from the back of the formation.

"You'll be leading the operation today, consider yourself the new platoon leader, congratulations. Sergeant Randal and I will provide tactical over watch and advice for you throughout the mission but you are in charge." The small Hispanic female gave a nervous nod, as sweat beads formed on her forehead. Her tiny, 5'1" 110 pound frame was dwarfed by most her fellow Marines. She had struggled to keep up with her peers throughout basic training and was currently ranked among the bottom three on the platoon order of merit list.

"Ye.. Yes Sergeant," she stumbled over her words. Kaleb was amazed at Hollis's decision to put her in charge of their final and most important mission. Surely there was someone else that was much better suited to handle the responsibility. Kaleb gave a look of disgust to his Alpha team leader, Private Robbie Hunt, his best friend in the platoon, which in turn Hunt acknowledged by shaking his head, agreeing with Kaleb's disapproval of Hollis's decision.

As Hollis began his mission brief to the platoon, Private Hunt leaned over to Kaleb and whispered, "I hope Sanchez isn't cramping up again, then we're really screwed on this mission." Kaleb smiled and tried to hold back his laughter.

Hollis caught a glimpse of what was taking place during his mission brief, "Private Hunt! Am I hearing things?"

Hunt looked up at the drill Sergeant with an expression of guilt, "Wh.. what do you mean staff Sergeant?" he answered sheepishly.

"I must be fucking hearing things because I know you weren't just carrying on a conversation in the middle of my briefing!"

"No Sergeant, I wasn't…"

"Shut up and start pushing, I don't need this bullshit going on before a major operation!" Hollis rebuked. Kaleb stiffened his stance and tried to look innocent as Hunt began to knock out pushups below his feet. Hunt was slightly smaller than Kaleb, at 5'9" 170 pounds with short, dirty blonde hair and blue eyes. Kaleb remembered him saying his parents were from the country of Canada back on Earth. He was a much more hyper individual compared to Kaleb but also was at the top of the platoon order of merit list. Like Kaleb, he was a colony kid, his family moved to New Sydney from Earth before he had been born. He joined up to get money to attend college after his service was up. His ability to find humor in any situation is what made him and Kaleb get along so well throughout the training. A good sense of humor is sometimes the best way to get through hardships like Marine basic training and the two of them shared many a laugh for the past nine weeks.

Hollis continued as Hunt pounded out pushups, "Now, as I was saying…. Your objective lies here, at this grid, it is an abandoned warehouse used to store weapons by mercenaries. Intel reports it is guarded by three dismount teams with small arms patrolling the outside of the building. The Raptors will touch down approximately five clicks to the northeast of the warehouse in this large crater so as to not give away our position and alert the enemy of our presence. You will reorganize and consolidate in a hasty security halt after drop off. Use your navigation data pad to guide you into the objective on foot. A primary and secondary route has already been pre-programmed into your nav system so there is no reason to get lost out there. Upon reaching the objective you will establish a support by fire position and conduct a flanking maneuver on the warehouse. Enter and clear the warehouse, consolidate any prisoners and equipment and call up a sitrep once the warehouse has been cleared. Now, be advised you will be operating in a zero oxygen environment and temperatures of negative thirty degrees Fahrenheit; the operation can only last as long as your oxygen does so plan accordingly. You'll have approximately four hours to execute the mission before your tanks are empty. If any of you experience any problems with your combat suit, oxygen flow and any other emergency while on ground, the exercise will stop and we will call for evacuation. Safety is the priority here, I don't want anyone trying to go cowboy on me out there, stay disciplined and work as a team. This is your first live fire assault exercise, the risk assessment for this training is high. Do not, I repeat, do not, under any circumstances fire your weapon until you have positively identified your target and intend to kill that target. Maintain muzzle discipline and ensure no friendly forces are in your kill zone at all times. Does everyone understand that?"

"YES SERGEANT."

"If there are no questions, Private Sanchez, you have thirty minutes for mission planning with your squad leaders, have the platoon loaded in the Raptors ready to go in forty-five mikes.

"Roger Sergeant," Sanchez answered quietly.

Sergeant Randal glared at the group of tense recruits, "Remember, this is your culmination exercise….. *everything* you've learned up to this point you will need to utilize to accomplish the mission. Marksmanship, individual movement techniques, radio operation, land navigation, ABAS operations, physical training, and most of all, teamwork. Things that will cause you to fail will be the following: failure to work as a team, leaving a Marine behind, getting lost, fratricide, and any other bonehead mistakes that you all should have worked out of your system by now. This is the time to quit analyzing and worrying about shit and just execute, let your training take over; it's just a reflex, understood?"

"YES SERGEANT," the recruits yelled back.

"Alright, we'll see you on the Raptor." The two drill Sergeants walked out of the ready room leaving fifty-seven Privates staring at Sanchez waiting for her orders.

Sanchez had not yet been placed in a leadership position and was at a loss for what actions she should take. She stared back at the platoon, laboring to put words in to sentences she spoke; "um… ok.. umm.. . squad leaders on me, e…everyone else continue to do mission prep." Kaleb paused for a moment, annoyed at Sanchez's lack of command presence.

He turned to his squad, "What the hell you waiting on first squad? Let's go, do your final mission checks and start to go through rehearsals while I get the brief from Sanchez." The other squad leaders followed Kaleb's lead and issued out similar orders. Once the other Privates began to go about their preparation duties Sanchez turned to Kaleb and the other two squad leaders.

"Wh… What am I supposed to do? I've never led a mission before! How am I supposed to know all this?!" she said frantically. Kaleb rolled his eyes at his fellow squad leaders, Privates Moore and Washington, both squared away Marines from Earth.

"Alright look, it's not that hard," Kaleb said in an annoyed tone. "Just look at the terrain around the objective and see what places look the best to attack from." Sanchez gave a blank stare to Kaleb signaling her failure to understand his last statement. He continued as he pointed to the 3-D terrain map; "Go back to Sergeant Hollis's mission brief, he said we need to set up support by fire on the warehouse, just like the platoon attack battle drill we learned in class."

"I was at sick call during that class I think," Sanchez shrugged her shoulders.

"Jesus, are you for real?" a frustrated Private Julien Washington blurted out.

"Hey… chill, let's just help her out and get this shit done, we don't have much time to figure this shit out," Washington countered in her Earth-born, New York accent.

Julien Washington and Tom Moore were polar opposites, Washington, a tough, extremely athletic, black female, grew up in the urban metropolis of New York City back on Earth and joined the Marines to get away from the gangs and drug dealers that plagued her neighborhood. She vowed to be the first person in her family to make something of herself. Her dream was to make enough money in the Marines to buy her mother a nice home outside the city away from the violence and gang wars.

Moore on the other hand was what some would call "trailer trash," growing up in what remained of the back woods of Arkansas. His red hair, freckles, and crooked teeth did not help to play down this stereotype. He was loud and brash and made sure to let everyone know he was a redneck. With most of Earth urbanized by 2150, typical southern American accents and country people became somewhat of a novelty as ninety percent of the world's population lived in urban areas. There were a few desolate areas left in North America and Moore ensured everyone knew he was from one. He dropped out of high school at sixteen, was kicked out of his mom's trailer at seventeen and was fired from his job at a turkey farm at eighteen for drinking whiskey on the job. He decided since he liked to shoot guns and the Marines didn't require a high school diploma, he'd go ahead and join up. These would become the USS military's best and brightest however as both had become molded into squared away Marines and it was no mistake that they were placed in their current leadership positions.

Kaleb, irritated by the circumstances, decided to help out Sanchez for the good of the team. "Alright look, see that hilltop about five-hundred meters to the southwest of our objective?" Sanchez nodded, "we can set up my squad there with the two sniper rifles we've got in order to take out any roving patrols on the outside of the warehouse just ahead of the assaulting force. Once my squad is set, then 2nd and 3rd can move up this dry canyon from the south that leads up to the warehouse. The canyon will provide cover and concealment on your movement up there. Once you're set give me the order to take out the roving guards. This rock outcropping one-hundred and fifty meters south of the warehouse will be the support by fire position, 3rd squad with heavy weapons can set up there once we've taken out the dismounts and cover 2nd squad's flanking movement. Moore, you can then take 2nd and continue up the canyon as it wraps around the eastern side of the building and levels out."

In his southern drawl Moore protested; "Now just hold on a minute there Napoleon. That canyon doesn't just go right up to the front door of that building, there's seventy-five meters of open terrain there, what makes you think I'm gonna send my squad across that with no cover while 1st squad sets their happy asses safe and sound on a hill five hundred meters away?"

Kaleb countered, "As I was saying, Washington's heavy weapons will provide cover fire for your movement up to the warehouse, once your squad is set, 3rd will lift fire and your squad can conduct enter and clear procedures on the warehouse. Once your squad is inside, 3rd can move up and provide reserve support for the clearing operation and tend to any casualties or enemy prisoners of war. Besides Moore,

I figured you'd want all the glory of being the main assault force, leading the platoon to victory against the sim robots."

Simulation Robots were inexpensive, mostly plastic machines in a humanoid shape that were controlled by an operator from a command post through remote and video image. They were utilized in live-fire training exercises by the USS military to add realism to the battle. The robots carried rifles that fired low-velocity rubber pellets filled with red paint at the recruits. When the rounds impacted on a Marines' combat armor they burst open, spreading red paint to simulate a wound. If a Marine was hit with one of these pellets, he would be designated as a casualty and taken out of the mission by the drill instructor.

"Hmm…Yeah…… I guess it would be best to give my squad the most important part of the mission," Moore scratched his head.

"Shit, I bet those robots pump your country ass full of rubber before you even step foot in that warehouse," Julien Washington chuckled. "Naw thas cool though, I'm trackin' the plan Taylor, sounds like it can't fail to me."

Sanchez looked up in amazement of Kaleb's quick assessment of the mission. "Um… where should I be during all of this?" she asked shyly.

"You should go with 3rd squad. From there you'll have the best picture of what's going on in all three locations. You'll also need to send up all the reports to Staff Sergeant Hollis on the radio net," Kaleb informed her.

"Ok, I can do that, channel 434 right?" Sanchez replied. Julien Washington reached across the terrain map and snatched the handheld radio out of Sanchez's hands.

"No no no, 454," she said as she adjusted the freq on the radio and gave it back to her.

"Ok, we've got ten minutes left for planning, Sanchez, you need to brief this to the rest of the platoon with what time we've got left, we'll help you through it," Kaleb commanded. He knew Moore would be quick and aggressive to execute the flanking maneuver while Washington, level-headed and disciplined would be able to hold position, provide steady support and be more patient in helping Sanchez with the radio and coordination.

Unknown to the recruits, from the deck above on the USSN Vancouver, Sergeants Hollis and Randal watched intently on a video screen as Sanchez struggled through her mission brief.

"Man she's got a long way to go before I let her graduate," said Hollis.

"Command will never let that happen, you know we have to meet our sixty-five percent pass rate, we can't afford to drop anyone else. Besides, you know they'll just assign her to a POG (*poh-g*) (People Other than Grunts) administrative unit," Randal countered.

Hollis let out a sigh, "Yeah I know about the political B.S., it just pisses me off that we have to pass some one that I don't think is up to standard."

Randal looked closely at the video feed, "Man....that Taylor kid sure has his head screwed on straight though, wish we had more like him."

Forty-five minutes later, Mars orbit

The Raptor assault transport that housed 1st and 2nd squad was packed to the brim with Marine recruits, weapons and gear. Kaleb could barely move his legs as they were jammed up against another Marines' knee and leg armor in the seat across from him. His right leg soon fell asleep as his circulation was cut-off from sitting in the uncomfortable position. Kaleb closed his eyes and imagined being someplace other than the crowded, hot, interior of the Raptor transport. The Raptor detached from the Vancouver with the sound of released air pressure and retracting of the steel latch connecting the fifty-ton transport to the cruiser. Its rocket boosters ignited, propelling it straight into the red planet.

At 15,000 mph the two Raptors entered Mars's atmosphere, heat from atmospheric friction began to create a red glow on the underside of the ships' heat shielding. The Raptors deployed their braking sails on the exterior of the ships which jerked the Marines inside into each other causing one Marine's rifle to knock Kaleb in his helmet visor. The transport shuddered as the titanium braking sails slowed the space vehicles to just under 3,000 mph, five miles above the Martian surface. Temperatures inside the carrier rose to an almost unbearable one-hundred thirty degrees from the high speed entry. The pilot's then deployed their parachutes from the rear of the ships which again slowed the Raptors down to under 1,000 mph, now one mile above the surface of the planet.

Standing up inside the cabin of Kaleb's Raptor, Sergeant Randal grabbed onto a handle above his head and shouted through the platoon intercom in the Marines' helmets; " Thirty seconds!..... get ready!" The Raptor pulled a swift banking maneuver and gracefully touched down inside the crater just as it had been briefed by Staff Sergeant Hollis. Kaleb's heart was pounding from adrenaline as the pilot punched the switch that dropped the rear exit ramp.

"GO GO GO!" yelled Sergeant Randal as the recruits scrambled out of the carrier onto the rusty surface of the foreign planet.

Kaleb was first out the ramp as he led his squad into the crater, the noise from the Raptor's engines drowned out all other sound therefore Kaleb utilized hand and arm signals to line his squad up in a defensive position, waiting the other squads to get set and receive Sanchez's orders. The sub zero-temperatures of the planet pierced through his ABAS and chills ran up and down his body. High wind gusts filled with iron oxide dust almost knocked a few Marines off their feet. Luckily, movement in his heavily-armored sealed combat suit was much easier as Kaleb felt considerably lighter in the Martian gravity which was only thirty-eight percent that of Earth's. Sanchez scrambled out of the Raptor, struggling to see out of her over-sized helmet. Kaleb waved her over to his position as the Raptors re-fired their rocket boosters and lifted off back towards space. The sound of the rockets was deafening, but not loud enough to block out Staff Sergeant Hollis screaming over the internal net inside Kaleb's helmet.

"Sanchez! Dammit, you better orient yourself and figure out what the hell is going on!" She performed a 360-degree turn, trying to locate all her squads, they were set up in a perfect triangular security halt formation; she was the only Marine not in the prone position pulling security.

Kaleb transmitted over the platoon net; "Sanchez, look at me, I'm waving my hand, meet me and the squad leaders in the center of the formation and we can orient our data pads and verify our ingress route." With Hollis screaming in her ear she hobbled over to Kaleb and the squad leaders who were kneeling in the center of the security formation. Struggling under the weight of her armor, she plopped down and pulled out her data pad. The data pad was a small, pocket-sized device that contained holographic digital maps, messaging capability, route planning, and overlays that assisted each Marine while on the ground.

Sanchez studied the route that had been programmed into her data pad, "Ok, it looks like we're here, right in the middle of the crater, just like we're supposed to be… and we need to head….. ummm…" she looked around in several directions and back down at the data pad, "we need to head one-hundred, twenty-four degrees for three point-four clicks and we should hit that canyon."

Surprised that she was able to figure out the route on her own, Kaleb smiled, "Roger Sanchez. My squad will take point; we'll get us to that canyon quickly and quietly."

"Alright let's move," Sanchez ordered with a hint of self-confidence that was previously non-existent.

The platoon moved across the barren Martian landscape, with forty mile per hour wind gusts blowing dust and iron oxide and negative sixty degree Fahrenheit temperatures, it was an extremely hostile environment to travel dismounted in. Normally, Marines would assault an objective like this from an armored tank or wheeled-rover. It was all part of the exercise however, the dismounted movement was designed to give the recruits confidence in their ABAS suits' ability to protect them from the harsh environments of foreign planets. Kaleb felt more chills through his suit as the winds gusted but overall he felt comfortable in his body armor system. After trudging through the red-tinted wasteland for over an hour they finally reached the shallow canyon.

"Okay this is where we split up. Taylor take that hilltop and give us that sniper fire, I'll go with 2nd and 3rd up the canyon," Sanchez commanded through the platoon net.

"Let's go 1st, Robbie, take point and bring us on top of the mountain," Kaleb said calmly to his friend. It took his squad another thirty minutes to climb the hill, which was more or less a giant iron oxide/sand dune, and get set in position. His squad had two of the Marine standard issue MR-40 sniper rifles, equipped with a variable thermal scope with pushbutton settings for 2-5-9 and 14x magnification. It was almost twice as long as the MR-6 assault rifle when it was fully extended but the rifle had a unique ability to mechanically shorten the barrel with the push of a button for short range combat or more efficient storage. The semi-automatic MR-40 "Hellbringer" contained a ten round magazine that fired a large, armor-piercing 9.45x 64mm center-fire round that could devastate any thinly armored target. Kaleb and Hunt were the best shooters in the squad and it was agreed that they should take the shots on any simulation robot patrols they encountered.

Looking through a pair of digital binos, one of Kaleb's squad members called out, "Ok, I've got the warehouse on scope…..don't see anything else….. wait…. Got movement……. Yeah I got two, no three sim robots patrolling together around the rear of the building. There's some kind of tower that wasn't on the briefing map, and…. Yeah there's a sim robot in there too, all armed with what looks like assault rifles." Kaleb and Hunt readied their sniper rifles from the ABAS suit's hard point on the back of their armor. The rifles expanded to full length and the two Marines pulled out the bipods from the underside of the rifles for extra stability.

Kaleb keyed the platoon radio net, "Alpha 6 this is Alpha 1, we are set in position and have visual on warehouse, break... have positive ID on three enemy dismounts patrolling the outside of the building and one in a guard tower just south of the warehouse, over." There was no response. "Alpha 6 this is Alpha 1, over.... .. Alpha 6 this is Alpha 1, over.....dammit she's not monitoring the radio," Kaleb said in anger.

"What the hell could she be doing? We're within range of radio comms, and we're on top of this hill; she has to be able to hear us," said Hunt.

"Alpha 1 this is Alpha 6," a faint voice finally came over the net.

"Six this is one, did you copy my last transmission over?" Kaleb answered impatiently.

"Umm.. roger... uh... there's a slight problem going on down here over."

"Six this is one, what kind of problem over?"

"Well uh...Washington and Moore are arguing with me over which direction to take," Sanchez quietly said.

The canyon they had been traveling up had unexpectedly come to a fork that was not indicated on their data pads.

Sanchez tried to speak up, "Hey guys, looking at the map I think we should take it to the left, I did a calculation on the range and bearing to our next waypoint and that should be the right way." The other two squad leaders gave Sanchez a look of contempt and continued arguing.

"Naw Sanchez, check it out, we need to go up the right side, can't you see that the warehouse to supposed to be right here," Moore pointed to a spot on his data pad.

"Sanchez you go left and we'll go right, see who gets there first," Washington stated in annoyed disagreement with the recruit platoon leader.

Kaleb, cursing to himself, keyed the platoon net on his in-helmet radio. "Alpha 2 and 3 this is Alpha 1, break... Listen, I don't give a shit whatever the hell you guys are arguing about down there, Alpha 6 is the platoon leader for this mission; do whatever she says and let's get this over with; we're running out of oxygen just sitting here."

"We need to go left, I'm telling you guys now let's go," Sanchez exuded a sense of assertiveness.

Both the squad leaders shook their heads, "Alright whatever, when we get lost it's you that's gonna fail not me," Moore sneered.

Fifteen minutes later and the two squads were right where they were supposed to be, the large rock outcropping lay just in front of them just above the shallow canyon where they were to set up their support by fire position.

"Alright.... Sanchez was right, guess you never should've doubted her Moore," Washington laughed.

"Shut the hell up you were just as wrong as I was," Moore answered. Washington moved her squad up to the boulders undetected as 2nd squad continued to move up the canyon closer to the eastern flank of the warehouse. 3rd squad set up their heavy weapons in the support position behind the boulders and awaited orders to fire, so far none of the Marines had been detected by the sim robots patrolling the warehouse. Sanchez settled in behind the boulder next to Washington and observed the warehouse by enabling the zoom feature on her helmet's heads up display.

"Alpha 1 this is Alpha 6, I have a visual on the enemy dismounts, you are cleared to engage, over," Kaleb could tell that Sanchez sounded more confident on the radio as the mission went on.

"This is Alpha 1, roger over." Kaleb and Hunt took careful aim with their sniper rifles zooming in to 14x magnification.

"Wind at twenty-four miles per hour blowing from west to east, range to targets four-hundred seventy-five meters," their spotter said as he looked through his view scope.

"Alright, take the two on the left side of the building, I'll take the one in front of the bay door and the one in the tower on my order," Kaleb said to Hunt.

"Wilco, I'm on target, whenever you're ready," Hunt immediately answered.

"Alright… take em out." In unison the two Marines fired their sniper rifles. There was a light blue flash followed by the deafening sound of the 9.45mm round accelerating at 4,000 feet per second towards their targets. The two sim robots disintegrated into a mess of plastic shards and sparking wires by the impact of such force. Kaleb quickly obtained a sight picture on his second target and fired, followed half a second later by Hunt. In less than four seconds all four of the patrolling sim robots had been destroyed.

"Solid hits on all targets," the spotter reported.

"Alpha 6 this is Alpha 1, all targets destroyed, 2nd squad is clear to flank over," Kaleb informed Sanchez.

"That was awesome dude!" Hunt elated through 1st squad's internal net while slapping Kaleb on the back.

Kaleb looked at Hunt and cracked a smile, "Yeah that was pretty sweet wasn't it. I don't think I've ever actually shot anything that blew up like that before," he laughed.

Washington ordered her squad to open fire on the warehouse exterior with her heavy crew-served weapons. They would suppress any enemy targets in the warehouse while 2nd squad completed its flanking maneuver.

"Alpha 3 this is two, we're at the edge of where the canyon levels out; we're going to bound up to the warehouse across the open area. Make sure you don't shoot our asses!" Moore transmitted over the platoon net as his squad crested the bank of the canyon. Sanchez peeked around the corner of the boulder she was behind to see what was going on.

"Lift fire Washington, Lift Fire!!" she yelled as she watched second squad's assault.

"I know, I know, don't worry we got this!" Washington yelled back in an annoyed tone. "3rd squad lift and cease fire, lift and cease fire!" The gunners slowly lifted their weapons so they shot over top of the warehouse so as to avoid hitting 2nd squad as they rapidly approached the building. "Cease fire, cease fire," Washington yelled.

At that same instant 2nd squad lined up on the wall of the warehouse preparing to enter and clear the building. The firing stopped and everything went quiet. Moore stacked his squad up on both sides of the door entering the warehouse. The squad's motion sensor picked up four more enemy sim robots patrolling the interior. The layout was a simple open bay with two catwalks hanging down from the ceiling.

"Chavez, get up here with that flash-bang," Moore ordered. The young Marine ran up from the back of the stacked formation and pulled out a flash grenade from his load bearing vest. "Alright, on three kick the door in through the grenade and get out of there." The heavy-set Private nodded nervously, adrenaline and excitement was pumping through all the Marines. This was their first realistic training mission and everything was going fairly well up to this point.

"One… two… three… " Chavez gave the door a solid kick on Moore's count and it quickly flew open revealing the interior of the warehouse. He tossed in the flash-bang as rubber pellets reigned down from the catwalks above.

"Get down!!" Moore screamed. Chavez tried to jump out of the kill zone but he wasn't quick enough as two paint-filled pellets exploded on his right thigh, spilling red colored liquid around the impact area. Sergeant Randal, who was following and evaluating 2nd squad, immediately chimed in upon seeing the positive hits on Chavez's leg.

"That's a hit! Private Chavez now has severe wounds to his upper thigh and femoral artery and cannot walk!" The flash bang suddenly went off inside the warehouse, disorienting the sim robots for a few quick seconds. Moore knew he had to clear out the building and eliminate the immediate threat before giving aid to Private Chavez.

"Go Go Go! Get in there!" he yelled at his squad as he pushed them through the doorway. The squad entered and quickly dispatched the two disoriented sim robots on the catwalk above with their assault rifles. Two more were in the back corner and were summarily obliterated by accurate MR-6 rifle fire from Moore's Bravo team. Everything went quiet inside the warehouse as no enemy was left standing. Moore immediately drew his attention back to Private Chavez who was still in the doorway lying down as a simulated "wounded" Marine.

"Alpha 6 this is two, I've got one urgent wounded up here, require immediate medevac!" Moore sent over the net as he kneeled over top of Chavez who was over acting his part as playing the wounded soldier.

"Oh god it hurts so much! Please help me!! I just want to go home!" Chavez chuckled.

"Shut up you ass clown, quick dickin' around," Moore yelled back. The rest of Moore's squad quickly moved to clear the rest of the warehouse and verified that all enemies were KIA. "Sanchez did you copy? I've got one wounded up here and four enemy KIA, the warehouse is clear, need medevac ASAP over!"

Sanchez fiddled through the menus on her data pad but could not find the frequency she needed for medevac extraction. "Umm, wait one over," she answered. "What's the frequency for medevac again?" she broadcasted over the platoon net. Staff Sergeant Hollis, observing 3rd squad and Sanchez throughout the mission stepped in, furious.

"You've got to be shitting me Private! You mean to tell me you're the platoon leader for this mission and you don't know what the goddamn medevac frequency is?!! Get your head out of your ass and figure something out, Private Chavez now has three minutes left before he bleeds out so you'd better find it and call it in!"

"Ye.. Yes Sergeant," she answered timidly.

Kaleb called in on over the platoon net; "Alpha 6 this is one, it's 984 Zulu, I say again 984 Zulu is medevac freq over!"

"Ro.. Roger Alpha 1, calling it in now," Sanchez replied. "Dustoff 1, Dustoff 1, this is Alpha 6 over…. Request urgent medevac at grid, Golf Lima three-four-two-two, seven-eight-five-niner, over." The pilot of the designated medevac Raptor patrolling their sector acknowledged the radio call and banked the ship ninety degrees to turn into their location.

"Roger, good copy Alpha 6, ETA two mikes, the pilot called over the radio."

"It's gonna be close!" exclaimed Washington. The Raptor flew over their heads a minute later at speeds over 800 mph, at only one-hundred feet above the planet's surface. The extremely thin Martian atmosphere made it easy for the Raptor to attain considerable speeds at low altitude. Its engines roared as it circled around the warehouse and slowed its speed down for landing. Private Moore tossed a green smoke grenade out from his position with the "wounded" Marine so the pilot could easily identify where the casualty was.

"Alpha 6 this is Dustoff 1, I'm tracking your smoke, moving into position now over." The Raptor swooped in with engines rumbling and pitched up at almost a ninety degree angle above the smoke in order to slow its speed to a halt. The vertical thrusters fired and leveled the ship out as it extended its landing pads. Four members of second squad hastily carried Private Chavez in a canvas stretcher over to the ship as it touched down to the ground. The ramp lowered in the rear of the ship and two Marines ran out to help bring in the "wounded" Marine. They grabbed the sides of the litter and pulled

Chavez into the transport as the ramp began to close and seal behind them.

Staff Sergeant Hollis observed the medevac from his location behind the rock outcropping with 3rd squad and Sanchez. Satisfied, he spoke over the platoon comm. "Alright Alpha element, that's a wrap, endex, endex, endex." Sanchez breathed a sigh of relief as the words "endex" were music to her ears. "Endex" was the universal military term for exercise complete and that meant they would all be graduating basic training in just a few short days.

"Private Taylor, get your squad down here ASAP and let's get on the Raptors. We will have our after-action review in the ready room of the Vancouver," Hollis ordered over the radio.

Kaleb gained accountability of his squad members and their equipment and walked the short distance down to where the Raptors had touched down. Private Hunt ran up next to Kaleb as they neared the transports and spoke over the squad net.

"Dude, you know how bad-ass we are...? I mean, holy shit, did you see how those things just exploded when we hit them? Four-hundred and seventy-five meter shots baby! Trained fucking killers man!"

Kaleb looked at Hunt like he was overreacting, "Dude, calm down, you're like an eight year-old on a sugar-high or something, did you take your Ritalin today?" Kaleb jested.

"Hah, go ahead, laugh it up. Shit, I have to get twice as excited about everything just to make up for your lack of enthusiasm," Hunt countered sarcastically.

9

USSN Vancouver, Mars Orbit, Two hours later

The Marine recruits filed out of the Raptor transports and into the narrow interior corridors of the Vancouver. Exhausted from the physical and mental stress of combat operations in a hostile planetary environment, the recruits plopped down in the few chairs and the floor in the ready room, awaiting Sergeant Hollis's AAR.

"Hey Sanchez, not bad for your first rodeo," Private Moore gave her a slap on the back of her combat suit.

"Yeah I had to admit, I thought we were screwed when you were giving out that mission brief. But you had your shit wired down tight Sanchez, overcome and adapt baby, that's what we do," Washington complimented.

Sanchez's cheeks blushed, "Well I mean I would've been screwed if I didn't have you guys helping me out… and Taylor's plan, that, by the way, worked pretty damn good," she replied.

Kaleb spoke up in a sarcastic tone; "That's what we're here for, to keep you out of trouble right?"

"At Ease!" Washington sounded off as Staff Hollis and Sergeant Randal entered the ready room. The recruits immediately stood up in unison and went to the position of parade rest. Staff Sergeant

Hollis, with his hands on his hips, surveyed the room full of recruits and nodded.

"Alright Marines, take your seats and listen up. Anyone that talks out of turn during this after action review is going to be doing two hours of flutter kicks with Sergeant Randal understood?"

"YES SERGEANT," the Marines replied as Sergeant Randal crossed his arms and grinned. Hollis clicked a remote control in his right hand, causing the 3-D terrain map to appear with their objective highlighted.

"You should all be proud of yourselves, you've all come an extremely long way since we first met back in the Amazon and you were all a bunch of worthless civilians. Now you're officially USS Marines. Less than point-five percent of people in the United Star Systems have ever done what you have just accomplished. You are all above average individuals, who have earned their right to call themselves citizens. That is something you can take with you for the rest of your life and I thank you all for your commitment and dedication to our service. Now, with that being said, there were definitely some things that could've gone better out there. For starters, Privates Washington and Moore, on your feet!" The two Privates reluctantly stood up at the position of attention as all the other recruits turned to look at them, waiting for Staff Sergeant Hollis to continue.

"Don't *ever* let me catch you getting into an argument during a tactical operation. The entire mission was jeopardized because the two of you, who were supposed to be squad leaders, screwed up your land navigation and then tried to argue about it with your platoon leader! First of all, the route wasn't your decision to make, Private Sanchez was leading the mission, she gives the orders, you as squad leaders follow and set the example for the rest of your squad. Does everyone understand that?"

"YES SERGEANT!"

"Washington, Moore….. You're both fired as squad leaders, time now." The two Privates sheepishly nodded and sat back down. "Sanchez!"

"Yes Sergeant," she shakily replied.

"Hell of a job out there for what you had to work with."

"Thank you Sergeant," surprised at the compliment, she nodded.

"Taylor… you're going give Sanchez a break from Platoon Leader, she's already proved herself today. You are now the Platoon Leader for the remaining week of basic training," Hollis ordered. Kaleb reluctantly nodded, acknowledging his new position even though he cared not for the responsibility that came with it. Hollis took a step back, "Sergeant Randal, take them through the tactical review."

"Roger Staff Sergeant." The shorter, stocky, blonde-haired Sergeant stepped up to the terrain board and began to talk about the tactical mistakes the Marines had made and how to fix them in the future. The after action review lasted about thirty minutes, Kaleb didn't really pay much attention to it. He was pissed off that Sanchez got all the credit for his plan and he had to save her ass again when she didn't have the right frequency during the medevac drill. *It doesn't matter anyways*, he thought. *One more week and I'll be out of here and into a real unit.* He'd no longer be a lowly recruit; he'd be an actual Marine. He'd come a long way since his time on Talos station. He now was more confident in himself than ever, he felt like he could accomplish anything he wanted in life. His thoughts drifted back to his parents as he continued to day dream through the AAR. Maybe now he'd have a chance to get back at the slavers. He'd heard Marines had been doing raids into Ares Alliance territory recently to destroy slaving and mercenary outposts, *hope I can get into one of those units after graduation*, he thought to himself.

"Taylor! Wake the hell up over there!" Randal yelled as Kaleb suddenly was jerked back to reality from his day dream.

"Huh? Oh, Yes Sergeant?" he answered. Randal annoyingly emphasized his words as he repeated his question that Kaleb apparently did not hear the first time.

"Do...you... have anything... else... to...add... platoon... leader?"

"Uh... no Sergeant, I thought it went pretty good," Kaleb replied not being able to think of anything intelligent to say at the moment. He was tired and just wanted to get some rest. The briefing had gone on long enough for him.

"Alright, well if that's it... everyone get below deck and get rested up... we're headed back to Earth" Randal ordered. The tired Marines in the room gave a couple cheers as to the news of the return trip to Earth. Mars wasn't exactly the most hospitable place in the universe; neither was being stuck on a small cruiser in space for that matter. Kaleb hated being on spaceships. He felt like he had no control, his life was in the hands of the helmsman and the Navy crew. He preferred to be on the ground with his rifle.

"Oh, and uh, Taylor," Randal stopped Kaleb as he was attempting to walk out of the ready room. "Staff Sergeant Hollis wants to see you in the NCO quarters, he's waiting for you."

"Roger Sergeant," Kaleb obediently nodded and split off from the rest of the Marines to the upper deck. *What does he need to see me for? Damn, I just want to go to sleep. It's probably some platoon leader admin bullshit I gotta do.* Kaleb trudged up two decks on the cruiser to the NCO quarters. He softly knocked on the door to Staff Sergeant Hollis's berthing area.

"Enter," he heard a voice from inside. Kaleb stepped in and stood at the position of parade rest. "At ease Private, take a seat." Hollis said, motioning to the single chair against the wall of the small, dark room. Kaleb slowly sat down. "So.... Private Taylor, hell of a mission wasn't it?" Kaleb tried to decipher Hollis's body language to figure out if he was here for an ass-chewing or a compliment.

"I thought it went well Staff Sergeant," he answered.

"Listen, the reason why I brought you in here is because I've got an opportunity for you."

Kaleb raised his eyebrow, "An opportunity Sergeant?"

"Yes that's what I said an opportunity. I've read your background files Taylor. You're a tough kid. Parents and sisters killed or MIA on the slaver attack on Hastati couple of years back, survived a face to face encounter with Darius Wendover, wanted slaver kingpin of the Septus Magnus Cluster, and you were the only person to come out of that rescued transport with no injuries."

Kaleb adjusted his position in the chair, uncomfortable with how the conversation was going and at how much the Staff Sergeant apparently knew about his history; "With all due respect Staff Sergeant, is there a point to this? I prefer not to relive my past as much as possible."

Staff Sergeant Hollis, ignoring Kaleb's question continued on as he flipped through pages in his military personnel record. "Top scores on the Marine physical fitness test, number one in the platoon in marksmanship training….. oh and by the way, I know that plan for that last mission Sanchez did was all yours. I watched on video screen from the upper deck as you took Sanchez step by step through the tactical planning process. You're one of the best Marines I've ever had the privilege to train Taylor, you're a leader and you've got a natural ability for this stuff. So, not to beat around the bush anymore, I'm recommending you for Marine Recon Training Taylor. I think you've got what it takes to be the best of what the USS Marines has to offer."

"Thank you Staff Sergeant," Kaleb answered, not knowing if he should be excited or dreading this new assignment. He had heard a lot of rumors about Recon training from his peers in basic. It was allegedly the toughest course to go through for the Marine infantryman. They were supposedly the elite Marine units, used only for the toughest missions. His buddy Hunt always talked about them and about how all he ever wanted to do since he was a kid was be Recon. Kaleb wasn't entirely sure if that was for him, just being an infantryman was hardcore enough at this point.

"Don't thank me yet Taylor, Recon School is some of the toughest training in the United Star Systems military. You're going to be going through twelve more weeks of advanced leadership, marksmanship, close quarters combat, land nav, and hand to hand combat training, just to name a few things. When you graduate, you will be a trained killer in the true essence of the word. Over the last three years only twenty percent of all initial Recon candidates actually make it to graduation. Once you do graduate you'll be on the front lines of any conflict the USS government gets itself into. It's a huge commitment and you have to be mentally prepared to do this Taylor. So, what's your answer? I need to submit the names today of who's going."

Kaleb looked directly at Hollis; "Sergeant if you think I can do it I will do it. If this gives me the best chance to kill the kinds of people that took my family from me then I know I won't fail."

Hollis smiled, "I figured you'd say something along those lines. Don't worry, I've seen a lot of Marines come and go and I know that you won't have any trouble making it through this training. I'll put your name forward today and I should have a class date by the end of the week."

"Thank you Staff Sergeant. I've learned so much these past nine weeks from you and Sergeant Randal. You guys changed my life," Kaleb replied.

"That's our job Taylor...Oh, and one more thing. I'm putting in Privates Hunt and Moore for Recon as well. They might struggle through the training. They are going to look to you for leadership and guidance when times get hard and one of them wants to quit. Don't let them. You're the leader of this basic training platoon, the rest of the Privates listen to and respect you. Whether you want the responsibility or not, that's just the way it is. Dismissed Taylor, get some rest."

"Roger staff Sergeant," Kaleb did an about face and walked out, contemplating his decision as he made his way first to the galley for a quick meal and then recruit quarters. *I guess this is what I need to do if I want to be the best. I don't understand why I always have to be the leader for everything though. It's so much easier just to follow orders than to give them.*

After stopping at the ship galley for a quick meal, Kaleb opened the small steel hatch and stepped into the recruit quarters of the Vancouver. Twenty small bunks stacked three-high lined the room with Marines' gear and weapons scattered everywhere. Moore ran up to Kaleb as he entered the room.

"Whoa! There he is!" Moore gave him a punch in the shoulder and then put his arm around Kaleb as they walked. "So Taylor, you hear the big news?!!"

Annoyed and tired Kaleb answered "No what's that man?"

"They want to send us to Recon training baby! Best of the best right here!"

"Yeah I heard, you, me, and Hunt right?"

Hunt interjected loudly as he lay in his bunk across the berthing area. "Naw man, Moore declined it, said he wanted to be in some POG admin unit so he can hook up with females and work in an office all day. He's a little bitch if you ask me, but hey, I won't be missing his redneck mouth."

Moore countered with a smirk on his face. "That's right assholes, I'm good enough to be Recon, but I declined. Here's why: while y'all are knee deep in some bullshit on a planet with no oxygen and freezing your asses off with no food or water, I'll be warmin' up with the finance and admin chicks up on a cruiser in orbit baby!"

Kaleb laughed and shook his head as he jeered at Moore "Yeah but I heard when Recon Marines get back from mission they steal all the women from the POG's and show them what it's like to be with a real man and not some bitch ass office jockey."

"Hah, keep tellin yourself that, you'll see. My cousin went Recon, said all he did was hump a hundred and twenty pounds a' gear all day and sleep in a cold ditch every-night. It ain't all it's cracked up to be," Moore shot back.

"Moore, it's ok if you're scared, I understand," Kaleb said with sarcasm as he walked over to his bunk which was directly across from Hunt's. He was intently reading the newest edition of Playboy Interstellar Edition magazine that had been circulating around the male berthing for the past two days. Kaleb climbed up to his middle bunk and put his hands on his forehead, breathing a sigh of relief knowing that basic training was all but complete aside from the graduation ceremony. He turned his head to look at Hunt.

"Dude, let me see that when you're done," Kaleb stated while lying in his bunk. "The pages better not be stuck together either."

Hunt didn't answer Kaleb's request, he just continued to stare intently at the pictures contained in the magazine.

"Hey retard, I'm talking to you," Kaleb taunted as he threw a pillow across the berthing, hitting Hunt's magazine and causing it to fall on to the deck.

"Whoa, what the hell man? I was reading the articles!" Hunt responded.

"So you're doing this Recon thing too huh?" Kaleb attempted to steer the conversation towards something a little more serious.

Hunt looked at Kaleb intently, "Uh, yeah. I mean, why the hell wouldn't I? I talk about it all the time. You're going too right? Don't be a pussy and bitch out like Moore is doing."

"Well, yeah... I mean.... I guess I've got nothing else to do. I figure we'll be in the same class again. Damn I'm getting tired of dealing with your shit all the time. Maybe I'll get put in a different platoon from you this time," Kaleb replied sarcastically to Hunt, trying to sound un-nerved about the upcoming training.

Hunt gave a mocking reply, "Don't worry, I'll be there to walk you through it all like everything else.….You know, you should like, pay me man, like every two weeks just give me a pay check."

"Pay you? What the hell for?" Kaleb inquired.

"Because… I always have to drag your ass through every single training event. Without me you'd probably be a colossal failure," Hunt jeered.

Kaleb reached down and quickly grabbed the porno magazine that was on the floor between the two of them. "No thanks, I'll just take this from you instead," Kaleb smiled as he opened up the pages of the magazine.

"Dammit, I wasn't done reading that one yet!" Hunt exclaimed.

10

Six years later, 2176- USSN Athens, United Star Systems Naval cruiser, presence patrol on the outskirts of the Pericles star cluster, 185 light years from Earth

"Taylor!" Corporal Robbie Hunt said as he shook Kaleb's shoulder with his right hand, waking him from a deep sleep. Kaleb grumbled and rolled over, attempting to delay the inevitable wake up call. "C'mon man, we got a company briefing in ten mikes!" Hunt tried to persuade Kaleb.

"Fuck off man…," Kaleb gave an angry reply and turned back over to go back to sleep.

"I'm serious dude, I think it's important this time; commander's called in all the leadership to the briefing room……" There was no response from Kaleb. "Whatever dude, suit yourself if you want to get your nuts crushed by Gunny Norton for not being there."

Kaleb grunted and reluctantly swung his legs off of his rack, his feet hitting the deck. He rubbed his green eyes and ran his fingers through his dark brown, medium-faded, military-style hair. His face looked slightly older than his current twenty-four years of age with a two inch long scar across the bottom of his chin that he received during the strenuous Recon training.

"Dammit," Kaleb mumbled to himself as Corporal Hunt slammed this door to the berthing. He sat up and began to throw on his dark blue/gray digital camo patterned duty fatigues over his lean, muscular, 6'0" 205-pound frame. The mirror that hung inside the door of his locker displayed six years of honorable service to the USS Marines upon his uniform. A Marine Recon tab was sewn upon the left shoulder of his uniform. An expert sniper's badge pinned on above his left chest pocket along with master planetary assault qualification insignia. Kaleb finished in the top three of his class at Recon School over five years ago and was now considered one of the best sniper squad leaders in the entire USS military. He advanced to the rank of Sergeant ahead of his peers and was under consideration for promotion to Staff Sergeant in the coming months.

Corporal Robbie Hunt had made it through the intense Recon training with Kaleb and they had pretty much become best friends ever since. They agreed to try to get assigned to the same unit after Recon training and after pulling a few strings with the human resources personnel they were able to make it happen. They both were promoted to Sergeant in the same month and had a healthy competition going on to see who could advance quicker than the other. Unfortunately for Hunt, a bar fight incident while on leave back on Earth a few months ago got him arrested and thrown in jail for several days. The resulting consequence was a demotion from Sergeant down to Corporal and relinquishing his squad leader position. The Marines would not tolerate a leader who couldn't control their personal life and they used Hunt as an example. He was now just a team leader in the platoon's 1st squad under Sergeant Yao, a fact that Kaleb was sure to taunt Hunt about on a daily basis.

After completion of Recon and scout sniper school, Kaleb was assigned to 1st platoon, Alpha Company, 1st Marine Recon Battalion, 26th USS Marine Regiment. Alpha 1-26 was one of the most elite Marine unit's in the short history of the USS military. As an entry requirement into the unit, all Marines had to have earned the Recon tab on their uniform. The 1ˢᵗ Marine Recon battalion was the only Marine unit to have this stringent qualification standard. Only the best Marine infantrymen were able to be assigned to the unit and Kaleb proved himself to be one of them. The unit hadn't seen much action since Kaleb and Robbie Hunt arrived as Privates four and a half years ago; a few skirmishes here and there with mercenaries and slavers trying to unsuccessfully raid USS colonies. The unit was mostly still green when it came to full spectrum combat operations.

The Conflict for Unification against the secessionist Ares Alliance had slowly dragged on for six more years since Kaleb entered basic training with no side gaining the upper hand. It was almost as if neither side wanted to risk a major offensive against the other and with the vast distances between the colonies it was easier for both governments to stay out of each other's way. It seemed to Kaleb that the USS government wanted the alleged "war" to continue so that the corporate defense contracting lobbyists could continue to turn a profit by producing war materials. It was assured to the people by the USS government that the massive defense budget was necessary to interstellar security, using the raid on Kaleb's home planet of Hastati as a source of justification.

Taxpayers in the major colonies had begun to grow weary of the unending war and the massive cost that it required. With new sources of cheap antimatter found on the moon of Alexander II within United Star Systems controlled territory, the purpose of the limited war seemed fruitless to more and more citizens on Earth and the rest of the major colonies. With new star systems and garden world colonies being discovered each year, public opinion shifted towards a strong anti-war sentiment. Kaleb hoped that the USS government would fall in line with the public opinion and end the war sooner rather than later. He was growing weary of the multiple eight-month long presence patrols in deep space that seemed to accomplish nothing. An eight months on, two months off work schedule didn't seem very fair to Kaleb. At twenty-four years old he felt he was missing out on what was supposed to be the best years of his life. Instead of having fun partying or going to a good college back in the colonies, he was constantly stuck out in deep space on endless patrols. Besides, the Ares Alliance mercenaries already knew the USS Navy patrol patterns by now. Space was a very large place and they easily found alternate routes around their presence patrols to their destinations. At Faust drive speed it was nearly impossible to track an enemy starship let alone obtain a firing solution on it. Needless to say, Kaleb failed to see the point of their current operation in the Pericles cluster. The Admiralty insisted however that a presence patrol "show of force" strategy was the best deterrent against Ares Alliance raids on USS colonies.

Why the hell are we having a briefing at 3am? (ship time) Nothing has happened in this sector for weeks, Kaleb thought to himself as he used an electric razor to trim his two-day old beard. *This better not be another bullshit safety stand down day.* (One of the Marines in another company broke his leg while trying to slide down one of the ship's deck ladders the day before). Any minor accident on board the ship usually resulted in an all-day safety class since the Marines typically had nothing else to do; given the lack of any enemy engagements on their current deployment.

Kaleb nonchalantly walked down the corridors of the Athens towards the briefing room. He'd spent a lot of time in space since joining the USS military and he'd become immune to the side effects of space travel. Most new recruits would come down with "space sickness" as it was called by the Naval servicemen. Living in artificial gravity, breathing recycled oxygen, and exposure to cosmic radiation takes its toll on the human body over time. Nausea, vomiting, headaches, stomach cramps and insomnia are very common in personnel aboard ship that aren't used to long periods in space.

Kaleb walked through the already opened hatch that gained him entry into Alpha Companies' small briefing room. Robbie Hunt waved his hand to signal his location to Kaleb amidst the small, poorly lit, 25x20' room crammed with over twenty Marines. Apparently, all of the platoon leaders, platoon Sergeants, and squad leaders in the company had been called in by the commander for this briefing. Kaleb found it very odd that the Company Commander was holding this meeting so early. Just as Kaleb sat down the lights in the room dimmed and a map along with satellite imagery and overlays popped up on the display screen. Captain James Williams, the Alpha Company Commander, opened the door to the room and confidently walked in front of the display.

"Company Commander!" the Alpha Company 1st Sergeant yelled as the Marines in the small room snapped to the position of attention, rendering the typical custom and courtesy to their commanding officer. Captain Williams was fairly tall, about 6'2" with thinning, cropped, black hair. A native of Earth, his descent was a mixture of several different races, a commonality among most humans in the 22nd century. He had a plain English, soft spoken accent; however his words always inspired and motivated the company. He had been in command of Alpha Company for just nine months and had established himself as a fair, respectable leader with a tactical prowess well above his peers. He was well-liked amongst all the Marines in the company including Kaleb and Hunt. Twenty Marines sat at attention as the room went silent, waiting for the commander to divulge the reason for him calling them in at such an odd hour. Kaleb pulled out his data pad and stylus, preparing to take any pertinent information down.

"Alright Vipers, (the company callsign) take seats," Captain Williams said as began the meeting.

Robbie Hunt smirked and whispered to Kaleb as the Company Commander continued on, "It's so damn crowded in here, how the hell are we supposed to take seats?" The two remained standing up in the cramped room.

"I'm sure you are all butt hurt about being called in here so early for no apparent reason. But guess what, we're in the Marines and sometimes you have do shit like this. I know this deployment has been uneventful and extremely boring for all of you up to this point. But it's time to reach down between your legs and grab both balls because we've got a high-speed mission coming down the pipe that has Recon written all over it. So pull out your data pads and take some notes gentlemen…..this one is for real," the room was silent as the Alpha Company leadership awaited this surprise mission brief from the commander.

Captain Williams began his brief. "Two hours ago, a United Star Systems Intelligence Office (USSIO) deep space research post dropped out of contact with our encrypted interstellar communications. Their last transmission stated that they were under attack from an unknown enemy force and had suffered significant casualties. The research station, located here, (Captain Williams pointed to a moon on the star map with his laser pointer) consists of several different modular facilities and bunkers on this dry, desert-covered moon called Gardner IV, which can be seen orbiting the gas giant labeled A330221 here. First instinct by Naval Command is that this attack was conducted by Ares Alliance mercenary forces from the Shinwar colony that discovered the research station's location during a roving patrol. That means expect any enemy forces to be well-armed and aggressive. Intel also believes the motive for their attack is not only to data mine the research station's computer files but also to take the scientists at the station as hostages and/or slaves. Being that the Athens is the closest ship within twenty-five light years to this backwater star system, 1st Recon Battalion has been tasked to infiltrate the moon under cover of darkness, rescue any hostages, and eliminate or capture any enemy forces. Since we have a reputation for being the best, Colonel West has tasked Alpha Company with the mission of entering and clearing these two separate bunker complexes that comprise the research facility, located at these grids," Captain Williams used the touch screen display to enlarge the graphics of the two fenced-in bunker facilities.

Kaleb leaned over to whisper to Hunt, "Holy shit, hostage rescue? Did you ever train for that?"

Hunt shook his head, keeping focused on the commander's brief, "Nope, not really, guess on the job training is the best way to learn though right?"

"Listen up Marines, this is what we've trained for, we're going in dismounted under the cover of darkness, if this doesn't get your blood pumping I don't know what will," Williams proclaimed to the group.

"OOO-RAH SIR!! Music to my ears!" Kaleb's big, stocky platoon Sergeant, Gunnery Sergeant Norton, yelled with enthusiasm upon hearing the words "dismounted." A few of the men in the room laughed as the commander continued.

"Huh huh… retard," Kaleb gave a fake chuckle and quietly mumbled to Hunt, mocking Gunny Norton's comment.

"Ok, the plan is simple Marines," Williams continued on. "All three platoons will conduct a high-speed Raptor orbital descent onto the moon's dark side hopefully avoiding detection from any enemy radar and thermal scanners…..Lieutenant Freeborn."

"Yes sir!" Lieutenant Travis Freeborn, the young 1st platoon leader acknowledged to his commander that he was paying attention.

"You will be inserted here, in this valley about six clicks from bunker complex number one. From there you will move dismounted north to the bunker, set up a cordon outside of complex, enter and clear this smaller, three-story underground facility, eliminating any enemy threat you encounter while rescuing any possible hostages along the way," Williams ordered.

"Roger sir," Freeborn quickly replied as he downloaded the coordinates of the facility to his data pad.

"Second and 3rd platoon will insert together here, five clicks west of the larger bunker facility shown here and do the same. Third, you will provide the outer cordon while 2nd platoon enters and clears this four-story bunker. I will be traveling with 2nd and 3rd platoon during the mission to provide command and control for both operations. Once our cordons are set in place, the 1st Sergeant, along with headquarters platoon and the XO will establish a Casualty Collection Point (CCP) at this grid, in between the two facilities for extraction of any hostages or enemy prisoners of war."

Williams cued up a zoomed-out view of the moon with statistical data displayed next to it on the screen. "The moon of Gardner IV consists of a desert landscape dotted with large, cactus-like vegetation. It gets very hot, even a night, and should be well above one-hundred degrees at the insertion zone. It does contain a thin atmosphere of nitrogen and oxygen along with a minimal set of carbon-based set of plant and animal life. NCO's need to make sure your Marines bring an oxygen tank just in case it gets too hard to breathe as it is well below the 21.8% oxygen that we're used to. Gravity will be a friendly 0.7 that of Earth's so shouldn't have any issues there." Williams then paused and surveyed the room of Marines. "Another thing, heat and radiation from the blue giant star will be too intense during the day cycle to conduct operations effectively. That means we need to get in and get out before sunrise so we don't get asses fried down there. Gentlemen, I also cannot stress enough the importance of stealth on this mission. It is imperative that we remain undetected as we move in dismounted to our objectives so as to not alarm any occupying enemy force. This could cause them to eliminate hostages or flee the site with sensitive intel gathered from the research station's computers." Williams looked up at the open hatch to the briefing room that Kaleb was standing next to.

"Sergeant Taylor, can you shut that door please," Williams said calmly.

Kaleb nodded and pulled the hatch shut, turning a lever on the right side of the bulkhead to seal it.

A stern look formed on the Captain's face as the hatch closed. "Gentlemen… it has been made extremely clear to me by Colonel West that this research facility holds some extremely sensitive material that is several levels above top-secret compartmentalized security. The USS government absolutely does not want the information getting into the wrong hands. Now, normally I would say just bombard the station from orbit and destroy everything, but the high-level spooks at IO want the facility left intact. So, the main objective is to ensure that no enemy forces are allowed to escape with this material alive, even if that means jeopardizing the lives of hostages. Elimination of the enemy threat is the priority no matter what the cost understood?"

The Marines in the room nodded in acknowledgement as some let out a quiet "Roger." Curious, Kaleb raised his hand in an effort to ask a question.

"Sergeant Taylor, what is it?" Williams said tersely.

"Sir, uh, any idea what this sensitive material is and where exactly inside the bunker complex it's located….just so we don't like accidently blow it up or something?" Some of the Marines in the room laughed as the atmosphere slightly lightened up.

"Not a damn clue," Williams said with frustration. "I asked Colonel West the same question and even he didn't know the answer. We're just the grunts that have to go in and do the dirty work I guess. Once we clear the facility of the enemy threat we are to call in a special reaction team from IO to secure the sensitive material and transport it to a new, undisclosed location." Williams paused again to look around the room. "Any other questions?" None of the Marines spoke as the room went silent.

"Alright, NCOs you're dismissed to go get your Marines ready to roll. I've got some mission details to go over with the platoon leaders and they will be giving their platoon briefs shortly. We should be in the orbit of Gardner IV in two hours, plan on Raptor load-up at 0445 ship-time roger?" Williams ordered.

The NCOs in the room including Kaleb and Hunt stood up in unison and saluted "Vipers leads the way sir!" they shouted as one unit and began to file out of the room.

Recon Marines were specially trained for light-dismounted operations, moving in on foot to an objective. They rarely had the opportunity for a dismounted mission however, as armored rovers and tanks dominated the modern battlefield. These vehicles could much more easily traverse long distances in harsh environments than a Marine on foot. A typical USS Marine Recon platoon consisted of two rifle squads, (1st and 2nd squad), a heavy weapons squad (3rd squad), and a sniper squad (4th squad). The setup allows the heavy weapons squad to lay down cover fire while the two rifle squads fire and maneuver on the target. The sniper squad provides accurate fire from cover and concealment surrounding the objective. The sniper squad usually split up into two-man sniper teams and surrounds an objective if possible. All Recon Marines were equipped with the latest in United Star Systems technology in combat armor, motion sensors, and heads-up display targeting systems. In addition, all Marines that volunteered for Recon had to sign a waiver, in which they agreed to undergo a series of genetic upgrades. Genetic augmentation for elite military units began after 2145, despite fierce opposition from right-wing political groups who believed the human condition should not be altered in any way. A relatively new technology, genetic upgrades in Marines had proven to be very successful and safe as long as they were implemented over time and in very small doses. It is estimated that only three to four percent of Marines reported serious side effects such as deformities and severe sickness or death. An acceptable figure for USS Military Command when considering the benefits gained though gene therapy. Over a six month period, all Recon Marines would undergo genetic augmentation therapy ending with an overall rate of twenty percent faster blood clotting, guaranteed 20/10 vision, twelve percent increase in reaction time, and a ten percent increase in bone and muscle density. A USS Recon Marine was the most elite ground troop that humanity had ever fielded and was far superior to any mercenary force employed by the Ares Alliance.

As for the 1st platoon leadership, Kaleb looked up to his platoon Sergeant, Gunnery Sergeant Norton, as his supervisor and mentor but disagreed with his brash, overbearing personality. A veteran of twenty years of service, Norton was lifetime Marine, he lived and breathed the corps and cared little about anything else. His leathery skin, polished and shaved head and raspy voice were a result of his long tenure of service as a grunt. His unbending personality and passion for being a Marine was sometimes his downfall, acting on impulses rather than thinking things out and developing a solid plan. Kaleb thought he was too old-school, making too big of a deal about petty issues such as uniform standards or customs and courtesies while ignoring the big picture. He and Kaleb had been in their fair share of arguments over the past few years and Kaleb felt that Norton treated his squad as second-rate simply because they were snipers. There were some in the Marines that looked down upon snipers as loners and somewhat cowardly, killing their enemies from over one thousand meters away from a hidden location, not acting as part of a coordinated fire team or platoon. Kaleb didn't let these stereotypes bother him or his squad however, and the majority of the platoon understood the necessity of the snipers and appreciated having them around, except for Gunny Norton it seemed.

His platoon leader, Lieutenant Travis Freeborn on the other hand was almost a total opposite of Gunnery Sergeant Norton. He was very young, twenty-four to be exact, and looked even younger.

A college kid, he had only two years of total service in the Marines. He was of average height with blonde hair, blue eyes, and a relatively thin build for a Recon Marine. He was sharp, intelligent, and a quick learner. What Kaleb liked most about him was that he listened to his NCO's when he needed to. Lieutenant Freeborn thought highly of Kaleb and would frequently consult him on tactical planning and advice. He had served as 1st platoon leader for over eighteen months now and Kaleb had full confidence in his ability to lead, despite his lack of experience.

Kaleb and Hunt stopped by the Athens' small galley on the way back to the berthing area for a quick meal before the mission. Kaleb sat in silence, staring at the wall as he shoved food into his mouth. Hunt looked up at him trying to get his attention.

"Hey... you alright man?" Kaleb gave no response as he continued to daydream, oblivious to Hunt and his surroundings. Hunt waved his hand in front of his face to get a reaction. "Hello... are you listening asshole?"

Kaleb looked back at Robbie as he broke out of his trance, "Huh... what's up?"

"Dude, are you alright, it's like your hypnotized or something. Usually you're bitching and complaining about shit right after we get out of a mission brief; today you haven't said a word."

Kaleb answered, "Yeah, I'm fine. I'm just thinking you know."

"Thinking.....about what?" Hunt replied.

"You know....thinking that maybe I got a score to settle on this mission. These Ares Alliance mercenaries from Shinwar; I mean, these have got to be the same group of people that killed my parents. This is the whole reason I became a Marine, to get back at these guys and this is my chance...I feel like I want to get up close to these cocksuckers and make them feel the pain I went through when they attacked my family."

Hunt shook his head. "I don't know man. That was like seven or eight years ago. Those slavers that sacked Hastati are probably long gone, and second, you know better than to let personal feelings get mixed in with a mission. You don't want to be acting on impulses down there. I'd just treat this like any other operation. You gotta be able to keep your composure down there."

Kaleb gave a lighthearted reply, "Man everyday that goes by you sound more and more like an officer. Are you sure you didn't put in for the selection board?"

"Alright fine, if you want to go cowboy on this mission and take out mercenaries' execution style be my guest, I'm not going stop you. And no, I didn't put in for the selection board. It's a sad day for the Marines when they ever make me into a goddamn officer." Corporal Hunt stood up and grabbed his tray, "Alright man, I'm going to go wake up my guys, you bringing your ass to the platoon brief on time or you going to be late as usual?"

Kaleb answered sarcastically, "Of course, you know the LT can't start without me, I'm the main effort of the platoon."

"Snipers? Main effort? More like puts out the least effort," Hunt replied as he began to leave his seat.

"Hey, watch your tone...*Corporal*," Kaleb said sarcastically.

"Yeah laugh it up, it's not my fault I got arrested, I was drunk. How can they demote someone for being drunk?" Hunt complained.

Suddenly the lighthearted conversation ended as the two bickering Marines couldn't help but take notice of the attractive female figure steadily approaching their table. The woman in her early twenties wore tightly-fitted flight suit coveralls and had her long bright, blonde hair neatly tied up in order to meet female Naval uniform standards. Her near perfect 5'6" feminine athletic build caused Hunt to give her an obvious look over as she drew closer. Her green eyes locked onto Kaleb's as she smiled and spoke in a playful tone.

"Hey guys what's going on?" asked Fight Lieutenant Jen

Thompson, one of the four Raptor pilots that were assigned to taxi Alpha Company Marines around for the duration of the current deployment on the Athens. She just so happened to be 1st platoon's pilot in particular. The Marines in Kaleb's platoon frequently talked about her as if she was some sort of playboy model, way too attractive to be serving on a USS Naval ship. Kaleb had spoken with her on frequent occasions throughout their patrol in the Pericles Cluster in an effort to find out if she was single or even interested at all but to no avail so far. Female Naval officers typically didn't pay much attention to enlisted Marines or even NCOs. He thought Lieutenant Thompson might be different though, maybe not as stuck up as the rest. She always came by to talk to the Marines she was flying around to try and get to know them, something Kaleb could appreciate. Plus her easygoing, happy-go-lucky personality helped to lighten things up before a mission.

Hunt's face turned slightly red as he blurted out a sentence with a slight laugh, "Not much ma'am. What are you doing up so early? You flying us out today?" Kaleb smiled back at her waiting for response to Hunt's statement.

"Yeah, totally, looks like we finally have a real mission to go on. I'm pretty stoked about it." She gave a lighthearted reply, continuing to smile at Kaleb.

Kaleb sarcastically shook his head, "Oh no, you're our Raptor pilot today? Damn, can you at least take it easy on the throttle this time? The guys in my squad were puking everywhere last time you took us out."

Thompson smiled and laughed. Kaleb's attempt at flirting appeared to be successful. "Haha very funny, come on, you know you guys like to fly with me the most. Besides, I found a way to broadcast music over the onboard intercom that you guys can listen to during the drop. Just give me what you want played and I'll hook it up for you. Now what other pilots would do that?"

"Uh oh LT, you trying to break the rules now? You know Captain Williams won't like that music interfering with his company radio net," Hunt replied in a playful voice, toying with the inexperienced Lieutenant.

"Hah, yeah but I don't have to answer to him; remember, I'm in the Navy, not the Marines like you guys," Thompson objected.

Kaleb responded to the Lieutenant before Hunt could open his mouth, "Don't listen to Corporal Hunt, he's full of shit, Captain Williams knows better than to hassle our platoon."

Thompson laughed once again and smiled, "Haha, ok, well, so yeah Sergeant Taylor, just send whatever music you want played to my data pad and I'll take care of it for you on the drop," she said as she tapped a few buttons to transmit her data pad email address to Kaleb's.

"Alright LT, I'll talk to the guys and pick out some good songs. Maybe the music will help you fly a little smoother this time," Kaleb teased again and took a sip from his glass of diet soda.

Thompson smirked and replied with sarcasm; "Keep talking crap and I'll just do barrel rolls the whole way down to the surface."

"Sounds like fun to me," Hunt blurted out as he chewed his food. Kaleb just shook his head.

"Hah, yeah you say that now....Well, alright guys, good talking to you, I'm going to eat this breakfast real fast and head to a pilot's briefing. See you on the Raptor in a few," Thompson stated as she walked off and sat at a table across the galley with several other pilots.

"Ok LT, see you later," Kaleb replied. He and Hunt closely watching her athletic figure as she turned to walk away. Two of the male flight officers sitting at her table gave them an obvious look of contempt from across the way.

"Dude, she's totally into you man, did you see how she was looking at you? If you don't get up with that then you're officially gay," Hunt sneered quietly once Thompson was a safe distance away.

Kaleb took one last bite of his scrambled eggs and replied, "Hah, yeah right, she's probably already hooking up with one of those asshole pilots over there at her table. What would she want with a lowly grunt- NCO like me?" he responded lightheartedly, despite the fact that he did feel some degree of attraction going on between the two of them.

Hunt threw his arms up and shook his head, "Whatever man, you're impossible. A hot flight-officer chick obviously wants you and you're too scared to give it to her." He picked up his tray and turned to go dump his trash. "I'm telling you, a girl like her doesn't want those soft ass Naval officer dudes, she's clearly into real men….like us, trust me."

"Yeah ok, like I'm really going to listen to advice about women from you," Kaleb answered back as Hunt walked to the galley exit. He took a final sip from his soda and followed Hunt out the exit hatch, ensuring to look back and wave at Lieutenant Thompson before leaving. She caught Kaleb's gesture out of the corner of her eye and eagerly returned the friendly wave.

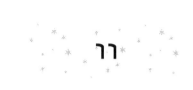

USSN Athens, en-route on Faust drive vector to Gardner IV

Kaleb opened the hatch to enter his sniper squad's berthing area. Taped on the door was a print-out that read: "4/1/A, Wolfpack," meaning 4th squad, 1st platoon, Alpha Company, "Wolfpack" being the platoon call sign. He flipped the switch on the bulkhead turning on the white lights in the compartment.

"Wake up snipers, let's get moving we've got mission in less than two hours. I want everybody's shit laid out for inspection in forty-five mikes, platoon mission brief is at 0415, Raptor manifest and load up is at 0445." Kaleb walked down each bunk corridor to make sure all his Marines were starting to get up and get moving. One of the brand new Privates, Private First Class (PFC) Landry, rolled back over and covered his head with his blanket. "Who is that? Hey! Wake the hell up you son of a bitch." Kaleb said annoyed. "Is that you Landry?....Of course, the fucking new guy."

The Private jumped out of his rack and stood at parade rest. "Sorry Sergeant, I didn't hear you."

"Get your shit together let's go," Kaleb ordered.

Corporal Headley, one of Kaleb's team leaders entered the berthing, already in his uniform, ready to go. Sweat beads were forming on the cleanly shaven head of the young Corporal and he seemed out of breath. He was relatively short and stocky, about 5'6" and a decent NCO, however Kaleb thought he was a little on the slow side and took everything a little too seriously. It always seemed everything was a priority with Corporal Headley. He wasn't exactly the brightest light bulb in the box either.

"Sarn't Taylor, Gunny Norton just stopped me in the corridor and he said our squad needs to clean the head and berthing areas before the platoon brief is started," he blurted out as he wiped his forehead with a cloth.

Kaleb turned slowly and looked at Headley as if he was an idiot. "Yeah ok Corporal; I'll put it on my to-do list right under inserting needles into my cock….Doesn't Gunny Norton know we have the most important mission this platoon's ever been on coming up in like two hours? And he's worried about cleaning the head? Our squad cleaned the heads yesterday! What the fuck?"

Corporal Headley gave a confused look to Kaleb. "I don't know Sarn't he just told me to tell you he wanted it done ASAP and he looked pretty pissed off."

"Whatever, I'll talk to him, just start checking your guy's gear…. and make sure you test your enviro-seals twice over, and attach spare oxygen tanks onto your combat suits."

Gunnery Sergeant Norton was famous for nagging his NCO's about trivial tasks at the worst times. Kaleb thought he was just getting out of touch with reality in his old age and couldn't really identify with this new generation of Marines. He was forty-two years old after all. Kaleb also didn't appreciate him going behind his back all the time and giving his team leaders orders instead of going through him first. He always seemed to have something against Kaleb's squad, constantly tasking the snipers out with any details that no one else wanted to do. Typically the snipers are the outcasts of a Recon platoon which Kaleb didn't mind. He did mind it however when the platoon Sergeant used that as an excuse to assign them the most frivolous tasks. *No way am I making my guys clean up the rest of the platoon's shit before a mission. Gunny Norton can fuck off for all I care*, Kaleb thought.

An hour later and Kaleb's squad was lined up in full combat gear inside the berthing area with their ABAS suits, weapons and equipment laid out ready for inspection by their squad leader. They stood at parade rest in front of their gear, hoping that it would meet their squad leader's standards. Kaleb meticulously checked each of his Marines' kit, making sure they were mission ready. If they weren't, it would be his fault. He lifted up a field pack that belonged to Private First-Class Kevin Smith, the youngest member in the squad at nineteen; he was a small blonde kid from southern California back on Earth.

Kaleb shook the pack, "Smith, what the hell? Where's your water source? You planning on not drinking any fluids for the whole time we're down there? You know how fucking hot it is on that moon?"

Smith straightened his stance and sheepishly answered, "No Sergeant"

"One-hundred and twenty degrees asshole, and that's at night, trust me, you're going to want some water down there. Come on now you know better than this. I shouldn't even have to check your guys' gear anyways, you're Recon Marines, we're supposed to be the best right?"

"Roger Sarn't," a few of the Marines replied.

Kaleb looked back at the Private, "Do pushups Smith." PFC Smith reluctantly began to pound out fifty pushups as he moved on to inspect the next Marines' set of gear.

At only twenty-four years old, Kaleb almost felt like a father to the Marines in his squad. Most of them were between the ages of nineteen and twenty-three years old, just kids really. As their squad leader however, he was responsible for their lives and welfare both in combat and in garrison. He had to know everything about his seven Marines, where they came from, their family situation, their strengths and weaknesses. If a squad of Marines wanted to survive in combat, they had to be like a family and they needed a good leader. Kaleb provided that leadership and loved being a squad leader, he felt like he had a chance to make a difference in his Marines' lives. Most of them came from broken homes and families like he did. The military became the only viable option for most of them. Kaleb knew he had to be hard on his squad at times to make sure they did their jobs right but he also made sure he was always fair. The Marines of 4th squad respected Sergeant Taylor for that and they knew he would always be there to take care of them no matter what the circumstances. Losing one of his Marines was Kaleb's worst fear. It would be like losing a brother and he vowed to do everything in his power to prevent that from happening.

Kaleb looked over Private Landry's weapon. The MR-40A2 "Hellbringer mark II" sniper rifle was the newest standard issue for Recon Marines. Its dark brown/green digital camo pattern and sleek appearance was true to its name. With a built-in laser range finder, thermal scope, and a wind and gravity meter, it was the latest in USS military small arms technology. Kaleb's Marines were armed with it, and the standard Marine sidearm, the MP-2 .45 caliber pistol which was worn on the right leg holster attached to the Marines' ABAS suit. Kaleb snatched the MR-40A2 out of Landry's hands and went through a full functions check.

"What the fuck Landry....." Kaleb peered through the scope on the weapon. "You've got all kinds of goo, or shit, or something clouding up your view scope. How the hell are you supposed to shoot somebody if you can't even see clearly through your damn sights?" Kaleb field stripped the weapon and examined the interior parts. "Look at this bolt and firing pin! What did you shove this thing up your asshole last night or something?! This thing's covered in dirt!"

The Private just looked at his squad leader, confused, not sure if he was supposed to answer the question or not.

"Well…. What do you have to say for yourself?"

Landry nervously cleared his throat, "Uh…I don't know Sergeant, I'll make sure it gets cleaned before the mission and I'll make sure I put my scope cover over it next time."

"Your damn right you will…." Kaleb looked around at the rest of his squad, "Jesus Christ guys, I hope I don't find anything else fucked up or I might have to tell the LT to just cancel the mission," Kaleb said sarcastically. He continued to go through the rest of the squad's gear, knowing that the faults he had found so far were very minor, but any deficiency could mean life or death for a Marine in combat. He completed the rest of his Pre-Combat Inspection (PCI) without finding anything else wrong and gave the squad a look of satisfaction, "Ok, everything else looks good to go. Headley, make sure everyone is in the platoon CP at least ten minutes prior to the LT's brief," Kaleb said, signaling the completion of his inspection.

0415 ship time, USSN Athens, Pericles star cluster

Kaleb checked the clock on the bulkhead of the cruiser as he made his way to the platoon CP for the LT's mission brief. He was ready to go. He felt confident in his squad's abilities and he was already beginning to feel some adrenaline rushing through his veins. He turned a corner and suddenly had his path blocked by Gunnery Sergeant Norton, who had his arms folded across his chest and an angry look on his face.

"Gunny Norton…. What's on your mind?" Kaleb said in somewhat of a smart-ass tone. He had a pretty good guess of what his platoon Sergeant was about to tell him.

"Sergeant Taylor…. Correct me if I'm wrong, but I do believe

I told your snipers that they needed to clean the head and berthing areas before this mission did I not?"

Kaleb let out a breath of frustration; *I don't need this bullshit right now.* "You know what, you're exactly right Gunnery Sergeant Norton... and I was just about to have my Marines do that. However, I felt that given the time constraints on this mission it was better that they focus on PCC's (Pre-Combat Checks) and rehearsals so that they are fully prepared to execute this operation successfully. I also recall that it was the sniper squad that cleaned the heads and berthing areas yesterday. So...if I'm not mistaken, we're supposed to be on a daily rotating schedule for cleaning of common areas so actually it would be...hmm let's see...1st squad's turn today."

The Gunnery Sergeant gritted his teeth and pointed his finger at Kaleb's chest, "Don't try and be a smart-ass with me Taylor, you snipers are a bunch of pre-madonnas who think they don't have to be part of the team. Let me tell you something son, you may think you're hot shit, but I've got my eye on your entire squad. You might think it's some kind of joke to bend the rules but when we get groundside you better have your ass wired tight Marine. There won't be time to question orders in the middle of a fire-fight, you remember that..." Norton gave a bleak stare at Kaleb, "I'll see you in the briefing room.....*Sergeant...* carry on," Gunny Norton sneered and walked off down the corridor.

Is this guy for real? He's getting more and more senile every day. He doesn't even make any sense when he talks. Kaleb shook his head and thought to himself.

Lieutenant Freeborn was glad to see Sergeant Taylor as he walked into the platoon briefing room. He immediately came up to him and shook his hand. "Sergeant Taylor, your squad ready for this?"

"Damn right we are LT, put us wherever you need us," Kaleb replied.

"Well that's what I was going to ask you. I've got everything planned out except for you guys. Looking at the imagery, I wasn't sure where the best spots are to place your sniper teams. Here take a look at it and see what you think."

Kaleb nodded and looked at the imagery the LT pulled up. Freeborn always asked Kaleb for his input, it was as if he needed his stamp of approval before going through with any mission briefs, another thing that also irritated Gunnery Sergeant Norton about Kaleb. Normally, a Lieutenant would consult with the platoon Sergeant on such matters, however, it was obvious that Freeborn held Kaleb's tactical prowess in higher regard than Gunny Norton's. Kaleb studied the 3-D terrain map for a minute and thought.

"Ok LT…split us up into four teams and we'll spread out in an L-shape at about two-hundred meter intervals along this rocky ridge on the west side. This will give us coverage of the north and west sides of the bunker. Third squad can cover the southern and eastern sides of the cordon from this boulder-field on the southern edge of the objective. The far north side sniper team will also be able to have eyes on 2nd and 3rd platoon's objective, and possibly provide cover for their operation simultaneously. Once 1st and 2nd squad are inside the complex you can call us in for back up if you need it. That work for you sir?" Kaleb asked respectfully.

"Yeah that's solid, thanks Sergeant Taylor. I'll go ahead and start the brief then, that puts all the pieces together," Freeborn replied.

"Sir, you ready to go?" Gunny Norton walked up and put his hand on Freeborn's shoulder while scowling at Kaleb, who was standing next to the LT.

"Yeah let's go ahead and knock this out," Freeborn said.

Gunny Norton turned and bellowed, "Wolfpack! Listen up, LT's gonna give his mission brief so pay attention and hold any questions you have till the end, understand?"

"Roger Gunnery Sergeant!" the platoon yelled in unison with a hint of over-enthusiasm. The Marines were fired up with adrenaline, for most of them it was their first large scale mission. They listened intently as Lieutenant Freeborn talked through the mission plan using graphics and complex overlays that outlined the platoon's assault. The plan was simple for Kaleb and his squad. Split off from the platoon after touch-down and move to their designated sniper positions. From there they were to provide over watch and covering fire for the assaulting force of 1st and 2nd squad who would enter the bunker and clear it while 3rd squad's heavy weapons covered the southern end of the cordon.

After about fifteen minutes, the LT had finished his brief. "Ok, Raptor manifest is in ten mikes, don't be late," Freeborn said as the platoon got up from their seats and saluted and then sounded off with a loud and thunderous "WOLFPACK!" The mission indeed briefed well, but Marines were always taught to expect no plan to survive past first contact with the enemy.

12

USSN Athens, Gardner IV orbit, Pericles Star Cluster

The Athens disengaged its Faust drive as it decelerated to under twenty thousand miles per hour, the moon of Gardner IV visible in the bridge front view port. By utilizing onboard heat sinks to minimize its chances of detection by enemy thermal scanners, the Athens was able to effectively dissipate the heat signature created by its Faust drive thrusters. The heat sinks held the exhaust and waste heat from the ship's drive engines for up to two hours, essentially making the ship invisible to enemy heat scanners, the primary method of target identification in space combat. The helmsman brought the cruiser around the orbit of the large moon at blinding speed. The Marines of Alpha Company were crammed into four separate Raptor transports strapped in and ready for descent to the surface onto the darkened side of the moon.

From inside 1ˢᵗ platoon's Raptor, Gunny Norton attempted to yell some motivational words over the rumbling of the Athens' drive engines operating at one-hundred percent throttle. "This is what we live for Marines! You can't do this kind of shit as a civilian baby! Everybody get fired up! I'll see you on the surface!"

Flight Lieutenant Jen Thompson sat in the pilot seat of her

Raptor which housed 1ˢᵗ platoon. "Separation in three, two, one," she stated over the transport ship's intercom.

A red light started to blink inside the cargo bay holding the Marines and a few seconds later the Raptor detached from the cruiser, fired its rocket boosters and accelerated towards the moon at maximum speed.

"Alright guys, here's some tunes to help get you focused on the mission; courtesy of Sergeant Taylor," Thompson transmitted over the intercom as she pulled up a holographic interface on her data pad. The onboard speakers came to life with techno/heavy metal hybrid type of music. The Marines of the Wolfpack platoon cheered and gave a few fist pumps at the sound of the trendy music before their mission. Kaleb smiled and acknowledged a few accolades given to him over the platoon net at the choice of songs.

The transport then began to shake violently as it entered the moon's thin upper atmosphere, slowing down to safe entry speed as it deployed its braking sails. Kaleb was used to the whole process of planetary assault by now, having completed sixteen successful orbital drops since basic training. He simply closed his eyes and went through the mission plan in his head amidst the music blaring from the speaker overhead. He war-gamed any possible scenario that might take place once they hit ground. The rumbling and shaking suddenly stopped as the four Raptors leveled out and flew along the moon's surface towards their landing zones. Three of the four transports broke off from the formation and headed towards 2ⁿᵈ and 3ʳᵈ platoon's landing zones, leaving 1ˢᵗ platoon on their own inside their single transport.

Lieutenant Thompson was no doubt an exceptional pilot and quite the reputation among her fellow pilots. She effortlessly maneuvered her Raptor just above the tops of the twenty foot-tall cactus-like vegetation that dotted the surface of the moon's desert landscape. She did this all while maintaining an air speed of over seven-hundred and fifty miles per hour while also ensuring to stay below enemy radar. She then pulled a hard ninety-degree left-bank, slowing down just enough to gracefully bring them over a small open area that would be their LZ (landing zone). The Raptor extended its landing pads and vertically touched down, simultaneously lowering its rear loading ramp, exposing the night sky of Gardner IV. A fraction of light reflecting off of the gas giant the moon orbited provided a small bit of visibility for the off-loading Marines.

Lieutenant Freeborn was the first to stand up. He motioned with his hand as if to say "follow me" and ran down the ramp into the darkened surface of the planet. The rest of the platoon followed quickly behind him with Kaleb's squad last to disembark the ship. Without any talk or coordination, the platoon moved quickly and quietly like ghosts into a triangular formation to set up its initial security perimeter. The LT passed down a hand signal for his squad leaders to bring it in on him for a final map check and coordination. Kaleb engaged his night vision image enhancement on his heads up display inside his combat helmet. As he moved towards the center of the platoon security halt, he glanced over at the Raptor transport while it lifted back off the ground and blasted away with a loud rumble. The platoon was now on their own for the rest of the mission. He came up to the LT and took a knee beside him, waiting for the other squad leaders to get there.

Kaleb listened in on the company net as Freeborn updated his commander. "Viper 6 this is Wolfpack 6, we are groundside and set over," the LT sent over his comm.

"Roger Wolfpack 6, keep me posted on ten minute intervals, and when you arrive at your ORP (Objective Rally Point), break…. Good hunting, Viper 6 out," Captain Williams replied as he moved towards his objective with 2nd and 3rd platoon over ten kilometers away Freeborn's current location.

Lieutenant Freeborn looked up at his squad leaders and spoke through his helmet's voice emitter, "Ok, we've got a three point-five click movement up to our ORP, 4th squad is going to break off from here and assume their sniper positions over the target…"

Gunny Norton interrupted; "That means you better move fast Taylor, we need you to be set in position *before* we get there." Kaleb nodded. *Ok Captain obvious, like I didn't already figure that out,* he thought.

Freeborn continued, "Once 4th is set, that will be the signal for me along with 1st and 2nd to begin our flanking maneuver to the western entrance of the bunker complex. Third squad will stay in reserve and be our Casualty Collection Point with Gunny Norton on the southern side of the bunker. S-2 Intel just sent me a text message on my data pad when we touched down. The Athens' scanners are picking up minimal resistance at our objective, they say the bulk of enemy forces are garrisoned at the second bunker complex where 2nd and 3rd platoon are attacking, so be prepared to pick up and provide support to their operation once we secure our target. Based on this moon's orbit, it should be getting light here in about….three hours and some change…that means we need to move fast to get to the objective before the sun comes up, any questions?" The squad leaders shook their heads, indicating the plan was clear and they were ready to execute. "Alright let's move," Freeborn said as his closed his data pad.

Kaleb formed up his squad of seven Marines in a fire team wedge formation and made the hand signal to move forward, splitting them off from the rest of the platoon. They were to move through the sparse cactus-like vegetation and make their way up a small ridge that would place them at about eight-hundred meters away from the bunker complex, overlooking the target. A fairly easy shot for a trained Recon sniper, as long as they could find a clear line of sight through the boulders and cacti along the ridge. The sniper squad moved quickly and silently through the darkness. The digital patterned smart-camo on their ABAS suits adjusted to a brown/ yellow sand color in order to blend in with the native surroundings.

Kaleb observed the environment around him, *pretty nice place for a moon, quiet and peaceful, too bad it's so damn hot out here,* he thought as sweat already began to drip down his forehead.

The scorching heat from the blue-cycle star, SB10023, was almost unbearable even with his ABAS suit's internal cooling system running at full power. Even at thirty times the distance from its sun than Earth was from Sol (modern name for our sun). Gardner IV's surface temperature was scorching hot due to the radiation and energy output of the blue giant star. It was impossible for a person to stay above ground for more than a few minutes during the daytime on the moon due to the intense heat and radiation exposure. The surface did cool off enough however during the night cycle to conduct above-ground operations. Kaleb's heads up display in his helmet visor showed a current surface temperature of one-hundred and twenty-eight degrees Fahrenheit. Despite the heat, they were able to move quickly as the gravity on Gardner IV was only 0.7 that of Earth's, making the Marines and their gear feel thirty percent lighter than they were used to.

After traveling about four uneventful clicks, they came upon the ridge where they would set up their sniper positions. The point man, Lance Corporal Burke, a young, fast tracking Marine from the colony of New Sydney, raised his arm up showing the back of his hand to the rest of the squad. Everyone halted in place and assumed security positions for their sector. Burke took a knee and peered up the ridge. Lance Corporal Burke was Kaleb's best point man; he was an excellent tracker and superb at land navigation. He motioned for his squad leader to come take a look as he continued to scan the ridge for movement. Kaleb quickly moved from the center of the fire team wedge up to the front and took a knee next to Burke.

"You see something?" Kaleb asked anxiously.

"Naw Sergeant, I heard something though, about a hundred meters up the ridge, past those jagged rocks," Burke whispered as he pointed in the direction of the sound.

"You sure? I didn't hear anything," Kaleb whispered back, failing to see any movement in the direction Burke had pointed in. Kaleb zoomed in on the area via his heads up display and engaged his thermal scanner in an effort to detect any nearby organic life forms. Suddenly a crash sounded and a dark, four-legged object ran across the top of the ridge visible on his thermal imaging. Kaleb quickly brought his sniper rifle up and gained a sight picture through a rock outcropping on the moving object ranged at one-hundred and twenty-five meters. He followed the creature through his scope, "What the hell is that?" he whispered.

Lance Corporal Burke looked through his view scope as well, "Ah, man, it's just some kind of native lizard or something. Looks like we scared it out from its nest. Want me to take it out Sergeant? I bet it tastes good," Burke whispered sarcastically.

Kaleb gave a faint grin as he lowered his rifle. "Good thing I'm not hungry right now, let's get moving. We've still got one more click to go and not much time to do it. Five-meter spread, no sound." Burke nodded and Kaleb stood back up, twirling his finger around in the air, signaling the squad to regroup and move out.

Once the squad crested the small ridge Kaleb gave a signal for a short security halt. He made a drinking motion with his hands to indicate for the squad to drink water. The Marines sucked down water through a built in tube in their helmet system that connected to a one-gallon container of water they carried on their backs. Kaleb was sweating profusely as the moon slowly rotated on its axis closer to the direct ultraviolet rays produced by the blue giant star. Short of breath after hiking up the ridge in the thin atmosphere, Kaleb switched on his extra oxygen supply. After a few breaths of oxygen he was back to normal breathing levels. Kaleb allowed a few minutes to pass as his Marines did the same following the vertical climb to the top of the boulder-laden ridge.

Corporal Headley pulled out a small brown cloth and wiped the sweat from his face under his helmet visor. "Man I been on some hot planets before but nothing like this," he said to his spotter, PFC Landry. Burke overheard his statement and countered.

"Come on Headley this isn't shit. Remember that operation on Atiah?"

"Trying to forget it," Headley quickly responded.

Kaleb checked the time on his heads up display. "Alright let's move," he spoke softly over the squad net. He again gave the signal to move out and squad quietly stood up from the kneeling position and continued on to their objective, the temperature on his HUD now reading one-hundred and thirty-one degrees.

He placed his first sniper team of Corporal Headley and Private Landry to overlook the southern end of the objective. The ridge formed an L-shape around the western and northern ends of the bunker with abundant cover provided by numerous rock outcroppings. Kaleb placed the rest of his two-man teams two-hundred meters apart along the L-shape, giving them sniper coverage over the entire objective area. Kaleb and his spotter, PFC Smith formed the last team at the far end of the L-shape, overlooking the northern end of the bunker. They set up in a crevice between two large boulders on the down slope of the ridge.

PFC Smith set up his spotting scope and scanned the area. "Sergeant, I've got the bunker complex on scope, single building, one floor above ground level, chain link fence with concertina wire on top surrounding the structure. Thirty meters of open terrain from the start of the fence to the entrance of the building.... No enemy forces present....wait...switching to thermal image enhancement......got movement......three times enemy dismounts....roving patrol around the outside of the bunker....they're definitely armed......No armored vehicles spotted."

Kaleb extended the bipod on his rifle and looked through his view scope, confirming Smith's assessment of the objective. He checked the clock on his data pad, *five mikes before the LT should be set*. "Wolfpack 6, this is Wolfpack 4 over." There was a long pause and crackling over Kaleb's comm unit.

"This is six send it," Lieutenant Freeborn finally answered.

"Roger, sitrep as follows break… Wolfpack 4 is set in position, eyes on target, break….single bunker complex surrounded by chain link fence with dismounted roving patrol present, break….thirty meters open terrain from fence to bunker entrance, no visible armor assets, break…recommend flank from western side using breach team on assault to neutralize fence obstacle, over." There was another long pause over the platoon net as Freeborn, along with 1st and 2nd squad, crossed a dry riverbed about 1,000 feet below Corporal Headley's position.

Climbing the other side of the large ditch, Lieutenant Freeborn keyed the radio in his helmet while breathing heavily, "Roger four, good copy….setting up 3rd squad in support by fire at this time, will begin flank to western side of complex in ten mikes…wait for my order to go hot, Wolfpack 6 out."

Gunnery Sergeant Norton had set up 3rd squad on the southeastern side of the bunker complex, hidden about one-hundred meters from the fence line in a boulder field. They set up their heavy support rifles that required a two man team to operate along with an anti-armor rocket team that that fired the self-guided, shoulder-fired Centurion missile, capable of penetrating six-inch thick rigid steel or titanium armor.

"Wolfpack 6 this is Wolfpack 7, support position and CCP set up and ready to roll. We've got a clear line of sight and will cover your assault over," Norton sent over the net to his platoon leader.

"This is six, roger…flanking team ready and waiting for go ahead from Viper 6," Freeborn replied after lining up 1st and 2nd squad along the base of the ridge. "Viper 6 this is Wolfpack 6, all squads in place, objective rally point established, waiting on your go ahead, over."

"Wolfpack 6, this is Viper 6 actual, roger, time hack as follows, you are cleared hot in eight mikes, Viper 6 out."

In approximately eight minutes, all hell would break loose upon the two bunker complexes as the entire company would begin their attack simultaneously, hopefully taking the enemy force by surprise. Kaleb scanned his sector again, zooming into to 14x magnification on his targets. The mercenaries in the roving patrols looked well-equipped as the intel brief described; top of the line combat armor and what looked like fairly advanced weaponry.

He keyed his squad internal net, "Corporal Headley, your target is the southernmost dismount, Burke, take out the nearside dismount, Corporal Martinez will cover the northernmost dismount, and I'll take back-up on any missed targets. Apply your silencers time now, how copy over?"

The team leaders replied in order, "Alpha team sights hot… Bravo, sights hot…Charlie team, sight hot."

PFC Kevin Smith zoomed in with his spotting scope on the dismounted targets. "Alright Sergeant, winds are calm, two miles per hour to the northeast, range to target eight-three-four meters, gravitational pull negligible, atmospheric pressure at point three-two."

Kaleb pulled his silencer out of his left leg assault pocket and quietly screwed it onto the end of his MR-40A2 rifle. He breathed in and out slowly as he brought his sight reticule between the eyes of his target. *Too easy* Kaleb thought, noticing that his prey was oblivious to the fact that his life would be at an end in a few short minutes.

"All Wolfpack elements this is Wolfpack 6, we are cleared hot, I say again we are cleared hot," Lieutenant Freeborn's voice broke this silence over the platoon net. Kaleb's heart rate increased upon hearing the go signal.

"Snipers engage time now," Kaleb calmly transmitted over his squad net. Corporal Martinez fired first; Kaleb just barely heard the "click" sound from his silencer two-hundred meters away. His armor-piercing round easily penetrated the helmet of the mercenary on patrol. Blood spewed out of his head like a fountain. The target hit the ground half a second after impact, motionless before the other guards even heard anything. Two more rounds fired from Burke and Headley's rifles in unison, quickly and efficiently knocking down the remaining two mercenaries in a silent but deadly barrage.

Corporal Headley hit his target a little low of center mass and the mercenaries' armor slowed the bullet impact to a degree. The target began to squirm on the ground, struggling to recover from the impact of the 9.45mm round on his lower torso. Kaleb zeroed in on the still-moving target and quickly pulled the trigger on his rifle hurling another tungsten round toward the helpless enemy at over 4,200 feet per second. The round impacted squarely on the head of the target, instantly killing the once heavily armed mercenary. All went quiet in the remaining darkness as PFC Smith scanned intently or any additional movement.

"All targets down Sergeant, no further contacts," Smith reported after completing his assessment.

"Wolfpack 6 this is Wolfpack 4, dismounted patrol neutralized, you have a clear path to the bunker, over," Kaleb immediately updated the LT.

"Roger four, we're moving in time now, good shooting, six out," Freeborn replied.

Lieutenant Freeborn moved 1st and 2nd squad out of the tree line in a bounding over watch movement. First squad moved up while 2nd squad provided cover, once they were set, the squads' switched roles and 2nd squad would move while 1st provided cover.

"Breach team go!" Freeborn ordered over the platoon net. A two man team ran up to the chain link fence and lit a small, blue-flamed torch. In one smooth, silent motion, one of the Marines cut a five-foot diameter hole in the fence. The platoon quickly filed through the precisely cut opening.

"First squad let's go! Get through the fence and stack on the entrance to the bunker! Breach and clear as soon as you're set... 2nd squad provide cover and move in after 1st squad clears the first room!" Adrenaline rushed through Freeborn's veins, training and instincts had taken over as he led the two squads toward the bunker. He could hear gunfire coming from 2nd and 3rd platoon's objective off in the distance; their timing of the attacks had been perfectly synchronized. Freeborn was surprised that no enemy forces had come out of the bunker to see why their roving patrols hadn't checked in. The demolitions specialist from 1st squad quickly ran up and placed a breaching charge around the corners of the steel door, it would take a several large blocks of plastic explosive wired together to blast through the entrance effectively.

Kaleb methodically scanned up and down his sector of fire over the valley attempting to locate any enemy reinforcements inbound. He saw nothing. The area remained calm. He then began to watch 1st squad's breaching operation on the bunker entrance through his scope. *Come on guys, hurry up and get in there.* Part of him wished he was down with the assault team, giving him a chance to fight Shinwar mercenaries up close. Something he had dreamed of doing ever since the loss of his family.

"On my mark, 3...2...1!" Freeborn commanded his demo specialist. Another deafening explosion sounded and the four inch thick steel door imploded into the interior of the bunker complex, hurling hot shards of metal inside the upper level of the structure.

"First squad go, get in there!" Freeborn yelled." The 1st squad leader pushed his Marines inside the smoke and dust filled room. The riflemen cleared all the corners of first large room they encountered. Corporal Hunt's heart was racing. Being the point man for 1st squad, he expected to be face to face with well armed mercenaries as soon as he entered. To his surprise, the room was empty, just a few storage lockers and a small table. Second squad moved into the room a few seconds later with Lieutenant Freeborn.

"This room's clear sir, not picking up anything on my motion sensor for this floor." the 1ˢᵗ Squad leader, Sergeant Yao, reported to his platoon leader. Freeborn looked at the next center-fed door that led into the main chambers of the bunker.

"Alright leap-frog it, 2ⁿᵈ squad stack and clear the next room, 1ˢᵗ maintain rear security." 2ⁿᵈ squad systematically stacked up four Marines on each side of the steel door.

"Flash and clear!" the 6'4" 280 pound second squad leader, Sergeant Maurice Chambers yelled to his squad. His Alpha team leader punched the pressure release button on the wall and the door quickly slid open. Sergeant Chambers pulled the pin on his flash-bang grenade and tossed it in. The Marines looked down and away from the door opening as there was a bright flash followed by an earsplitting concussion. The Marines filed in quickly with their weapons up and ready to lay waste to anything hostile inside the room. Again the Marines found no hostile forces. To Chamber's surprise, all was quiet as the smoke from the flash-bang dissipated. He flipped off his night vision image enhancement and surveyed the room with his weapon light.

"Holy shit…..LT….looks like we got a lot of bodies in here. There was a firefight, lots of brass casings on the floor……looks like we got some members of the science team here in lab coats, couple of IO agents, and I guess some of the Ares Alliance assault force, all dead from gun-shot wounds." Chambers reported over the net.

"Ok, grab whatever intel you can off the bodies and let's get this floor cleared and move down to the lower levels, there's got to be someone left alive in here." Freeborn ordered as he entered the room to inspect the carnage. He kneeled down next to one of the dead Ares Alliance mercenaries. "Wait a minute," Freeborn said as he turned the body over. "These aren't fucking mercenaries, these are

Ares Alliance special ops commandos. Check out the insignia on his left shoulder," he said to Chambers who was standing over him.

"I thought that armor they're wearing looked like high grade military shit. No way mercenaries are getting their hands on this type of equipment," Sergeant Chambers replied in agreement.

"Something big must be going on here. Whatever that sensitive data is, the Ares Alliance wants it pretty fucking bad to send these guys after it," Freeborn replied, standing back up. "C'mon, let's get moving. We still have to get this bunker cleared. Everyone keep your shit wired tight, it looks like we're up against Ares special ops now."

"Roger sir, we'll take point and make our way down to the second floor," Sergeant Yao, 1st squad leader, acknowledged over the net.

Sergeant Yao was a native of Earth, born in the country of Vietnam within the Asian Union but raised in America. He was small in stature but a lifetime Marine and an exceptional squad leader. He was older than most of the Marines, not joining up until he was twenty-four. Now thirty years old and happily married to his wife back on Earth, he served almost as a father figure to the younger Marines in the platoon.

*   *   *   *

"I can't believe they haven't made contact yet, something can't be right," Kaleb whispered to Smith. Just as he finished his sentence he heard a faint noise off in the distance coming from the other side of the ridge.

"What the hell is that?" PFC Smith asked apprehensively. Kaleb looked down at the bottom of the ridge where a dirt road led north away from the bunker.

"It's a vehicle, its coming from the trail below, sounds like it's pretty big," Kaleb answered calmly. A plume of dust rose up from the trail as a large, twenty-ton 4x4 armored rover approached the complex at high speed. He quickly looked through the scope on his rifle and zoomed in. Jutting out from the turret were two large caliber barrels, some sort of coaxial machine gun along with a grenade launcher. Kaleb's eyes widened and he immediately keyed the platoon net. "Wolfpack 6 this is Wolfpack 4 urgent traffic over!" he said frantically. There was a pause for about ten seconds before Lieutenant Freeborn replied.

"This is six, send it."

"Roger, I've got eyes on an enemy armored vehicle closing in on the bunker complex fast. It'll be on top of you guys in thirty seconds over!"

Upon hearing the news Freeborn stopped in his tracks as the two squads just entered the bottom floor of the complex. Behind him, the steel blast door they just entered suddenly sealed shut without warning.

"It's a trap! Everybody get down and get cover now!!" Freeborn screamed at the Marines who had just begun to clear the 1st of four laboratory rooms on the bottom floor. Suddenly, several shrill explosions shook the interior walls of the bunker. Shrapnel flew aimlessly throughout the corridors of the 3rd floor. Lieutenant Freeborn was hurled to the deck as a proximity mine detonated just above his head on the ceiling of the corridor. Several large pieces of shrapnel dug into his right leg and abdomen, penetrating his ceramic armor. He yelled in pain and cringed at the sight of his own blood. He looked up only to see his Marines being ambushed by what appeared to be at least twelve to fifteen Ares Alliance commandos that ran out into the corridor from the three remaining un-cleared rooms. Sergeant Chambers and Sergeant Yao yelled out commands to their Marines to take cover and return fire. Corporal Hunt turned around in order to fall back behind a large metal crate for cover. He stumbled over his feet as several rounds impacted and ricocheted off his back plate armor. Hunt leaped behind the steel crate and regained his composure, that's when he noticed that the LT was hit.

"Sergeant Yao the LT's hit!" he screamed at his squad leader over the automatic gunfire. Hunt ran back to where Freeborn lay about ten feet behind the steel crate. He grabbed him from under his arms and dragged the Lieutenant behind the safety of cover. Hunt fumbled through his first aid pouch, pulling out his battle dressing and morphine syringe. After frantically detaching Freeborn's chest and leg armor to expose his wounds, he ripped open the packages and spread the dressing over the LT's wounds, helping to stop the bleeding and ease the pain. Sergeant Yao looked back at Hunt giving first aid and then to his overwhelmed force of Marines.

"Fall back! Fall back top-side now!" Sergeant Yao screamed, realizing that the enemy had them at a severe disadvantage.

"Wolfpack 6 this is Wolfpack 4 did you copy my last transmission?" Kaleb anxiously called on the radio for the third time after no response from the LT. The enemy rover pulled to a stop just outside the west entrance to the bunker where 1st and 2nd squad had entered. It lowered its rear ramp and to Kaleb's surprise, four more heavily armed Ares Alliance commandos trudged out of the vehicle. The gunner sitting inside the turret of the rover began to scan the boulder field to the south with a massive spotlight.

"Wolfpack 4 this is Wolfpack 7, be advised we have eyes on the enemy rover and are engaging at this time over," Gunny Norton blurted over the net. Before Kaleb could get a shot off on one of the mercenaries exiting the rover, a hail of gunfire engulfed the armored vehicle from 3rd squad's position. The four enemy soldiers immediately ran inside the bunker for cover as the rounds ricocheted off the rover's titanium armor.

"Wolfpack 7 this is four, your small arms fire is ineffective on the rover, you need to engage with anti-armor rockets, over!" Kaleb yelled over the net. Third squad had given away their position with their machine gun-fire muzzle flashes that brightly lit up the pre-dawn darkness. The gunner of the rover instantly rotated his turret and locked onto their position with his grenade launcher.

"Wolfpack 7 get out of there, he's zeroed in on your location!" Kaleb yelled again at Gunny Norton as he watched the scene unfold from his sniper position atop the ridge. *Thump, Thump, Thump,* a three-round burst fired from the rover's grenade launcher, hurling 40mm high explosive rounds towards 3rd squad's position. A Marine from 3rd squad took aim from the kneeling position with the squad's Centurion anti-armor rocket launcher. Just as he was putting his finger on the trigger to fire, three consecutive explosions detonated on the rocks just in front of him, knocking him to the ground unconscious from the concussive blasts. Sergeant Gallo, the 3rd squad leader, leaped over a large rock and grabbed the unconscious Marine, hoisting him up and over behind the safety of cover.

"Fall back! Fall Back!!!" Gunny Norton screamed, realizing he had given away his position. *Thump, Thump, Thump,* the rover fired another three-round grenade burst at 3rd squad.

"Wolfpack 4, this is seven, we're falling back to cover, hold your position until I can get reinforcements from Viper 6 over!" Norton yelled as he ran back towards the insertion zone, three more grenades detonating twenty meters behind the squad as they sprinted away to the south.

That dumb motherfucker, why didn't he open up on the rover with the Centurion?! Now he's falling back and leaving the LT to get ambushed by those mercenaries! What the hell is he thinking?! Kaleb thought angrily. He looked down at the bunker, then back up at PFC Smith.

"Fuck that, we don't have contact with the LT, there are four enemy dismounts about to ambush them and an armored vehicle waiting for them right outside their egress point. We've gotta get in there and do something!" Kaleb said out loud.

A confused Smith pondered the situation for a split second then spoke quickly. "Sergeant, I'm carrying two blocks of remote plastic explosive, we can sneak up on the rover and disable it. We'll come down the ridge and they won't see us because they think the threat is coming from 3rd squad." The plan sounded good enough for Kaleb and they were running out of time. He got back on the platoon net.

"Wolfpack 7 this is Wolfpack 4, negative on that order... break... I'm going in with two teams to disable the armored vehicle and regain contact with the LT inside the bunker, over." Gunnery Sergeant Norton switched back to the platoon net after attempting to contact Captain Williams for help.

"Goddammit Sergeant Taylor hold your position! We've lost the advantage! You *will* hold your position until further guidance, is that understood?"

"Negative seven, we don't have time to wait for Viper 6 to bail us out. I'm moving down the ridge now, Wolfpack 4 out." Kaleb switched over to his squad net, cutting off any further transmissions from an irate Norton. "Corporal Martinez, get your team down the ridge and link up with me and Smith at the breach point on the perimeter fence. We're going to rig the vehicle with explosives and find out what the hell happened to 1st and 2nd squad. Headley, Burke, hold position and give us cover while we assault the vehicle." All sniper teams acknowledged Kaleb's orders over the net as he and Smith double-timed down the ridge towards the bunker.

*   *   *   *

"Open that door now!" Sergeant Yao screamed at Corporal Hunt as the Marines inside the bunker attempted to fall back. Hunt fumbled with the blast door controls. A red light on a wall control panel indicated it had been sealed from the other side, the only way through was to try to blast a hole through the four inch-thick steel door.

"I can't, it's sealed! The door controls are locked and encrypted from the other side!!" Hunt yelled back.

Sergeant Yao desperately called over the platoon net, "Any Wolfpack element, this is Wofpack 1, we are trapped in an ambush inside the bunker, need assistance ASAP…the LT is down, I say again, the LT is down, over!!" There was no response to Yao's distress call. "Any Wolfpack element, do you copy?!......Shit! The blast door must be blocking our signal," Yao shouted back at Hunt.

The two squads struggled to find cover behind the few metal crates in the main corridor of the bottom floor. They fired controlled bursts from their assault rifles, pushing back the attempted advancements of the Ares special ops forces flowing out of the different lab rooms. The Marines managed to eliminate several of them in the opening salvos however the close- quarters battle was now at a stalemate. Sergeant Yao ducked down behind a crate to change out the magazine in his assault rifle. He looked over at Lieutenant Freeborn; he lay by the squad medic's side across the hallway.

"How's he doing?!" Yao yelled over more gunfire.

'He's stabilized I think, he lost a lot of blood but he'll be alright!" the medic replied.

One of Sergeant Yao's Marines held his assault rifle above his head over the top of a metal crate, spraying covering fire throughout the hallway. An Ares Alliance commando swiftly returned fire, several rounds hitting the Private's weapon and blowing off his right index finger in the process. The Private screamed in agony as he dropped his weapon down to the deck. He covered his right hand to try to stop the blood from gushing out of his severed finger.

"Fuck! My finger!! Holy shit it hurts!!" the Private yelled frantically. The medic tending to the LT heard the Private's call for help and immediately ran across the corridor with a battle dressing.

With bullets whizzing over his head the medic wrapped the dressing around the Private's hand to stop the blood.

"You're gonna be ok!" yelled the medic over the gunfire. "Shoot with your left hand from now on! I gotta get back to the LT!" The Private nodded and picked his weapon back up with his remaining good hand, putting himself back into the fight.

Sergeant Yao looked back at Corporal Hunt by the door. "Corporal Hunt! Our only way out of here is to blast that door! Start rigging it with a breach charge! In the meantime we'll see if we can gain a strong point and out flank these guys!"

"Roger Sergeant I'm on it!" Hunt acknowledged.

*   *   *   *

The enemy rover stayed in place, blocking the exit to the bunker. Its gunner scanned the southern tree line, searching for 3rd squad. Kaleb, Smith, Martinez, and Lance Corporal Colby, Corporal Martinez's spotter, quietly linked up at the hole in the perimeter fence.

"Alright, you guys stay here and cover me and Smith while we rig the vehicle with explosives." Kaleb ordered. The two other Marines nodded, taking up defensive positions.

"Let's go Smith!" Kaleb said as the two quickly moved across the fifty meters of open terrain, approaching the right flank of the vehicle. The gunner and driver that remained inside the rover had limited visibility through the small view ports that existed on the turret and front of the vehicle. So long as the gunner did not rotate the turret towards Kaleb's direction, they would never see them coming in the cover of darkness. Kaleb and Smith kneeled down behind the rover and began to rig up the remote charges. PFC Smith placed one inside the exhaust port and Kaleb crawled underneath the vehicle to place the other one on the thinly- armored underside of the rover. The charges easily stuck to the vehicle with their built-in adhesive. Kaleb immediately crawled back out from under the rover and checked the direction the turret was facing. *Still in the clear* he thought as he grabbed Smith and ran thirty meters to the rear of the vehicle. Smith pulled out his detonator and the two Marines took cover behind the backside of the bunker.

"Hit it" Kaleb said quietly as he looked Smith in the face. Smith pressed down on the remote detonator switch, in a split second the rover was engulfed in a brilliant bright-orange flash followed by black smoke and a loud explosion. Kaleb watched as the gunner's body parts flew out of the destroyed turret and spread over the ground below. The driver opened the top hatch and attempted to crawl out, flames had engulfed his body. He jumped off the side of the vehicle, screaming as the flames melted his armor to his skin. Smith raised his rifle to put him out of his misery but Kaleb reached up, grabbing the top of the weapon, pushing it back down.

"Let him burn...fucking mercenary," Kaleb said quietly in a sinister tone as he stood up from behind the bunker wall and motioned to Martinez to bring his team up. They met up at the blast door where 1st and 2nd squad had entered. *This is my chance to settle the score with the type of people that raided my home all those years ago,* Kaleb thought to himself.

The Marines linked back up at the blasted out entrance to the bunker, "Ok, Smith will take point. We'll go floor by floor clearing each room till we find and kill those mercs. We've got to move fast before they catch 1st and 2nd by surprise." The three Marines nodded and stacked up on the first door, waiting for their squad leader's command.

13

United Star Systems Intelligence Office (USSIO) headquarters building, London, England

USS Intelligence Office agent Ryan Inlow checked his watch as he nervously power-walked down a long hallway that led to a large conference room. His black dress shoes tapped the tile floor quickly as he increased his speed. Sweat beads ran down his forehead as he went over in his head what he was supposed to say in the upcoming briefing with USS military high brass. He wore a jet black suit with a black tie which was the typical uniform for IO spooks at the time. His small stature, balding head, and oversized glasses gave him a passive, negligible appearance to most individuals. Despite his lack of physical prowess, Inlow was an extremely clever man who had quickly moved up the ladder at IO since he signed on fifteen years ago. Since then he had been involved in the darkest and dirtiest black ops one could imagine. The extreme levels of compartmentalized security didn't even allow the President of the USS government to be privy to his work the majority of the time. Whether it was the staged false flag attack orchestrated by IO agents during the Goshen incident to start the war against the Ares Alliance, or his current assignment regarding the attack on the Gardner IV research station, Inlow was very good at keeping secrets. His ability to keep these secrets currently put him in charge of IO's Extraterrestrial Intelligence Division (EID). Known for having a calm and collected demeanor, this was the first time Inlow could remember being so nervous before an intel brief. *Why am I sweating so much? Why are my hands shaking? Feels like there is a huge knot in my stomach.* He thought to himself. Maybe it was because the file he held in his right hand had information in it that would change the course of mankind forever. Perhaps it was because he may have single-handedly compromised the integrity of the most important discovery in human history.

Since the inception of the United Star Systems interstellar government and military, the Intelligence Office branch quickly gained power in the size and scope of its operations. Many members of the USS Parliament questioned the amount of power given the IO Director in regards to secrecy of important interstellar security matters. The IO Director for the past twenty years, the honorable Michael Romanoff, had a track record of failing to divulge sensitive top secret information to Parliament or the President when they requested it. Romanoff had engineered a complex pyramid power structure within the Intelligence Office. He had spies, covert operatives, disinformation specialists, and double agents in almost every arm of the USS government and media. This was all unbeknownst to the current President as well as most of Parliament of course. Many in the USS government and media have stated that Michael Romanoff is one of the "most dangerous" and "influential" men in the entire interstellar community. His power structure made it impossible for any audits or investigations to turn up any substantial evidence against Romanoff and the IO regarding corruption or the withholding of sensitive information to key members of Parliament. Several congressional hearings were held in the past in an effort to oust Romanoff from his current cabinet seat. Only to be proven unsuccessful due to deep cover IO operatives nested within the government. The existing puppet President of the United Star Systems knew better than to challenge Romanoff's position when he was elected and decided to keep him assigned as IO Director until the end of his term. Romanoff had effectively created a "Men in Black" army of spies and operatives to enforce his will and provide a shadow government that steered the USS Parliament's policies on almost every major issue.

Ryan Inlow was one of Romanoff's most loyal "Men in Black," or so Romanoff thought, which perhaps could be why he was chosen to lead IO's most important division. Inlow questioned the morality of IO's operations and secrecy practices from time to time, however he was in far too deep to start looking for a new career field at this point. In addition, IO had a history of making people "disappear" that tended to ask too many questions.

Mr. Romanoff called an emergency meeting with the head of Naval Intelligence, Rear Admiral Falasad, to discuss the recent events taking place on the moon of Gardner IV. The moon currently housed the most top secret research project in IO history, in which Inlow was in command of. He had primarily been managing the assignment from IO headquarters back on Earth while periodically visiting the research facility to check on progress, leaving his second-in-command at the actual site full-time. Inlow knew that he was in for a thrashing from Mr. Romanoff and the Admiral in the upcoming meeting. He obviously had not properly garrisoned the moon with defenses to protect the secret project and now it had become compromised by Ares Alliance forces.

Will I be fired? No, I know too much, Romanoff would probably just hire some agents to "erase" me. Oh well, no turning back now, he thought to himself. Ryan Inlow approached the sealed off conference room and showed the two armed guards out front his Top Secret Compartmentalized level seven ID badge. The guard nodded in approval after meticulously inspecting the ID badge under his scanner.

"Good morning agent Inlow, please step forward to the line and look into the retinal scanner," the balding, heavy-set security guard said without emotion.

Inlow stepped forward and stared into a small scanner attached to a robotic arm that moved in front of his right eye. A laser crossed over his pupil and a green light lit up on the security guard's computer.

"Looks like you're good to go sir. Mr. Romanoff is waiting for you inside." The guard informed Inlow.

"Yes, I'm sure he is," Inlow said despondently as the guard opened the thick metal security door, motioning with his hand for Inlow to enter.

"Agent Inlow, so nice you could make it," an ominous voice came from the head of the conference table, it was Mr. Romanoff. Dressed in his usual black, pin-striped suit with a green tie, he leaned back in his chair and smiled at Inlow as he entered the room. Romanoff undeniably had a suave appearance to him. At fifty-seven years old, he looked much younger, more like he was in his early forties. His black, slicked-back hair and dark brown eyes gave the onlooker the impression that he was constantly plotting something against them. Inlow positively did not trust the man yet had always remained loyal to him over the years. A fact that Inlow hoped Romanoff would take into consideration when choosing punishment for his recent failing with the Gardner IV project.

Agent Inlow took a seat at the far end of the table, close to a projector screen. He gave a phony nod and smile to all the members of the conference table as he pulled out the all-important file he carried in his right hand and began to flip through the documents inside. As expected, Admiral Falasad sat on the corner of the table next to Romanoff, the rest of the seats were filled with Falasad's staff and lackeys; a few Naval Intelligence Captains and a Lieutenant who apparently served as the Admiral's aide de camp. The guard outside sealed the heavy security door and the lights in the room dimmed slightly as the projector screen lit up.

"Alright Mr. Romanoff, now that your assistant is finally here I want some damned answers," the Admiral of Earthborn, middle-eastern origin spoke forcefully. "My men at Naval Intel knew you had something going on with extraterrestrial intelligence, but my question is just what the hell is it we are dealing with here and why is it about to fall into the hands of the Ares Alliance military?!"

Romanoff slyly leaned back in his large black office chair and casually lit up a cigarette. Ensuring to take a heavy drag off of it before he evenly answered the Admiral. "My apologies Admiral, I was unaware that it was my responsibility to defend USS interests against attacks from the Ares Alliance. Normally that duty does fall under the Navy and Marines does it not?" The Admiral, taken aback by Romanoff's defiant comment swelled with anger, however, before he could rebuke the IO Director for his disrespect, Romanoff continued. "But that doesn't matter right now. There will be plenty of time to shift the blame around. What matters is that your Marines are currently in the process of securing the sensitive material and soon my agents will be transporting it to a much more....*secure*.... location," Romanoff knocked the ashes off his cigarette as smoke filled the room.

"Goddammit I want some answers! I didn't come here to play catch me fuck me games with you Romanoff. You people at IO are way out of hand here. The President continuously gives you a blank check so now you think you can just do whatever the hell you want. What gives you the right to withhold information of this magnitude! My Marines are down there risking their lives for something no one in the USS Navy even knows about!" The Admiral became heated and pounded his fist on the conference table. Inlow jumped slightly at the unexpected impact, taking him out of a daydream.

Romanoff took another drag off of his cigarette, "Admiral, I understand your concern and right now we are going to have to work together to get this unpleasant situation resolved. That is why agent Inlow here, my project leader on Gardner IV, is about to give you full disclosure on what we've found there." The Admiral seemed to calm down slightly after hearing the words "full disclosure."

"Mr. Inlow, if you would please," Romanoff motioned to the projector screen signaling for Inlow to begin his brief.

"Very well sir," Inlow began. The projector screen cued up a 3-D image of what looked to be a large, black, obelisk-like structure containing strange markings on the bottom half and an eerie red glowing orb at the very top. "Gentlemen, what you are looking at, is what we at IO believe to be a device of intelligent, extraterrestrial design…..." the room was dead silent as the Admiral's aide de camp's jaw suddenly dropped in amazement. Admiral Falasad put on his glasses and leaned forward, peering intently at the image. "During a routine deep space exploration mission six months ago, one of our Recon ships detected an anomaly on the surface of Gardner IV. What they found upon further inspection was this device here….." Inlow flipped to a zoomed-in image of the strange structure."

"Jesus Christ Romanoff, six months ago!! Six months ago and you wait until now to tell anyone else about it!!" the Admiral yelled furiously.

"Admiral please, you're not making this process any easier, like I said, we can shift the blame later. Right now IO is asking for the Navy's help in this matter," Romanoff attempted to calm the Admiral down. "Dr. Inlow please continue."

"Yes sir…upon IO's discovery of this alien device, the Gardner IV research station was immediately constructed in order to study what we have been now calling codename Project 'Contrivance.' This dark black, obelisk-like object stands over twenty feet tall, is three feet wide at the base and comes to a sharp point at the top where this small glowing orb is attached. Once we moved it to the underground research station it began to emit an intermittent electro-magnetic pulse as well as an ultra-high frequency radio signal. Attempts to decipher the signal by our cryptologists have failed up to this point. But we are assuming it is a type of communications relay or navigation transponder perhaps. We are unsure of what material it is made of however initial analysis suggests it is an extremely light as well as durable metal alloy compromised of several unknown elements. We also are unaware of what powers the object which enables it to produce such a high energy radio signal and electromagnetic field." Inlow explained.

The Admiral shook his head, "So what you're telling me is, you've had the damn thing for six months now, and…and you don't even know one thing about it?"

"That assessment is not totally inaccurate sir….without any type of basis to go off of… it is difficult to discern just what exactly 'Contrivance's' purpose or origin is," Inlow replied sheepishly.

The Admiral countered, "So how do you even know that this isn't some kind of…top secret weapon or encrypted communications device developed by the Ares Alliance? Just because it has some weird symbols on it doesn't automatically mean its alien in nature."

"Rest assured Admiral, we have considered that possibility heavily. There is no doubt that this….we'll continue to call it 'Contrivance,' is not of human design. The elements surveyed from the metal alloy are nothing we've ever seen before. The symbols have been cross referenced with every colonial writing, Alphabet, and number system in use and nothing matches up. The radio frequency also exists on a bandwidth never before used by any human organization," Inlow further explained.

"Well, I guess my next question is, how in the hell did the Ares Alliance find out about it?! Why leave the damn thing undefended way out in deep space? You should've brought it back to a secure location on Talos or Earth where it could be properly studied. And unless our Marines can pull off a miracle out there on that moon, it looks like the Ares government is going to be the new owner of it," Falasad asked angrily. "What a goddamn mess. You should've told someone Romanoff, you should've asked for our help earlier," Falsad continued his tirade.

Inlow looked across the conference table at Romanoff, hoping that he would answer the Admiral's question. Romanoff gave a slight nod to Inlow and spoke reluctantly, "I believe it may have been someone inside of my organization. It is the only way the information could've leaked. Ares Alliance intel must have offered one of my agents a fortune to defect with this information."

The Admiral threw up his hands in disgust. "Well that's just great Romanoff. Not only does IO unlawfully keep secrets from the USS government, you can't even keep your own people in line!"

Romanoff put his cigarette out in the ash tray on the table. "It was… an unfortunate setback Admiral. One that I can assure will never happen again at IO," he gave a stern look across the room to Inlow as he spoke. "As for keeping Project Contrivance on Gardner IV, we felt it would be reckless to risk traveling over a hundred light years with it and placing it on one of our most strategic colonies. We don't know enough about it, what its purpose is; who or what put it there. What if it was broadcasting its location back to whoever built it through that radio frequency? Bringing it back to Talos or Earth could've revealed the location of the center of humanity to a technologically superior and hostile alien race. Is that a risk you would be willing to take Admiral?"

"On the verge of the greatest discovery of humankind and we just let it slip right through our fingers," Falasad said quietly as he looked down at the table, shaking his head. "Let's hope those Marines can get the damn thing back…."

"Admiral, if we are unable to recover Project Contrivance and the Ares Alliance gains possession of it….We will have to destroy the facility on Gardner IV and deny any involvement in order to save face politically. And I would suggest… Admiral…that this issue remain only within the upper echelons of IO and Naval Intelligence. At least until we know what transpires on Gardner IV and the fate of the alien artifact," Romanoff stated in a grave tone.

The Admiral thought for a second and then nodded his head. "For once I agree with you, Mr. Romanoff. It is imperative that neither the President nor anyone in his Cabinet is notified of this situation until we have a complete resolution."

"Very well, Admiral. In the mean time, I currently have my best double-agents infiltrating the Ares Alliance government to find out how much they know and how we will go about getting Project Contrivance back into our possession, if your Marine operation should fail," Romanoff declared confidently.

"I would sure hope you've got something planned Romanoff, because if any of this leaks out, you'll be the one taking the fall, not me. I'll send you an update on the recovery operation as soon as I get it from the Marine commander on the ground." The Admiral said as he stood up from the table, shuffling his papers. "No more secrets Romanoff! Your people need to share *everything* with Naval Intelligence on this matter understood?"

"Of course Admiral, Naval Intelligence will have full disclosure," Romanoff responded in somewhat of a sardonic tone as the Admiral and his staff began to leave the secure room. He leaned back in his chair again, lighting up another cigarette, staring intently at the image of the strange alien device.

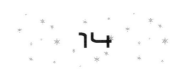

14

Surface of Gardner IV, Pericles star cluster, IO research facility

Marines from 1st squad brought down three more Ares Alliance commandos in a hail of gunfire as they attempted to overrun the two squad's positions in the corridor. Sergeant Yao noticed that this created an opening to a hallway that could allow his Marines to flank the remainder of the enemy forces.

"First squad! Bound forward, get a foothold in that far room! Hunt, what's the status on the door breach!?" Yao said forcefully.

Hunt turned and yelled back. "Give me two more mikes and we'll be ready to blast a hole through it! We've got to clear out of this corridor though. The detonation radius will be at least fifteen meters!"

"Roger that…Chambers! We've got to push everybody forward out of this corridor to that far room, time now!" Sergeant Yao relayed to his fellow squad leader.

"Roger, bounding forward now," Chambers sent his squad into action. The Marines systematically moved from crate to crate out of the corridor and into the adjacent science lab room, one team provided cover fire for the others as they moved. They were beginning to push the enemy commandos back, isolating them into one small corner room. The Ares Alliance special ops team had now lost their initial advantage. Corporal Hunt keyed up his remote detonator for the breach charge attached to the steel blast door that would be their exit. A green light indicated the charges were linked and set. He picked up Lieutenant Freeborn and threw him over his shoulder fireman's carry style, running into the science lab that 1st squad had just cleared and established a foothold in.

"Sergeant Yao, do you want me to blast the door?" Hunt transmitted over the squad net as he carefully lay the wounded Lieutenant Freeborn down on the deck.

"Not yet, we're gaining the advantage! Clearing the last room at this time! First squad flash and clear!" Sergeant Yao yelled.

*   *   *   *

Kaleb followed right behind PFC Smith as they quickly maneuvered down the first two floors inside the darkened bunker. They snuck quietly around the halls and corridors using their night vision image enhancement on their head's up displays. Corporal Martinez and PFC Colby fell in line directly behind them, covering their backside.

"Look at all the bodies…" PFC Smith said quietly as they made their way down the bunker.

"I don't see any of ours, that's a good sign, just keep moving," Kaleb answered. They had been unable to locate the team of four special ops commandos that entered the bunker ahead of them. As they descended down the long stairwell to the bottom floor they began to hear a faint sound of gunfire.

"Shit, you hear that? They're in a firefight down there!" Corporal Martinez stated in his Mexican-American accent.

"Shut up and stay alert. This should be the bottom floor, those enemy dismounts have to be down here," Kaleb whispered back.

They came up on a dark corner and began to hear the sound of a low-pitched voice grumbling on and on over what sounded like an open radio net. Kaleb held up his fist to indicate for his team to freeze in place. Slowly, he peeked around the corner, his green-tinted night vision made out a large human silhouette standing with his back to him just a few feet away. Kaleb froze. His heart felt like it was pounding through his chest.

The Ares commando in front of him had his assault rifle at the low ready, luckily facing away from Kaleb at the time, talking into a handheld radio. Kaleb slowly reached up with his right hand towards his combat-knife sheath located on the upper left chest of his ABAS suit. He gently gripped the handle of his ten-inch long, serrated edge, Marine standard issue field knife. Pulling the knife out of the sheath, Kaleb took one faint step towards the still oblivious enemy commando who continued to rattle on over his radio net.

"Yeah, this is Ziggs.....no.....nothing yet....did you find the access door? Negative...ok...I've got our rear covered....keep me posted-....."

Suddenly, in one swift motion, Kaleb reached around the Ares Alliance commando's helmet with his left hand, pulling as hard as he could, wrenching the enemy's neck and head to the left side, exposing a gap in his armor between the neck collar and helmet. Almost a half a second later, Kaleb forcefully dug his field knife into the exposed, right half of the commando's neck, burying the blade all the way to the hilt. The ten-inch blade sliced through the man's main arteries with ease and stuck itself into his upper vertebrate, paralyzing him instantly. The commando let out a faint grunt as his final breath of life expired a few seconds later. Kaleb carefully grabbed the man's body, quietly laying it down on the deck so as not to make any noise. He turned back and motioned with his hand for the rest of his team to move up, the hall was clear.

One down, now just need to find the other three, Kaleb thought as he led his three Marines further down the hall to what appeared to be another corner that wrapped the corridor around to the right. Once again, Kaleb slowly peered around the concrete wall down another dark passageway. Standing by a large blast door at the end of the thirty meter-long passage were the remaining three Ares Alliance commandos that Kaleb witnessed dismounting from the armored rover earlier. They were standing in an un-guarded posture, attempting to override the security lock on the blast door. One of the men anxiously punched the keys on his data pad, attempting to decrypt the access code.

The two other men paced back and forth, cursing. "Goddammit, I knew we should've left more men down here. How the hell did we not pick up their drop ships on radar?" one of the men said angrily at his counterpart.

"Calm down and get ready, I've almost broken the security code. They shouldn't expect us to come in from behind them. Where's Ziggs? Tell him to stop guarding the hallway and get back over here." the one holding the data pad whispered back.

Kaleb reached down to his assault belt on the waist of his ABAS and pulled out a high explosive grenade. He twisted the top, activating the five second fuse. "Frag out," he whispered to his team behind him. Kaleb took a step around the corner and with his left hand he side-armed the grenade down the corridor towards the blast door. The sound of the grenade bouncing off the concrete floor alerted the Ares Alliance commandos to his presence. All four of them turned in unison towards the sound, assault rifles pointing down the corridor towards Kaleb. The grenade rolled to a halt just below one of the commando's right foot.

"Grena….!" The enemy soldier didn't have time to finish his words as the high explosive detonated beneath him, shearing his body into pieces. Standing in a tight cluster, the other two men were immediately thrown against the concrete walls of the corridor, plopping down on the ground after the impact, killing at least one more of them. The surviving commando proceeded to get back up on his feet, stunned from the concussion but protected by his high-grade body armor. He started to reach for his weapon but not before Smith, Martinez, and Colby shot out from around the corner and took aim with their sniper rifles at close range. Three consecutive bursts from the Marines' MR-40A2 rifles echoed through the hallways as they knocked the enemy commando back down to the floor, blood began to spew out of the holes pierced in his chest-plate armor by the 9.45mm rounds. By this time Kaleb had readied his rifle and fired three more quick shots into the lifeless bodies of the special ops soldiers. The deafening sound from the rifle salvos echoed throughout the halls of the bunker complex.

Corporal Martinez grabbed Kaleb's shoulder, "Sergeant Taylor, they're dead already....you ok man?"

Payback for what you guys let happen on Hastati.... Kaleb thought to himself as he let out a deep breath, clicking the safety back on his rifle. "....I'm fine, come on, let's get that door open."

*   *   *   *

First squad stacked on the wall adjacent to the open door to the final un-cleared room. Three Ares Alliance commandos were all that remained from their initial ambushing force of fifteen men. Sergeant Yao's only concern right now was getting all of his Marines out alive. He gave a nod to the point man stacked beside the door. The Marine pulled out a flash-bang grenade and activated its timer. He cooked off the grenade for three seconds and tossed it in the small room. The three commandos inside were hidden behind a few desks and a file cabinet, ready to make their last stand against the Marines. They heard the grenade roll into the room and immediately focused their attention on it. Before they had a chance to identify what it was it was too late. A bright flash temporarily blinded all three men, their eardrums ruptured from the concussion that followed. First squad filed into the room, clearing the near and far corners. The first three Marines from Yao's Bravo team entered the room half a second after the thunderous report of the flash-bang. They instinctively acquired their targets through the image enhancement on their heads up display. Three controlled, five to six round bursts from their assault rifles sent multiple 6.8mm armor-piercing rounds through the stunned Ares Alliance special ops commando's armor. They dropped like rag dolls to the deck, bleeding out in seconds. The Bravo team Marines scanned the darkened room for any other enemy threats.

"Sergeant Yao, three hostiles KIA, room clear...hold on...what the hell?" The Bravo team leader stated over Yao's squad net. He shined his weapon light into the corner of the room, discovering a pitiful looking man in a white lab coat, cowering in a chair, his hands bound together with flexie cuffs. "Sergeant, looks like I've got one live hostage as well, repeat, one live hostage."

"Roger, Wolfpack 1 coming in," Yao responded as he turned the corner to walk into the lab. "Somebody find the fucking light switch I can't see shit in here." One of Yao's Marines found a switch on the wall and flipped on the fluorescent lighting. Sergeant Yao looked over at the handcuffed scientist. "Alright get those cuffs off and search him." Two Marines went over to the shell-shocked man and cut the flexie cuffs, helping him to his feet. The scientist's face had been badly beaten and covered in blood and bruises; his right eye was swelled shut. They patted him down just to make sure he wasn't carrying a weapon. Sergeant Yao walked over to the terrified man and removed his combat helmet in order to get a clear look at the scientist.

"Get me a medic in here! You're with the IO science team right?" Shaking horribly, the man struggled to nod, acknowledging Yao's assessment. The 1st squad medic ran in the room and began to treat the wounds on the man's face. "It's alright, we're going to get you out of here and back to a medical bay," Yao reassured the man. The scientist began to raise his left hand up, slowly pointing to a what appeared to be a heavy vault door that was slightly cracked open in the back of the room.

"Oh shit, another room!" the Bravo team leader yelled. Yao turned immediately towards the heavy steel door, his weapon at the ready. "Goddammit, clear that room quick!"

The team leader motioned with hand and arm signals for a stack on the door. It took four Marines aggressively pushing to open the massive door, three more ran in as soon as a large enough opening was created with their weapons up. They swiftly cleared the corners of the large vault room.

"Nothing here Sergeant, just a big room with probably a thirty-foot high ceiling, totally empty." The team leader reported to Yao.

Sergeant Yao let out a sigh of relief and looked back at the scientist. The man sat back down in the chair and spoke softly while staring at the floor. "They…..they took it…..I wasn't fast enough….. they took it."

"Took what? Are there any other survivors? Is the sensitive data secured?" Yao questioned with annoyance.

"Project Contrivance….the commandos took it, killed my science team. You weren't fast enough….. I'm the only one left alive. I….I was in charge of this lab….I failed….they tortured me…tried to get me to decrypt our data files on the project…..I wouldn't give it to them…doesn't matter though…they…they don't…underst….. don't know it's purpose…..it's power…must get it back….before… before it's too late…" The scientist began to drift in and out of consciousness.

"Whoa, take is easy man, we're gonna get you out of here. Sergeant Chambers let's get this guy on a litter and get the hell out of here." Yao ordered. Chambers nodded and had his squad medic place the deranged scientist on the portable stretcher.

"Hunt, whenever you're ready, blow that door so we can get topside and get in contact with the rest of the platoon," Yao relayed to Hunt who was in the next room over, placing the LT on a another portable stretcher.

"Roger Sergeant!" Hunt pulled out his remote detonator and walked out into the corridor to get a clear signal to the charges. He lifted his thumb over the green activation switch. Suddenly, the door control light flashed from red to green and the four-inch thick steel barrier slid up into the wall, revealing four Marines standing on the other side of it.

"Taylor!....What are you doing down here! Holy shit, I was half a second away from blowing the hell out of that door!" Hunt yelled down the hallway.

Kaleb slightly smiled, "I figured coming down here and opening it would be a little easier for you guys."

"Sergeant Yao! Fourth squad is down here… they just opened the door from the other side, they said the bunker's all clear!" Hunt excitedly transmitted over the comm. "

"Well I'll be god-damned, nice to see someone finally came to bail our asses out. Come on let's get topside now!" Yao ordered.

The Marines quickly made their way back up through the bunker complex towards the surface, four of them carrying Lieutenant Freeborn and the rescued scientist on stretchers. As they entered the top floor of the bunker they made their way towards the entry door, stepping over the bodies of the former science team members and Ares Alliance commandos.

"How's the LT doing?" Kaleb asked Sergeant Yao.

"The doc says he'll be fine, he took quite a bit of shrapnel when we got ambushed, lost a lot of blood but we clotted him up and he's stable now." Yao answered.

"That's good to hear, he the only casualty?" Kaleb said surprised.

"Yeah, except for one of my guys getting his finger shot off that's it. Looked bad at first; they set demo charges and ambushed us, but the guys fought hard. We eventually were able to gain a foothold in one of the rooms and started picking them off one by one. Thanks for coming in to get us man, those guys would've torn us apart if they had a chance to hit us from behind….Shinwar mercenaries my ass, looks like intel dropped the ball again, these were Ares Alliance special ops…" Yao was explaining Kaleb when he saw four dark figures enter the bunker in front of them.

PFC Kevin Smith was on point and drew down on the unknown men with his assault rifle. "Identify yourself or I'll blow your fucking heads off!" he tensely yelled. The rest of the platoon took cover, not knowing what to expect. The four men appeared to be unarmed as they emerged from the shadows wearing strange, dark black fatigues that Kaleb did not recognize.

"Hold your fire, we're the United Star Systems Intelligence Office special reaction team, we're here to investigate the site. We heard the bunker was secure." One of the men spoke as they entered the faint light of the room.

PFC Smith walked up and checked their ID badges, "Special Agent John Smith huh?" the Marine skeptically asked. "Guess we're not related…. they look clean Sergeant," PFC Smith reported back in a condescending tone.

Kaleb walked up to the man that spoke, "How did you know it was secure? We've been out of radio contact."

"That doesn't matter Sergeant. We're here to take custody of Dr. Rothberger here and conduct an analysis of the research station. Your platoon is outside waiting for the rest of you. You did a great job Marine. You neutralized the enemy force as the mission required. But now it's our turn to do our job. Please step aside and give us the doctor." the tall, pale faced, dark haired IO agent spoke without emotion.

The platoon medic stepped forward in between Kaleb and agent Smith, "he needs urgent medical attention; we have to get him to an infirmary now."

"Don't worry, we have everything under control, we will see the doctor is treated once we debrief him. Now your orders are to report to your platoon outside and proceed to the extraction point. You will be debriefed on your mission onboard the Athens. IO has taken control of the operation at this time." the man mysteriously spoke.

Kaleb looked at Yao shaking his head, "Whatever, right now we need to get out of here and get the LT back to the Athens. Let these spooks do their thing." Yao nodded in agreement.

"You heard Sergeant Taylor, let's move, leave the scientist," Yao ordered. The IO agents, without sympathy, forcefully grabbed the frightened doctor and disappeared to the lower floors of the bunker.

$$* \qquad * \qquad * \qquad *$$

The Marines reached the outside of the bunker to find Gunnery Sergeant Norton and 3rd squad investigating the burning rover that Kaleb's team destroyed. A faint light began to shine on the horizon, signaling that daybreak was near on the moon. Gunny Norton locked eyes on Kaleb and stormed over to him as the Marines filed out of the entry point.

"Taylor what the hell do you think you're doing!" he screamed while pointing his finger at Kaleb's helmet visor. "You jeopardized the entire mission because you didn't want to follow orders! You're relieved of your squad leader duties, time now…. Corporal Martinez!"

"Yes Sergeant!" Martinez looked up, confused.

"You are my new 4th squad leader!"

"First of all, you better get your finger out of my face before I shove it up your ass," Kaleb calmly stated, rebelling against Gunny Norton's authority. Norton fumed with anger at the comment. He reared back and smacked Kaleb across the front of his helmet with the butt of his assault rifle, knocking him back a few steps.

"You son of a bitch! You are done, you hear me! Done! Nobody talks to me like that!" Norton screamed at Kaleb.

Sergeant Yao ran in between the two NCO's, holding back Norton from going after Kaleb again, "hold on now Gunny, Sergeant Taylor just saved our ass; we would've been ambushed from our six by Ares commandos if it wasn't for him!" Sergeant Yao attempted to defend Kaleb.

Gunny Norton turned to Yao, "You shut your mouth Marine, this is between me and Taylor, and where in the hell is your LT anyway?! I've been trying to reach his sorry ass on the net for the last forty-five minutes! Doesn't he know I need to be kept in the loop, Viper 6 is gonna fry his ass for not sending in a sitrep!"

Kaleb, after regaining his stance and composure, rolled his eyes at Norton, "He's right there, on the litter, maybe if you weren't such a certifiable asshole you would've noticed that."

Norton's eyes fumed at Kaleb's comment. "That's it. I don't have time for this shit. Our orders are to report back to the extraction point ASAP. Taylor, you can rest assured that I'm gonna get you court-martialed as soon as we get back onboard the Athens. Sergeant Yao! First squad takes point! Now let's move out!"

The platoon of Marines just stood and stared at the Gunnery Sergeant, in awe of what just transpired. Their cohesive unit had been broken down in a matter of seconds. "Goddammit I said move out!" Norton again yelled after no one moved. The Marines reluctantly began to form up and walk back to the extraction point. Martinez came up to Kaleb with a puzzled look on his face and whispered.

"Sergeant Taylor, what the hell is going on? We don't need to follow Norton, that dude's crazy man. I'm behind you 100%, you're still my squad leader." Martinez said.

"It'll be alright, we don't want to play that game, just do what he says and get the squad back to the extraction point. Things will sort their way out once we get back on the ship and the LT gets better, I promise. You're squad leader right now, take us home." Kaleb explained to the Corporal, patting him on his shoulder.

Martinez nodded, "Alright Taylor, I trust you, let's get off of this shit hole moon."

"Hey! Cut that chatter back there! This isn't social hour! Martinez! Get your squad in line!" Norton screamed back at the Corporal, shining his helmet spot light in his face as they entered the gloomy, pre-dawn canyon that led to their extraction point.

"So much for light and noise discipline," Sergeant Yao mumbled to himself, disgusted at Gunny Norton's outburst during a tactical movement.

*   *   *   *

Michael Romanoff sat at his marble desk in his darkened 72nd story office at IO headquarters in London. He couldn't stop studying the images taken of the alien device his men called the "Contrivance." *How could I have been so foolish to let it be compromised? My chance to be the first human to make contact with an intelligent alien race could very well have slipped through my fingers. So foolish it was to have given Agent Inlow so much responsibility on the project. I should've personally supervised the operation. Perhaps it was Inlow himself who leaked the Project Contrivance's location to the Ares Alliance? Would my most loyal agent so treacherously betray me? I **will** find out, it is inevitable. One thing was for sure, this would be the last time I trust anyone other than myself.*

Romanoff's encrypted video terminal blinked red indicating an urgent, real-time interstellar message. He flicked on the video screen on his desk, hoping for the good news he'd been waiting for from his agents on Gardner IV. The stern, steely-eyed face of special agent John Smith appeared.

"Mr. Romanoff sir…..we've lost positive control….."

Romanoff clenched his fist and strained to hold back an outburst of anger. He took a deep breath and then hastily lit up a cigarette, taking a heavy drag off of it before speaking.

"Find it, agent Smith, find it now before I make you disappear, understood?" Romanoff said through clenched teeth.

"Yes sir, immediately," the IO agent replied. "I do have one lead for you Mr. Romanoff. Doctor Rothberger, agent Inlow's second in command. He is still alive and we have him in custody. He says an elite Ares Alliance special forces unit infiltrated the facility and knew exactly where the vault holding Project Contrivance was located, had the access code, everything. Said they had it transported back to the Ares colony two hours before our Marine rescue force even arrived. Some of the Ares Alliance special ops team stayed behind to scour the rest of the facility and interrogate the doctor regarding the data files he had on the project. Luckily our USS Marine force made fairly short work of them though."

"Well, at least somebody can do their damn job…..so, what did the doctor tell them?" Romanoff asked angrily, anticipating the worst.

"Nothing sir, at least not according to the lab's video surveillance footage we have of his interrogation. They beat him up pretty bad but the audio tape confirms he didn't divulge anything to them. One other thing sir…the Ares commandos…..somehow they had prior knowledge of the access codes to the Project Contrivance secure vault. Dr. Rothberger and agent Inlow were the only ones on the project that knew the access code to that vault. If Rothberger didn't give them the code…..well that only leaves one person sir."

"That little cock sucker! I knew it!" Romanoff yelled as he pounded his fist on the desk in front of him. "Good work John. Find everything you can about where that special ops team took Contrivance on Ares and send me an update as soon as you have something. In the mean time....I'll deal with our friend, agent Inlow, accordingly."

Romanoff cut off the transmission, not wanting to hear anymore. He paused for a moment to think, and then pushed the intercom button on his desk to hail his secretary. "Janet, I need you to get Mr. Velasquez of internal affairs on the line for me, tell him we have an urgent matter that needs to be discussed."

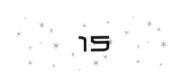

15

USSN Athens, Talos station Orbit, three weeks after the mission on Gardner IV

The large Naval cruiser, Athens, slowly orbited the massive USS Naval space station waiting for clearance to dock and have services conducted on the ship after its recent mission into deep space. It was a long trip back to the USS Naval headquarters station. The ship had to travel through four separate Faust drive wormhole legs and twelve days of travel at ninety percent of light speed to reach the station. During that time, Lieutenant Freeborn's shrapnel wounds had begun to heal and he was back on his feet. He was still confined to the medical bay onboard the ship for a few more days however. Gunnery Sergeant Norton and Kaleb had not spoken since the incident on the Moon. He knew that Norton had put him in for a court-martial; he just didn't know what had become of it. Kaleb figured he'd find out today as he was to report to Captain Williams' office in a few minutes. Until then Kaleb's mind was focused on the upcoming two month long shore leave and his plans to travel to Earth for a couple of days with Sergeant Yao, Corporal Martinez, and Robbie Hunt to check out the party scene there. He lay in his rack in the NCO berthing onboard the ship, checking out an internet advertisement for Cancun, Mexico, the "party capital" of Earth as it was now labeled.

"Dude check out the chicks is this picture! It says here that at this one bar in Cancun, you can take body shots off of hot topless girls for five credits all night!" Hunt exclaimed to Kaleb while he surfed the same internet site from his data pad as well.

"Hah, I don't have to pay to take body shots off of hot women. In Cancun they'll be begging to take body shots off of me," Kaleb jested. "Women are just naturally drawn to me, I'm not sure what it is, but they just are."

Hunt laughed out loud, "Yeah too bad Sergeant Yao won't be getting any chicks down there; his dumb ass went and got married."

Yao responded sarcastically while he wiped down his assault rifle. "Yeah and if I catch any of you assholes trying to tell my wife I'm going there with you guys, I'll cut your fucking balls off in your sleep."

Corporal Julio Martinez butted in, "Man, white people don't know nothing about Latino women. You have to wine and dine them if you want to get in their pants. The women are civilized in Mexico. All you need to do is follow my lead. Besides, I've been there like five times already, I know where all the hot bitches are."

Kaleb responded, "Whatever man, I guarantee that if any of us don't get any action it will be you. See there is this thing called 'game' and it's something that you definitely don't have any of." The four Marines laughed out loud at Kaleb's statement.

"Fuck you Taylor, I've got more game than anyone here. You don't know how I operate at the club," Martinez protested.

Kaleb stood up and walked towards the berthing hatch, "Martinez, I'd love to stick around and listen to more of your bullshit but unfortunately I've got to run. I've got my meeting with Viper 6 in five minutes where I'm probably going to take it up the ass for disobeying Gunny Norton's orders."

"Hey Taylor, don't let them mess with you man, we're all behind you, one hundred percent. If they try to do a court-martial or some bullshit, I'll testify against Norton." Yao said in a serious tone.

"Yeah I appreciate the thought but let's just see what happens first. I don't want to create a division within the platoon or anything." Kaleb replied as he walked out of the berthing area.

*   *   *   *

Kaleb knocked on the door to Captain Williams' office onboard the Athens. "Enter!" the Company Commander yelled from inside. He walked in and stood at attention in front of the commander's desk. To his surprise, he noticed that Lieutenant Freeborn and Gunnery Sergeant Norton were also seated in the small room.

"Sergeant Taylor reporting as ordered sir," Kaleb saluted and went to the position of parade rest. Lieutenant Freeborn sat in the corner in front of Taylor and gave him a nod. A set of crutches were resting at Freeborn's side. Gunnery Sergeant Norton sat in the other corner behind Kaleb with a scowl on his face.

Damn, the commander looks extremely pissed, Kaleb thought after seeing the look on Captain Williams' face.

"Ask me why you're here Sergeant Taylor," the commander said calmly.

Surprised at the question, Kaleb responded, "Uh...say again sir?"

"Ask me why you're fucking here!" the Captain yelled back, pounding his fist on the desk in front of him.

"...Why am I here sir?" Kaleb replied in a confused manner.

"I'll tell you why you're here. You're here because two of my most experienced and respected Non-Commissioned Officers came to blows with each other in the middle of a fucking mission! I mean, what kind of example is that for your Marines? The most important operation this company has ever been involved in and you want to act like goddamn Privates out there! I ought to have you and Gunnery Sergeant Norton reduced in rank and transferred out of the 1st Recon Battalion right this second! This is a goddamn embarrassment is what it is! An embarrassment!" Kaleb stood motionless with no expression on his face, ignoring the spit flying out of Williams' mouth that landed on Kaleb as he yelled. It was the first time he witnessed the normally calm and collected Company Commander screaming at someone. "Well!...Sergeants!...what do you have to say for yourselves?"

Gunny Norton stood up and spoke in an annoyed tone, as if he felt he had no reason to be there. "Sir, Sergeant Taylor disobeyed a direct order while the platoon was under fire. If that's not evidence enough to court-martial him, I don't know what is."

Kaleb, showing no emotion, spoke his rebuttal, "Sir, I have no excuse for my actions and will take any punishment that you see fit to in order to rectify the situation.... In no way did I mean to jeopardize the lives of my Marines and it was unprofessional of me as an NCO to disobey my supervisor in front of the rest of the platoon."

Captain Williams was surprised at Kaleb's response. He quickly looked over at Freeborn sitting in the chair. "Very well....Lieutenant Freeborn, you're the platoon leader, what course of action do you recommend?"

Freeborn sat forward and cleared his throat, not expecting to be put on the spot by his commander. "Uh...sir...uh... It is my assessment that Gunnery Sergeant Taylor made a tactical error by not immediately employing his Centurion missile system against the armored rover that attempted to ambush the platoon.... This endangered the mission as he gave away his position and was forced to pull back several clicks for cover, essentially taking 3rd squad out of the fight as myself, 1st and 2nd squad were trapped and out of radio contact inside the bunker. In my opinion sir, Sergeant Taylor acted with bravery and selflessness when he took the initiative to flank the vehicle and destroy it. Knowing that we had fallen out of contact, he then took his team into the bunker, neutralized an ambushing force of Ares special ops soldiers, and was able to link back up with his platoon and ensure their safe egress from the objective. Based on the events that occurred on ground, Sergeant Taylor is the only reason why we were able to accomplish our mission….. and do so without taking any serious casualties. I'd also add that Gunnery Sergeant Norton acted in an unprofessional manner when he struck Sergeant Taylor with the butt of his rifle and should be punished accordingly. I believe that Sergeant Taylor should be exonerated of any charges of misconduct and if anything, his courage and valor under fire should be rewarded."

Norton, infuriated at the LT's comments, abruptly stood up and glared at Freeborn, "You little sack of shit! How dare you! I was a Marine while you were still pissin' your pants in pre-school!"

Captain Williams interrupted, "Gunnery Sergeant Norton! Stand down! You are addressing an officer! Show some respect and keep yourself professional or I will gladly boot your ass out of the nearest airlock, understood?!"

"Yes Sir," Norton gulped and went to the position of attention, realizing his outburst was way out of line.

The office was silent for several seconds as Williams tapped his fingers on the desk in front of him, going over thoughts in his head. After a long pause, he lifted his head and spoke. "Norton, I'm re-assigning you to Marine Training Command. Your service to the Recon has been impeccable up to this point, but I can't have you in my unit anymore Gunny. You've lost the edge needed in combat. I believe that your skills and experience would greatly benefit in the training of future Marines. I'll have the 1st Sergeant get with personnel services to get your new orders cut….Dismissed Gunnery Sergeant." Gunny Norton slowly saluted in disbelief with a broken look on his face, confused as to what just happened. He ducked his head down, and nodded, did an about face and walked out of the office, ensuring to give Kaleb a death stare as he passed by him.

"Sergeant Taylor!" the commander yelled.

Kaleb straightened his stance, "Sir!"

"You should be thankful that your platoon leader thinks so highly of you. Were it not for his counsel I would've had you castrated and assigned you to some rear echelon supply unit! However, the LT spoke to me on the details of what happened on the mission before I called you in here and I hold his opinions in high regard," Captain Williams lowered the tempo of his speech.

"Well, now that we've gotten the ass chewings out of the way I'll give you my personal assessment of what happened down there...... To put it bluntly, the way I see it, your actions saved the lives of your fellow Marines and are in keeping with the highest traditions of the USS military. Therefore, I'm putting you in for a battlefield promotion to Staff Sergeant, and you are to be awarded the Marine Commendation Medal for your bravery in the face of battle. You did what you had to, *Staff* Sergeant Taylor. Taking initiative and finding a way to accomplish the mission is a quality much admired in the USS Marines. You handled the situation with Gunnery Sergeant Norton as best you could and now that he has been reassigned, that makes you the new 1st platoon Sergeant. Congratulations Wolfpack 7, you've got a lot more responsibility on your shoulders now." Captain Williams firmly shook Kaleb's hand.

Kaleb was taken aback by the commander's response, "Uh.. Thank you sir," he nodded. "I will perform the duties of platoon Sergeant to the best of my ability." Kaleb got a queasy feeling in his stomach as he reflected on what just happened. *Is this really happening? Here was the orphaned farm colony kid with no future, now a senior NCO in an elite Marine unit, earning commendation honors for valor.*

"Well I'm sure you and your LT have a few things to go over with each other, I won't keep you two any longer, hell of a job down there gentlemen, dismissed." Freeborn got up with his crutches and began to hobble out of the commander's office.

Kaleb followed his LT out into the ship's corridor. "Man LT, that was pretty intense in there. I thought for sure I was going to get busted down in rank the way the commander started off. I appreciate you sticking your neck out for me like that. I honestly didn't expect you to come to my defense so easily," Kaleb admitted.

"It was the right decision. Gunnery Sergeant Norton was incompetent as a leader. He needed to be transferred for a long time. He was totally out of line and risked getting Marines killed. Besides, you know the guys all look up to you for leadership, hell even I do. You're the most capable NCO in the platoon, that's why you got the job. Corporal Martinez is ready to take on 4th squad, he'll do fine under your mentorship. We'll have a platoon meeting tonight to break the news to the guys before we all head out on leave. Training room at 2000 hours sound good?" Freeborn asked.

"Roger sir, I'll let everybody know…..I'll catch you later, have fun with those nurses in the med bay." Kaleb teased.

"Yeah I should be stuck here just two more days, I can walk fine but the doc will freak out if he sees me trying to get around without these damn crutches. Don't worry, I'll be back in the fight soon enough," Freeborn replied.

*   *   *   *

Ryan Inlow sunk down into the seat of the overnight high-speed rail train that would take him to Leipzig spaceport in Germany. There he was to board a Private shuttle that would transport him one-way to the colony of Ares. His newly created identity should keep Romanoff's hired goons off of his tail long enough for him to reach his contacts within the Ares intelligence apparatus. Since he'd been on the inside of the intelligence field for so many years, it was easy for Inlow to make himself disappear. He had the right contacts inside the system to help him along the way.

I don't have any regrets for betraying Romanoff. After all, the man was downright evil; with a god complex and a craving for so much power, the man was a danger to everyone. The seven-hundred and fifty million credits that the Ares intelligence branch wired to my bank account two weeks ago is surely helping to ease the feelings of guilt. I've been a slave to Romanoff and the IO for long enough. It was time I looked out for myself, he thought as he looked out the window of the hydrogen powered train and into the darkness of Northern France. He looked at his watch, *1:30 AM, might as well get some rest,* he thought. Only one other person was in his rail car, an old woman reading a book, *no threat there* Inlow thought as he began to dose off.

Twenty minutes later, two well dressed men in black suits and ties entered from the forward rail car. The sound of the sliding door closing that connected the two cars startled Inlow, waking him from his sleep. He looked up to find the two strange men in black suits staring right down at him.

"Ryan Inlow?" One of the men spoke in a deep, ominous voice.

Inlow sat up, his heart pounding, "Wha...What? What are you talking about? That's not me," Inlow objected, even though he knew playing dumb was fruitless at this point.

"Of course it's not you...Ryan Inlow is dead," the man said back. In an instant, the man's partner standing next to him pulled out a small, silenced, 9mm pistol. Inlow made an attempt to reach for his own personal weapon inside his trench coat pocket. Before Inlow could get his hand on his pistol, Romanoff's agent fired four quick rounds into his chest *pew, pew, pew, pew,* and a fifth into his head, *pew.*

16

Two weeks later, Cancun, Mexico, North American Union, Earth

"I propose a toast, to our first night out in Cancun, and to my future wife, Anna here," Robbie Hunt stated in a drunken slur. He held a bottle of tequila in one hand and his other arm around an attractive South American girl he had just met on the dance floor.

Kaleb, Hunt, Martinez, and Yao had just arrived at their resort hotel on the beach of Cancun to start their two month-long shore leave a few hours ago. It didn't take long for the four of them to find the nearest bar and start pounding drinks. They were currently at "El Bar del Bandido," a beachside watering hole that featured karaoke and wet t-shirt contests. Tiki lights were strewn about the wooden ceiling of the outside bar and the latest electronic dance music could be heard playing over the sound of waves crashing against the sand on the nearby beach. The four Marines had managed to meet up with a group of local girls and were already developing their game plan on how to bring them back to the hotel for an "after party."

"I second that, and I toast to Earth so far being awesome! They sure don't have places like this in the colonies," Kaleb replied with an attractive brunette girl sitting on his lap whose name he had already forgotten. "Still glad you got married Yao?" Kaleb smiled and gestured towards the women around them.

"Fuck you Taylor" as far as she knows I was never here. It's going stay that way too," he answered as the rest of the Marines laughed.

They all raised their glasses with the girls and took down another shot of liquor, their seventh one of the night.

"Man, I don't know if I can go back to the fleet after all of this," Yao said with a hint of nostalgia. "I mean, we almost got ourselves killed back on Gardner IV. Makes you start to wonder."

"Hah…yeah that was pretty awesome wasn't it? Talk about the ultimate adrenaline rush man!" Hunt blurted out. "Heh, Sergeant Yao was like, 'Open the damn door man!! And I was like 'but its fucking locked dude!!'" Hunt nearly fell off of his barstool as he tried to re-enact what happened in the bunker on Gardner IV. Everybody laughed hysterically except for Yao, who downed another shot, grimacing at the flow of more tequila hitting his taste buds.

Sergeant Yao wiped his mouth and stood up from his barstool, grabbing Kaleb's shoulder. "Hey man I think I'm going to head back to the room before I do something I'll regret. I'm pretty freakin' wasted right now."

Kaleb gave a surprised look, "What?! You serious? The party's just getting started."

"Yeah man, I'm old and married remember? People like me have to go to bed early," Yao countered.

"Pussy!!! Hey everybody, Sergeant Yao's gotta go put on some vagisil, he'll see you tomorrow," Hunt yelled in the background.

"Yeah, yeah, laugh it up jerk off," Yao decided he didn't have enough energy to make up a witty comeback. He turned to Kaleb and spoke with a more serious tone. "Hey Taylor…what you did on Gardner IV, standing up to Gunny Norton like that. That's high speed shit man. I respect that, not many people would have the balls to do that. You probably saved our lives back there. Just wanted to say thanks, I guess," Yao explained to Kaleb.

Kaleb smirked, "C'mon man, don't get all emotional on me because you've had a couple drinks now."

"Naw, I'm serious, thanks. Let me tell you something, the guys in the platoon, they respect you. They'll follow you anywhere. You're the platoon Sergeant now, we trust you. Keep taking care of us like you have been and we'll be right behind you every step," Yao continued on in his somewhat slurred speech.

"Well, thanks, I appreciate it…do you need help getting back to the room at all?" Kaleb asked as Yao stumbled slightly.

"Screw you man, I'm a lightweight but I can handle my shit, I'll see you in the morning, peace out," Yao said as he wandered off back to the hotel.

∗　　　∗　　　∗　　　∗

The rays of sunlight from Sol beamed into the hotel room from the balcony window as Earth's sun rose from the eastern horizon. Kaleb slowly woke up to his data pad ringing off the hook on the bedside table next to him. He turned to look at the clock, which read 6:02AM.

"What the hell?" he mumbled as he cringed from the hangover that had set in from the previous night's festivities. *Ring, Ring, Ring* the data pad continued to signal an incoming call. Sergeant Yao, in the other hotel room bed across from Kaleb grumbled and rolled over upon hearing the incessant noise.

Kaleb reach for the data pad and looked at the screen. *The LT? Why the hell is he calling me right now?* He hit the answer key on the touch screen, "Hello," Kaleb reluctantly said.

A tense voice came over the speaker, "Staff Sergeant Taylor, its Lieutenant Freeborn. There's been a mass recall of leave for the entire battalion, we're ordered to report back to Talos station immediately, I need you to call all the squad leaders and let them know, first muster is in seventy-two hours, we've got to…."

"Whoa whoa whoa hold on LT, what are you saying now?" Kaleb was still trying to get his bearings after being abruptly woken up after a long night of heavy drinking.

"There's been an attack, I'm not sure of the details but it is pretty serious, we need to get in contact with the rest of the platoon…"

"Ha….haha, you're very funny LT. But for real, don't fuck with me sir, its 6:02 in the morning here," Kaleb responded, still feeling somewhat buzzed.

"I'm not fucking around here Sergeant Taylor, turn on the news and see for yourself if you don't believe me, it's on every station. Now get your ass up and get the platoon recalled back to Talos station. We have company formation on the Athens in seventy-two hours."

Kaleb grabbed the remote from the bedside table and turned on the holographic projector screen in the hotel room. A frightened looking female newscaster appeared with a backdrop of a burning city behind her.

"…As I said these are initial reports, but it is confirmed that the capital city of the Ares colony has suffered a devastating attack from what appears to be an unknown number of extraterrestrial star ships. Casualties at this point are said to be in the hundreds of thousands and the whereabouts of top-level Ares Alliance government officials is unknown at this time….." Kaleb's jaw dropped as he listened to the news report coming in. He looked back at the data pad as the LT was still talking through it.

"Staff Sergeant Taylor? Are you still there? Can you hear me?"

"Uh…yeah, yeah LT I got you. Holy shit you're not kidding," Kaleb replied in shock.

"No Sergeant, I'm not, now get the platoon together ASAP and meet me back on board the Athens in three days Earth time, roger?"

"Yeah...ok...yes sir, I'll have them there, don't worry," Kaleb answered quietly.

"Roger, out," Freeborn abruptly ended the call.

Kaleb looked around the room at his friends who were still passed out; oblivious to the conversation he just had with the LT. Hunt was sprawled out on the floor of the hotel room with a random girl lying beside him. Martinez was nowhere to be found, probably still at the strip club. *Goddammit why does this have to happen now?* Kaleb thought, rubbing his head. He stood up and cleared his throat,

"Hey! Assholes!! Wake up!!....We've got a mission."

17

Twenty-four hours later, Talos Station, Naval Intelligence briefing room

Fifteen of the highest ranking military and intelligence officials sat around a large, oval-shaped conference table. Inside the main Naval intelligence briefing room were a dozen view screens feeding information from all of the colonies on the unprecedented attack that just occurred on the colony of Ares. There was a somber atmosphere inside the room as aides and secretaries quietly updated the USS military high brass that sat around the table, attempting to come up with a course of action. At the head of the table sat the President's chief of staff, Ms. Sharyn Borders, next to her was Fleet Admiral Beck, now commander of the entire USS Naval fleet. On the other side was the burly, gray-haired General Austin, commander of all USS Marine forces. Rear Admiral Falasad, head of Navy Intel, sat at the other end next to none other than, IO Director Romanoff.

The middle aged, professional looking, female chief of staff, Sharyn Borders, stood up from the table to call everyone to attention in a forceful tone of voice. "Alright everyone listen up. We've got to get something going here or we're all going end up like those people on Ares," the sidebar conversations tapered off as the high ranking officials turned their attention to the woman at the head of the table. "Director Romanoff, I understand you have several agents implanted throughout the Ares Alliance feeding you reports, what can you tell us?"

Romanoff stood up and lit his usual cigarette before speaking. "Very well…ladies and gentlemen….. We all knew that we would eventually make first contact with an intelligent, space faring civilization. Unfortunately for us, they are unmistakably hostile…." Romanoff took another drag off of the cigarette. "Here's what we know. Twenty-six hours ago, the Ares Alliance Navy detected a large number of unidentified star ships suddenly entering the Ares star system from an unknown origin. Their routine patrol frigates attempted to make contact unsuccessfully with the vessels. Upon closing distance with the ships, they received direct fire from some sort of high energy laser originating from several of the alien ships. The three patrol frigates were utterly destroyed upon impact with this laser weaponry. The Ares Alliance fleet was notified and moved to engage the enemy force. A short inter-system engagement took place, and it was reported that the Ares Electro-Magnetic Accelerator primary weapons were largely ineffective against the alien craft. They proceeded to then launch several tactical nuclear missiles which may have destroyed only a few of the alien ships. The Ares Fleet was quickly overwhelmed however, taking at least eighty-five percent losses….."

"Jesus," one of the Marine Generals sitting at the table said under his breath at Romanoff's report.

The Director paused, then continued on; "The enemy fleet then bombarded the colony's entire surface defense grid from orbit with these high powered lasers, while also knocking out all of their satellite communications within a few hours. With their fleet decimated, communications offline, and surface defense towers destroyed, the colony is now a sitting duck. The rest of what we know is that the enemy force released what we'll call 'drop ships' from its fleet onto the surface of the planet in its major cities after the bombardment. The drop ships contained the extraterrestrial 'entities' that have been captured on film on the surface of Ares. These aliens have a sleek, carbon-based, humanoid appearance. Their heads slightly larger than a human's with smooth, brown skin, and resembles a reptilian-like appearance with large yellow-colored eyes, with black slits for pupils. They also appear to be seven to eight feet in height, move very quickly, and are considered to be vastly our technological superiors."

"These entities captured on film by my agents are shown here;" Romanoff pointed to a projector screen that showed a low-quality video feed, "freeze the video please… here, and here, is what can be called their 'soldiers.' They are wearing some sort of integrated combat suit or armor. Their right arm appendages seen here; are apparently replaced by smaller versions of their high-energy laser weapons. This shiny, dark black armor here looks like it is permanently affixed to their bodies. However, this is all just speculation at this point….. We do also believe they communicate telepathically and may have the ability to control other humans through this method, but like I said it's merely speculation."

Admiral Falasad chimed in, "We don't know the purpose of their dismounted forces that are on the ground. If they wanted to destroy the colony it seems they could easily do it from orbit with their ships. While these 'soldier' entities have been killing any human they encounter, we believe they are also searching for something. There may be something on Ares that they want. What it is and for what purpose they want it, we as humans may never understand."

Chief of Staff Borders scoffed at the Admiral's remarks. "Listen Admiral, we don't have time to come up with theories on why they are here in human space. What matters right now is that what remains of the Ares Alliance government is asking the USS President for our urgent military assistance. Just before their interstellar communications went down, a Deputy Director Rhenquist of the Ares Intelligence and Science Department relayed an emergency priority request for us to send in our fleet to try to save their colony. We believe he may be one of the only surviving members of the Prime Minister's cabinet and is most likely now in command of the situation there. Now I think it is our duty, not as members of the United Star Systems government, but as fellow humans, to do whatever we can to help them."

General Austin vehemently protested; "have you lost your mind ma'am?! Did you not just hear what Director Romanoff said? The Ares fleet was decimated. Their ground forces are in the process of being destroyed! If we send in our fleet it would be like leading cattle in to slaughter! I won't sacrifice thousands of my Marines in a haphazard attempt to save a colony that we are currently at war with!"

Romanoff interjected, "It would in fact be rather reckless to send our entire defense force over one hundred light years away to attack a technologically superior enemy we know absolutely nothing about. Not to mention, it would leave Talos, Earth, and our other colonies wide open to attack. They could have other fleets of ships just waiting to descend upon all of our colonies for all we know. I think the practical course of action would be to keep on the defensive for now, wait and see what we can learn about them, perhaps find a weakness in their fleet that we can exploit or find out what it is they are looking for."

"Thousands of People are dying Mr. Romanoff!" Chief of Staff Borders said expressively. Her aide suddenly approached the table and began to whisper something into her ear. She nodded as the aide passed on what appeared to be an urgent message. The Chief of Staff looked up and spoke in a grave voice, "Well, it doesn't matter anymore. I've just been informed that the President has made his final decision. We mobilize all available fleet assets to Ares immediately."

General Austin threw his hands in disgust, shaking his head. "Suicide! Complete madness."

Borders continued, unhindered by the General's outburst. "Admiral Beck, how quickly can your forces be ready for an all out assault?"

Beck, showing no emotion regarding the current crisis, responded in his deep, raspy voice, "I can have third and seventh fleet ready for combat operations in less than forty-eight hours. That will be a force of over sixty-five assaulting star ships. Second fleet is currently undergoing re-fit in New Sydney, it may take Admiral Fairchild slightly longer to mobilize his forces there. But, that would be an additional twenty-seven star ships."

"Very well, we begin the planning process now, I'll inform the President of our timetable, in the meantime, let's hope those poor bastards on Ares can hold on," Borders stated. The room erupted in sidebar conversations and arguments on the President's decision to attack.

Mr. Romanoff turned to Admiral Falasad and whispered, ensuring he wasn't heard by the surrounding staff, "It's that damned alien Contrivance we found. Those sons of bitches stole it and took it back to Ares, now these damn aliens are back looking for it."

"I think you're spot on. We need to find out where in the hell the Ares government is storing that thing, re-capture it, and either destroy it, or maybe somehow try and give it back to the alien forces." Falasad suggested.

Romanoff nodded, "Don't worry Admiral. I've got one of my best agents already on the ground there. He's currently infiltrating the Ares Alliance Intelligence communications network. As soon as he finds something solid, we'll act upon it. So long as he can survive down there long enough."

18

Two days later, Talos Station, main muster hall

The large mustering hall inside the station was filled with ranks of Marines and Navy servicemen. Kaleb stood at the position of parade rest in from of his platoon toward the back of the hall. It was hell trying to recall a platoon of Marines right after they were sent on shore leave. None of his men were happy about it but they all understood the gravity of their current situation.

He couldn't even see the front stage where Fleet Admiral Beck was supposed to give them some sort of rallying speech before they went into the unknown. Kaleb was still in total disbelief of what had transpired in the past three days. He felt as if he was in a really long dream, waiting for someone to pinch him so he could wake up and be back in Cancun on vacation with his friends. Somehow he had gone from his quiet life on Hastati as a kid to being on the front lines of an attack against some extraterrestrial race. He daydreamed while standing in formation, thinking of his family and working those long days on the farm. *Everything was so simple back then. Why can't I just be a naïve sixteen year old kid again?*

"*Task Force!....Atten....tion!!!*" Kaleb snapped out of his daydream as someone called the hall to attention. Fleet Admiral Beck appeared on the stage in front of a podium. Kaleb could barely see him from way in the back but he thought he looked much older than when he first saw him on the USSN Raleigh. The same Captain that rescued him from slavers was now the commander of the entire USS fleet, *strange coincidence*, Kaleb thought.

Admiral Beck had a large, dominant appearance that automatically commanded respect. He looked around the room for a few seconds at his Marines and servicemen.

"Men and women of the United Star Systems military....before us, lay the most paramount crusade ever attempted in human history. As we speak, our human brothers and sisters on Ares are being mercilessly slaughtered by an unknown alien race. This is why we are here. We all took an oath to defend humanity in its entirety against any outside threat. This was the founding principle of the United Star Systems military. Once our sworn enemies, the Ares Alliance is now in dire need of our help. We must unite all of humanity against this outside abomination and drive it from our galaxy. We do not know what will happen upon engagement with this new enemy. We will rely on our human qualities of honor, courage, and ingenuity to win this fight. The cost of failure is unbearable.....we have no choice.... fight, and win....or be utterly destroyed. May the great Creator, the bearer of the light, shield us in the upcoming battle. Leave no one behind!.....Commanders! Assemble the fleet!" Beck yelled. The hall erupted in cheers and battle cries as Beck proudly walked away from the podium and out of the large chamber. Little did the Marines and servicemen know about the hell that soon awaited them.

Kaleb did an about face and turned to face his platoon. "Alright listen up! In one hour the Athens leaves dock and is headed for Ares. If you've got anyone you need to call and say goodbye to, now is the time to do it. I want all of you in the Wolfpack briefing room at 0745 ship time ready to roll, understood?!"

"Roger Sergeant!" the platoon yelled.

"Dismissed," Kaleb said. As his Marines fell out of formation to conduct their business, Kaleb turned to walk through the masses of servicemen and women towards the Alpha Company command post. On his way out of the mustering hall, he couldn't help but notice a familiar set of bright-blonde hair that belonged to Flight Lieutenant Jen Thompson amidst the crowded hall of Marines. She stood in confusion, as if looking for someone in the crowded chaos. He walked up behind her and lightly tapped her on the shoulder.

"Hey LT, you look lost, help you find something?" he inquired.

Thompson turned around with a distressed look on her face that quickly turned to a smile once she saw that is was Kaleb. "Hey you! What are you doing here?! Is this not crazy?!"

Kaleb shrugged his shoulders, "Ma'am, I'm still waiting for someone to wake me up from this nightmare, how about you?"

"Tell me about it, I feel the same way right now. By the way, you can call me Jen, none of the 'Ma'am' stuff anymore." Lieutenant Thompson replied.

"Roger ma'am...just kidding...I mean Jen." Kaleb responded sarcastically. Thompson let out a giggle, appreciating a little humor to break the tension. "So what are you doing here still? I'm sure you pilots have tons of mission planning to do right now to get ready for this crazy counterattack," Kaleb asked above the loud echo of hundreds of conversations going on at once inside the muster hall.

Thompson frowned again as she held up a paper document for Kaleb to look at, "I just got transferred to Delta Company, I'm looking for their 2nd platoon leader, I'm supposed to be flying them in for their drop this time."

"What?! They transferred you out of Alpha? What the hell for?" Kaleb asked, obviously frustrated at the sudden change in Raptor pilots for his platoon.

"I know, I know, its total bullshit. I loved working with you and your guys. All I know is there has been tons of shifting around of spacecraft and personnel for this mission because of some changes in operational parameters. Apparently Delta needed additional assets or something, way above my level of decision making," Jen tried to explain.

"Well damn, if you're gone who's supposed to be my platoon's pilot?" Kaleb wondered. "Maybe that means we don't have to go on this mission and I can just go back on shore leave."

"Hah, yeah right, I doubt that is happening. Honestly, I wish I knew. This huge mission and having over a third of the fleet still making their way back from shore leave recall has thrown everything into chaos it seems like," Thompson said as she watched the crowds of Marines and servicemen run about the muster hall issuing out orders to subordinates.

Kaleb shook his head and looked around the hall. He raised a hand up and pointed to a short, dark haired, Marine Lieutenant about twenty feet away from the two of them. "Hey, over there is Lieutenant Hashburn, 2nd platoon leader, Delta, that's going to be the guy you're looking for," Kaleb said unenthusiastically.

"Oh wow, thanks, I didn't even know what he looked like...I better catch him before he leaves....Listen, I'm going to miss you guys in 1st platoon....it might get bad out there on Ares....if I don't see you before the fleet heads out, well...." Thompson leaned in close to Kaleb and gave him a soft hug, wrapping her arms around him and laying her head on his shoulder for a few seconds, then pulling away. "You guys just make sure you make it back that's all... I wanted to say.... I guess...."

Kaleb gave a slight laugh as he stepped away from the hug and smiled, "Don't worry about it LT, we always make it back in one piece. Besides, I still don't believe in aliens....live ones anyway."

Thompson laughed and she turned to walk over to the 2nd platoon leader, "Always joking around as usual. Give me a call if you can't find your new Raptor pilot, I'll come back and make two trips down to the surface if I have to. Tell your platoon I said hi and wish I was still flying them."

"Alright Jen, we'll see you when we get back," Kaleb waved and smiled as she walked off. As she turned her back to him his smile quickly turned to a grimace. *Yeah right, if we even get back.*

✳   ✳   ✳   ✳

Eight hours later, Whetmore, capital city of Ares colony

A loud crash impacted on the roof of the Ares Alliance Intelligence and Science headquarters building. Special Agent John Smith covered his head and jumped under a desk, avoiding a large chunk of concrete that flew through the window towards him. He had set up his counter-intelligence operations in the now abandoned congressional building adjacent to the Ares Intel and Science headquarters across the street. Since the attack, Smith had been relaying reports when he could to Mr. Romanoff back on Talos station via his portable interstellar communications box,; a high-tech device that was able to relay encrypted messages across the galaxy within only a few hours.

A fierce battle waged in the streets outside between the tired soldiers of the Ares Army and the alien ground forces. The capital city of the Ares colony, Whetmore, had been under siege for twenty hours now. Thousands of Ares citizens had been massacred in the streets by the ruthless onslaught of this unknown extraterrestrial enemy. By this time the alien soldiers, clad in their near impenetrable, glossy, obsidian-like battle armor and menacing high-energy laser systems, had reached the outskirts of the capital city center. What remained of the Ares Alliance army valiantly tried to hold defensive positions around the remaining government buildings that held key officials of the Ares congress and cabinet who hopelessly tried to maintain some form of emergency government amidst the chaos.

Agent Smith had successfully infiltrated the Ares Alliance Intelligence apparatus in the weeks following the capture of the alien "Contrivance" on Gardner IV. After tapping into the Ares local communication network, he fed daily reports to Mr. Romanoff about what the Ares government did with Project Contrivance since its capture.

This could be my final report, better make it count, he thought to himself as his carefully set up his interstellar communications interface from under the protection of the desk. He would try to get one last message to Romanoff before the congressional building he was in was either destroyed or captured by alien forces. The building shuddered following an impact from one of the alien laser weapons. *Come on hurry up you son of a bitch,* Smith said to himself, waiting for the communication box to obtain a signal.

*   *   *   *

There were only a few survivors remaining in the basement of the Ares Intelligence and Science headquarters consisting of Deputy Director Rhenquist and a few of his staff. They huddled in a dark, emergency command post several floors down in the basement. His staff analyzed the few remaining projector screens that fed them mission reports from Ares Army commanders on the ground outside. Most of their headquarters building had been destroyed by the bombardment from the alien starship in orbit. They were unaware that agent Smith had been tapping into their communications and feeding reports to the USS government from the next building over. Deputy Director Rhenquist and his staff tried to war-game a counteroffensive strategy to retake the capital in a futile attempt to maintain some semblance of control over their situation. Covered in dust and surrounded by rubble, the aged, gray haired, Rhenquist, peered through his glasses at the situational awareness display on the wall in front of him. It showed icons of enemy alien forces surrounding their location and closing in.

"Do we have confirmation of the arrival of the USS fleet yet?!" Rhenquist frantically asked his staff as he studied the screen. He had come to realize the gravity of his current situation. He knew that the defending Ares army would not be able to hold their position much longer.

"No sir," one of his staff answered.

"Gentlemen…we may have to come to the realization that our colony is lost. We can either try to come up with an escape plan, or hold out here until the end," Rhenquist stated in a hopeless manner.

"Sir, I believe an evacuation attempt would be fruitless at this point. Our inter-system communications are down and they have us completely surrounded. All we can do is hold out here as long as we can and hope the United Star Systems fleet can mount a successful counter-offensive," another of his staff members replied.

Rhenquist sighed as he looked up at the enemy icons closing in on the screen. "Unfortunately, I have to agree with you….we'll hold out here until the bitter end gentlemen……let's just hope the USS Navy gets here before it comes to that. We should've destroyed that damned abomination when we had the chance. Now look where it's gotten us," the Deputy Director shook his head in despair.

*   *   *   *

Three hours later, Talos Station Naval Intelligence war room

"Sir, I have urgent interstellar communications traffic from Agent Smith on Ares!" Michael Romanoff's nerdy looking assistant shouted as he ran over to the intelligence Director. Romanoff sat at a table in his war room with General Falasad and few of his closest staff on Talos station, waiting for the USS counter-attack to begin.

"Finally!....I'll take it on my secure data pad," Romaoff said excitedly. The assistant nodded and tapped a few keys on his holographic computer console. The small screen on Romanoff's data pad lit up with a time-delayed video message from agent Smith. Smith's distressed face appeared on the video message, covered in dust and small cuts. The audio on the message began:

"Mr. Romanoff sir...agent Smith here....this may be my last transmission as the alien forces have closed on my position in the city center. By the time you get this my location will most likely be compromised and it is imperative that the USS fleet acts on the following information..." Smith said in a desperate tone as piercing explosions could be heard in the background. The video feed became very static and was cutting out every couple of seconds.

"The Deputy Director of Ares Intelligence is currently in a sealed underground command post in their headquarters building. They are trying to make a last stand against the aliens in order to hold out until our fleet arrives but their defense and communications grids has been knocked out. Sir...they somehow activated the alien Contrivance found on Gardner IV while trying to study it. Their scientists activated it and apparently they believe that's why these extraterrestrials showed up....I don't know how or why, but the aliens sir...they want it back. I intercepted conversations back and forth from Deputy Director Rhenquist and his staff. They think the aliens are not even from our galaxy, inter-dimensional maybe. They think the Contrivance may have opened some kind of portal in nearby space to a parallel universe. He ordered to have Contrivance destroyed but his message didn't make it through to his staff at their secure facility in time before all Ares communications were knocked out. Project Contrivance is located in a deep underground military base only about fifteen miles outside of the capital city of Whetmore at the following grid...Alpha Golf, Hotel Sierra, two-..."

The transmission abruptly cut-off before Smith could give the complete grid location of the device. A loud explosion was heard in the background as it appeared that the building he was in was collapsing around him. After a few seconds of loud crashes and screaming from agent Smith, the desolate sound of static was all that remained on the audio of the message.

"Goddammit!" Romanoff yelled, distraught at the fact that he had come so close to learning Contrivance's location. "Son of a bitch got himself killed before telling me the goddamn grid."

Romanoff looked up at Admiral Falasad and spoke quietly, ensuring no one else in the room could hear him. "Admiral….we have to find that underground base…. find Project Contrivance. It could be the only key to defeating these things. Destroying it could possibly close this portal that Rhenquist is talking about…or maybe cause them to lose their purpose for being here."

The Admiral thought for a moment; then spoke in a skeptical tone. "Attempts to communicate with anyone on the ground from the Ares government have been unsuccessful. Until we can open up a communications channel with a surviving member of their government that knows just exactly where this thing is…we don't have very many options."

Romanoff pulled a silver-plated Zippo out of his pocket and in a well-rehearsed motion, lit another cigarette, then spoke, "There is one other option Admiral…a long shot, but an option…."

"And just what would that be Romanoff?" Falasad said in a tired voice.

"Send in a task force of Marines…if they can somehow be inserted near the capital center…they could try to get to where that intel official, Rhenquist, is hiding. Rhenquist knows the location of that underground base. If we can get to him and he is still alive… we get the grid location. Then we send in a quick-reaction team in to secure Contrivance, and possibly deactivate or destroy it."

Falasad reluctantly shook his head, "It would be pure suicide….

the capital center is crawling with those alien beings…they have total control. We don't even know if our fleet will be able to even get close enough to the damn planet to launch Marines. They could get blown out of space just like the Ares Alliance Navy did….." The Admiral despondently continued, "Deactivate it? Just how the hell are we supposed to know how to do that? The thing could be indestructible for all we know and there is no guarantee that will cause the aliens to even leave the system. *If* our Marines can even get to him, Rhenquist will most definitely be dead by then. You heard your agent's message. The aliens have already occupied the capital center." Falasad let out a sigh, rubbing his tired face, then looked back at Romanoff. "But…Mr. Romanoff….I'm afraid I think you're right…we don't exactly have any other options do we? I will approve the mission and send word to General Austin….He won't like it, but he'll have to understand."

*   *   *   *

USSN Athens, ten minutes from entry into Ares Alliance space

The Wolfpack platoon was already loaded up into their Raptor orbital assault transport. Forty-two Marines were strapped in tightly in four separate rows that ran lengthwise along the cargo bay of the small transport. The platoon had finally been assigned a new spacecraft and pilot for the mission. The cramped, hot, interior of the Raptor left little room for Lieutenant Freeborn to walk up and down the aisles as he briefed the platoon. The entire USS Fleet was inbound to the Ares colony. The plan was straightforward; conduct an all out assault on the enemy ships orbiting the planet to in order to buy enough time for Marines to be launched down to the surface. Hopefully, the USS fleet, led by Admiral Beck, could stave off the alien ships long enough for the Marine divisions on the ground to liberate the largest cities of Ares and cause the aliens to withdraw.

The 1st Recon Battalion's mission remained vague at this point. They were tasked with driving out all enemy ground forces from the capital city center. Trying to organize a fleet of over sixty ships complemented with over 10,000 Marines in less than forty-eight hours was a monumental task. It was utter chaos from when Kaleb arrived on Talos station. The platoon's mission had changed at least seven times. They loaded and off-loaded their Raptor on three separate occasions as intel briefs changed by the minute. The chaotic environment of uncertainty toyed with the Marines' heads. They just wanted to get out there and get on the ground. Kaleb was sick and tired of being cooped up on a ship. His Marines didn't know what to expect once they landed on Ares. They were given four different intel descriptions of what the aliens' looked like and what type of weaponry they used. Kaleb didn't really care what they ran into at this point. All he knew was, if it didn't look human, he was going to take it down. Kaleb's platoon was suited up in their ABAS's ready to roll. Luckily, Ares was a lush, largely tropical, garden-world with a nitrogen-oxygen atmosphere as well as slightly less gravity than Earth allowing the Marines to ditch their extra hazardous environment equipment. *If they even made it to the surface of the planet before getting vaporized by aliens,* Kaleb thought to himself. As he conducted random spot checks of his Marines gear around the inside of the Raptor, Lieutenant Freeborn began his en-route mission brief:

"Listen up Marines!" Lieutenant Freeborn yelled over the roaring engine noise from the Athens' Faust drive. "We've got another change in mission," the platoon grumbled at the news of yet another change in mission parameters.

"This mission just came down straight from General Austin himself so pay attention! First Recon Battalion is now the main effort in the assault on Ares. Our mission is now to conduct a high-speed orbital Raptor insertion directly into the capital city center. With support from the 46th Heavy Armored Brigade as well as air assets from 12th Fighter Wing, we are to secure a HVT (High Value Target) inside the Ares Alliance Intelligence and Science headquarters building located in the Ares Governmental Courtyard Center. The man we are to secure is their Deputy Director of Intelligence that goes by the name, Rhenquist. Mission reports state that he is fortified in an emergency command post deep in the basement of the headquarters building. Our job is to go in dismounted, get in there, secure the HVT and get him back to the Raptor for transport to the safety of our fleet. We are told that he has information that is vital to the success of the entire USS assaulting force. Wolfpack… failure is not an option here. We very well may be fighting for the existence of all humankind down there. The only way we are going to get through this is if we stick together and remember our training, understood?!" Freeborn stateed firmly above the engine noise.

"Yes sir!" the platoon answered in unison.

"Good, we should be entering the engagement area in less than ten mikes, I will see you all on the surface! Staff Sergeant Taylor, you got anything?" Freeborn turned to Kaleb as he ended his brief.

"Yeah LT, just one thing. Listen up! Here's your rules of engagement; if it doesn't look human down there, light it the fuck up, understood?!" Kaleb yelled in a confident voice at his Marines.

"Roger Sergeant!" the platoon acknowledged, nodding their heads with a smile. They were ready. They had waited in the confined space of the Athens cargo hold for hours. It was time for the Wolfpack to unleash hell upon this new enemy.

"Whoooooo! We gonna fuck some shit up baby!!" Corporal Hunt screamed. The platoon cheered at the statement, the men yelled a series of battle cries as the USS fleet came out of Faust drive speed and into real-time space about 600,000 miles from the alien fleet that orbited Ares.

*   *   *   *

The USS fleet slowed to combat attack speed, the fleet of sixty-five ships was arrayed in a wedge-shaped battle line. The fast attack cruisers and frigates formed the front lines, with the four, Jupiter-class battleships behind, screened from enemy fire. In tight formation behind them were the three massive USS Naval fighter carriers, containing a complement of eighty small, one-manned assault fighters each.

Admiral Beck stood on the bridge of his flagship, the battleship, USSN Cairo, analyzing reports from his crew. The scanners operator chimed in as the fleet closed with the Ares colony. "Admiral Beck sir, I've got the enemy fleet on scope, looks like they are unaware to our presence, they're holding a static orbit around the colony, about 10,000 miles from the surface."

"Understood chief, I need numbers, how many ships," Beck countered in his calm tone.

"Aye sir, I'm picking up what looks like twenty to twenty-five battleship to carrier sized vessels sir. About 800 to 1200 meters in length each," the scanners chief said nervously.

Beck threw a wad of tobacco snuff in his mouth upon hearing the report from the chief. "Very well chief...at least we've got them out-numbered......Weapons officer!"

"Sir?!" the weapons station Lieutenant answered immediately.

"Time and distance to Primary EMA range?" Beck asked as he studied the situational awareness monitor above him.

"Sir, Battleship EMA's will be in range in forty-five seconds, distance to nearest target two-hundred point three-four," the young Lieutenant responded.

Beck walked over to the communications station on the bridge. "Patch me through to the battle group Lieutenant," he spoke dryly.

"Aye sir….ok you're good to go," the female communications officer replied.

Beck spit some tobacco into a plastic bottle and spoke into the mike, addressing the entire fleet. "Attention to the fleet, this is Admiral Beck….All battleships engage targets with primary EMAs at this time, all cruisers launch nuclear rockets, hit them with everything we've got before they know we're here. Wait for my mark to launch fighters…" Beck ordered the commencement of the attack.

A massive salvo of electromagnetically propelled tungsten projectiles hurled their way to the alien fleet at incredible speed. The interior lighting of the USSN Cairo dimmed as it fired its two massive EMA canons. The ship shuddered from the release of kinetic energy and the helmsman applied full forward thrust to counteract the recoil of the weapons. A few seconds followed as over forty cruisers opened their missile bay doors and fired multiple nuclear tipped missiles to complete the monumental barrage. The tungsten projectiles would meet their targets first, taking just seconds to traverse the vast distance between the two fleets.

The fleet of alien ships suddenly conducted a brilliant evasive maneuver, each ship simultaneously rotating on its axis one-hundred and eighty degrees. The smooth surfaced, jet black ships were indeed alien in appearance. There were no visible propulsion systems or thruster ports. Just a sleek, three-dimensional diamond-like design with no visible outer control surfaces, they moved almost effortlessly through space, quickly traversing a few hundred miles, throwing the EMA firing solutions off course.

"Sir, enemy ships are taking evasive action, five seconds to first salvo impact," the weapons officer stated to Admiral Beck.

The first half to the EMA tungsten projectiles missed their targets by a few miles due to the rapid maneuver by the alien ships.

"Sir, the first salvo overshot the targets, second salvo impact in six seconds," the weapons Lieutenant continued to update Beck.

The four remaining projectiles launched from the Jupiter-class battleships impacted with astounding force on the alien warships. Massive explosions penetrated the hulls of two of the large black craft but they continued to maneuver unhindered by the damage.

"Sir, we have solid hits on two enemy vessels, it looks like their fleet is moving to engage,' the weapons officer stated.

"Very well, Task Force; close in and engage at will, loosen combat formation and launch fighters, follow the Cairo's lead!" Beck ordered across the battle-net. "Helmsman! Make a hard burn for Ares orbit! We've got to give our Marines a chance to get to the surface!"

The volley of intersystem nuclear missiles from the USS fleet's cruisers closed in and acquired their targets. In multiple brilliant flashes of light the warheads detonated amidst the alien fleet of ships. The incredible energy expended engulfed the fleet in a massive explosion.

"Whoohooh sir! Direct hits with all warheads! I think we got 'em sir!" the over-enthused weapons officer exclaimed to Beck.

As the nuclear blast area cleared from the space around the alien fleet, the scanners chief's jaw dropped. It became apparent that the barrage of atomic weapons did little to slow the advancing alien fleet. The ominous diamond-shaped vessels emerged from the nuclear storm largely unscathed and continued to close on the USS fleet.

The cheers and high-fives around the bridge of the Cairo's ceased as the scanners chief gave his report. "They're still there sir…. I still show at least eighteen of twenty-three original ships closing in to engage. A few of their ships were destroyed but the bulk of the fleet remains sir," the chief gave a somber update to Beck.

"Jesus….how the hell can their armor withstand that…." Beck said quietly to himself as he watched the alien fleet closing in on the visual display. "Very well chief, continue to close with the planet and ready close range weapons systems."

The chief continued to feed the Admiral reports, "Sir, detecting unknown energy spike originating from the alien fleet, I think they are preparing to engage sir!"

Beck's eyes widened as he witnessed the view screen showing the alien ships' opening some sort of bay doors on the side of their hulls. A bright flash of yellowish light began to emit from inside the bays.

"Fleet! Conduct evasive maneuvers! Prepare for counterattack!" Beck ordered over the fleet battle-net.

In a desperate attempt to shift course, the helmsman of the Cairo steered the lumbering vessel into a ninety degree turn. The other ships in the USS Fleet conducted similar evasive turns and then attempted to re-acquire their alien targets. Swarms of USS fighters flew past the Cairo towards the alien fleet to engage at close range. The eighteen remaining alien ships fired a bright yellow high-energy laser beam from inside their hulls towards the large USS fleet. The solid beams of concentrated light-energy tore through the USS vessels with pinpoint accuracy. The lasers melted through the human ships' steel/titanium armor plating like a hot knife through butter. The Cairo's sister ship, another Jupiter-class on its left flank, was ripped into two pieces, shattering its Faust drive core. The ship erupted in a massive explosion, sending a fireball and shrapnel hurling towards the Cairo.

"Brace for impact!" The scanners chief on board the Cairo yelled as the collision alarm sounded over the shipboard intercom. Large hunks of the destroyed battleship plowed into the Cairo's hull, damaging several decks of the vessel, the explosion blasted the massive ship off course from the rest of the fleet.

The cruiser, Athens, holding the Wolfpack platoon, stayed on course, making a bee-line for Ares orbit. The ship Captain's primary objective was to first drop off his Marines, then worry about engaging the alien fleet. Other cruisers and frigates erupted in fireballs around the Athens. The first salvo of the alien heavy lasers had decimated the USS fleet. Inside the cargo hold of the Athens, Kaleb and the Wolfpack platoon were jumbled around the interior of their Raptor. The Athens performed a series of evasive, high-speed maneuvers in order to weave its way through the onslaught of the alien laser attacks.

Admiral Beck pulled himself back to his feet on the bridge of the Cairo and ran over to the battle-net mike. The battleship had taken some damage but was still functional, which was more than over half of the original USS Fleet could declare. Beck looked out of the side view port of his flagship to see most of his fleet in ruins.

"Fleet, hold position and re-engage! Give our cruisers cover and get those Marines on the ground now!" Only thirty ships of the original sixty-five remained after the alien counterattack. "Weapons officer! Level our bow on that alien flagship and hit it again with primary EMA's! Something's got to be able to take that son of bitch down!" Beck yelled across the bridge.

The remaining twelve fast-attack cruisers fell into formation with the Athens as it entered close orbit with Ares. Explosions surrounded the task force as USS fighters and frigates attempted to give them cover while they dropped their Marine carrying Raptors down to the surface. The remaining bulk of the USS fleet had now become entangled with the alien battle group. The two opposing forces began to slug it out at extreme close range of less than a few hundred miles. Three more tactical nuclear missiles detonated on the hull of an alien vessel, causing it to rupture and implode in on itself.

A green light lit up inside the interior of the Wolfpack platoon's Raptor. The Athens' cargo bay opened up, revealing the surface of Ares to the transport's pilot. A pressure lock released and the Raptor engaged its thrusters at full power, separating it from the Athens. Several of the Wolfpack Marines inside vomited from the extreme jostling around that resulted from the high-speed maneuvers. The platoon's Raptor accelerated towards the atmosphere of Ares at blinding speed. As the other cruisers began to launch their orbital assault transports, three more yellow colored, high-energy beams sliced through the USS ships attempting to make their drops. Two of the alien cruiser-sized vessels had swung in behind the human drop ships and mercilessly launched salvo after salvo of laser beams at the assaulting force. Four of the cruisers were vaporized by the laser blasts. The Raptor with Kaleb's platoon dove to the surface of the planet, just barely escaping the assaulting alien vessels and entered the atmosphere of Ares. Only a small fraction of the original landing force of Marines would make it through unscathed. The carrier that held the 46th Heavy Armored Brigade's tanks that were to support the 1st Recon Battalion's assault was utterly destroyed in the opening volley of the starship engagement. The 12th Fighter Wing was caught in an engagement in high orbit with the alien fleet. The Recon Marines would now be on their own when they hit the ground.

19

Planet Ares, Capital City of Whetmore, alien occupation zone

The Wolfpack platoon's Raptor tore through the thick nitrogen-oxygen atmosphere of Ares at incredible speed. A bright orange fireball formed on the nose and hull of the assault craft due to the extreme heat from friction. Temperatures rose to an unbearable one-hundred and sixty degrees inside the ship. Kaleb could barely breathe as he sat helplessly strapped into his seat, unable to move his arms or legs from the ever-increasing g-force. Sweat poured over his face and eyes as he attempted to peer through his fogged helmet visor at his platoon. It appeared half of them had either fainted or were passed out from g-lock while the pilot tried to level out the Raptor and gain control over their high-speed descent.

"Goddammit don't put so much pressure on it! We're going in too hot!" the Raptor's co-pilot yelled at the pilot seated next to him.

The pilot struggled to pull back on the control stick of the Raptor, gritting his teeth, "Shit!...We've got company! Coming in on our six!" The scanners showed two unidentified craft closing in behind the Raptor at high speed.

Two small fighter drones of alien design acquired the Raptor as it entered the lower atmosphere, heading towards the city of Whetmore. The kite-shaped, obsidian-black craft looked similar to the alien starships currently engaged in orbit, however on a much smaller scale. These small fighters were only thirty to forty feet in length and did not appear to be piloted by any organic being. They maneuvered effortlessly at over 1,500 mph in behind the Raptor as it neared 20,000 feet above the surface of Ares.

The pilot of the Raptor conducted a half barrel-roll and pulled back on the stick, placing it into a near ninety-degree dive toward the surface. The two alien fighters immediately followed suit and easily stayed on track behind the Raptor despite the pilot's gutsy maneuver.

"Shit! I can't get them off our tail!" the pilot yelled as he continued evasive maneuvers. The Raptor transport was slow and bulky in the thick atmosphere and was an easy target for the alien fighter drones which appeared to be un-hampered by gravity or atmospheric friction. Two small, yellow beams of light fired from the noses of the alien fighters as the engagement neared just 5,000 feet above the surface. The accurately placed laser fire impacted on the port side of the Raptor, tearing through its lightly armored hull.

"We're hit! We're hit!...I've lost pitch control!" the pilot screamed upon feeling the shudder and explosion coming from the rear of his ship. The fireball engulfed the left side of the cargo area inside the Raptor where Kaleb's 3rd squad was seated. Black smoke filled the cabin and a hole was torn into the side of the ship, revealing a large tropical forest on the ground just 2,000 feet below. Body parts, weapons, and gear flew around the inside of the ship as nearly all of Sergeant Gallo's squad was enveloped within the blast. Several Marines screamed as the vacuum created from the opening in the ship sucked them out of their seats and through hole only to plummet to their death on the ground below. Kaleb watched in horror as he saw almost one-third of his men die right in front of his eyes. He cursed himself, unable to move or help them. He tightly grasped the handles above his head and closed his eyes, preparing himself for what seemed like the end for him and his platoon.

The pilot hopelessly attempted to steady the burning ship as the immense capital city of Whetmore came into view through his windshield. "I can't hold it! Prepare for impact!..." He yelled over the Raptor's intercom.

Kaleb looked out the six-foot by six-foot hole blown out of the hull on the opposite side of the craft and saw another Raptor full of Marines going down in flames. *Well, I guess this is it.* Kaleb thought to himself. He again closed his eyes and relaxed, picturing his family and life back on the farm when he was just a kid. He smiled at the thought of possibly reuniting with them in the afterlife amidst the screaming and explosions around him. Everything then went black with the sudden impact of the Raptor's hull with the ground in a thunderous crash.

$$* \qquad * \qquad * \qquad *$$

"Taylor!.....Hey, Taylor!!...Wake up man!!!...You're not dead....Wake the hell up!"

Kaleb heard a faint, muffled voice as he started to regain consciousness. His vision was blurry but he could make out a human-figure standing in front of him, slapping him on the side of his helmet. He lifted up his head and tried to focus his eyes.

"Wha...where, am I?..." he said slowly, disoriented from the crash.

Corporal Hunt unbuckled the harness straps around Kaleb's shoulders and legs that fastened him securely to the Raptor. The ship had crashed on one of the downtown streets of Whetmore, there was still a fire burning inside the cabin and mangled bodies lay everywhere.

"You're inside the Raptor, we crashed man....you gotta get up quick," Hunt said frantically as he continued to fool with the harness straps.

"Holy shit...." Kaleb said quietly as his vision cleared and he looked around the inside of the Raptor. It was pure carnage, bodies, blood and fire surrounded him. Hunt pulled Kaleb to his feet and handed him his assault rifle.

"We need to move now, this thing is going up in flames fast," Hunt said urgently. Kaleb nodded and followed Hunt through the hole in the side of the Raptor.

What remained of the platoon was taking cover behind a large pile of concrete and rebar about fifty meters from the crash site. Kaleb looked around at his surroundings. It appeared that the once beautiful capital city of Whetmore had been reduced to rubble. The majestic, ancient Roman and Greek-inspired style of architecture the city was known for throughout space was now barely recognizable. Fires and blown out structures encompassed the platoon's position. He could hear sounds of gunfire and explosions off in the distance. Smoke and dust filled the air above them, blotting out a large portion of the midday sunlight. Kaleb peered into the cockpit of the Raptor. Blood was splattered all over the windshield, the pilot and co-pilot lay face down on the controls. He took a knee beside a group of 1st squad Marines near the pile of rubble and shook his head, trying to clear out the cobwebs after being knocked out for several minutes from the crash. Sergeant Yao scrambled over to Kaleb, making sure to keep his head below the cover provided by the concrete rubble.

The city of Whetmore was what used to be the crown jewel of Ares Alliance space. Its well planned, symmetrical streets and structures were intermixed with the native tropical vegetation of the region creating a sustainable, eco-friendly urban zone. The founder of the city proclaimed to have been a descendant of Julius

Caesar himself and modeled the city after ancient Rome, with 22nd century upgrades of course. The citizens of Ares were always known to be fiercely independent and self reliant, taking great pride in their colony and its capital city. Now the city of over one million inhabitants was devastated by the alien orbital bombardment and subsequent invasion.

"Oh shit, Staff Sergeant Taylor, thank god man...we thought you were dead" Yao said in a jittery tone.

"Naw, not quite, just took a bad hit to the head I guess. What's our status? Where's the LT?" Kaleb said, irritated from the pounding still going on in his head.

Sergeant Yao looked at the ground and shook his head dejectedly. "Pretty sure we found a few pieces of him scattered around the crash site. Poor bastard was on the side that got hit with along with 3rd and 2nd squad."

"God-damn," Kaleb whispered as he looked up in shock. "Who else?"

Yao shook his head once more in defeat. "Best I can tell, Sergeant Gallo's squad got completely wiped out when the Raptor got hit. Sergeant Chambers has only got two men left from 2nd, the rest died in the crash....he took some bad shrapnel to his right arm though, can't even hold his weapon, he's in a lot of pain.... 1st and 4th are full up. We got lucky being on the starboard side away from the blast. So we're looking at twenty Marines left Staff Sergeant."

Kaleb looked around for a second and thought. Sergeant Chambers was sitting against a wall with a bloodied battle dressing wrapped around his heavily lacerated arm, grimacing in pain. With Lieutenant Freeborn gone, it was now on him, the platoon Sergeant, to lead these men out of the hell they had just dropped in to.

"Ok...Yao have your guys gather up whatever ID tags they can find off our dead. Martinez, you and 4th cover them while I figure out where the hell we're at." Kaleb ordered as he pulled out his data pad and keyed up the 3-D terrain interface. Sergeant Yao and Corporal Martinez nodded and moved out. Kaleb looked over at Hunt as he manipulated the data pad.

"Have you had any contact with the enemy yet?" Kaleb asked.

"Naw, nothing so far, you were only out for a few minutes after the crash, you know about as much as I do. I'm guessing we're somewhere in the middle of Whetmore." Hunt answered.

"Ok, waiting on a nav fix…try to get comms with Viper 6 actual….or anybody at least so we can get some situational awareness," Kaleb said, focusing on his data pad.

Corporal Hunt set up the platoon's long range communications box, which was capable of transmitting a radio signal over a sixty-mile radius, attempting to contact any units over the company and battalion nets in the background.

"Any Viper element, any Viper element, this is Wolfpack one-Alpha….." Hunt transmitted the radio traffic several times, only to be answered by static.

Kaleb's data pad blinked green as the navigation interface engaged. "Ok…got us a grid. According to this we are about two and a half clicks from the capital city center…. I'm going to look for a good LZ (landing zone) where hopefully we can get someone to pick our asses up and get the fuck out of here. At less than fifty percent strength we are combat-ineffective….you agree?" Kaleb asked Hunt while he was trying to work the radio.

Hunt took his ear off the hand mike for a second and nodded at Kaleb's question. "Yeah man, the company must be spread out all over the place, no way are we going to be able to do anything down here… Only problem is we got no comms with anybody…I tried company, battalion, and regiment, nothing." An earsplitting explosion nearby shuddered the ground below the Marines' position, causing Kaleb and Hunt to immediately hit the deck mid-conversation. The dust soon cleared and Kaleb got back up on a knee.

"Well shit, keep trying…that radio is our only way out of here right now," Kaleb declared forcefully.

Hunt nodded and continued to call over the net. Sergeant Yao and 1st squad had completed rounding up ID tags and assumed a triangular defensive position with 4th squad around Kaleb and Hunt. Yao moved over to them in the middle of the security formation, trying to catch his breath.

"Ok, we got what we could. The Raptor's about the burn to the ground, salvaged as much out of it as possible….We able to get anybody on there?" Yao pointed to Hunt and the long range communications box.

"Nope, nothing….just static-wait a second…getting something… yeah, wait one….ro-roger sir….roger…we are 1st platoon…1st Recon Battalion…hang on sir let me get our seven element on here for you…" Hunt looked at Kaleb and handed him the small hand mike. "Dude, it's the Regimental Commander, Colonel West…he wants to talk to you….guess somebody heard us," Hunt said with a surprised look on his face.

Kaleb grabbed the mike, "This is Wolfpack 7, actual, over……"

A commanding voice with a southern accent came over the net. Hunt and Yao leaned in towards Kaleb to listen in. "Roger Wolfpack 7, I read you Lima Charlie (loud and clear)….this is Pegasus 6 actual….what is your position and situation over?"

"Pegasus 6, this is Wolfpack 7, roger we are two-point-five clicks south-southwest of the city center, break…..I am at fifty percent strength and I am unable to make contact with any other friendlies in my vicinity, break…our Raptor has crashed and we are combat ineffective, requesting immediate extraction over…."

After a few seconds of static the command voice came over the net again, "Negative Wolfpack 7….1st Recon's mission is the main effort at this time, your platoon is the closest combat asset we have to the city center….you will proceed to your objective on foot and secure the HVT as instructed, is that understood, over…."

Kaleb reluctantly keyed the mike, "R-roger sir…what about any reinforcements…or air support…over"

Loud crashes and explosions could be heard on the Colonel's side of the net, "Negative on air assets…26th Regiment is spread to hell all over this place and engaged in force with the enemy on the eastern side of the city….your are all that's left of the 1st Recon Battalion Sergeant….get the job done and report back to me on this net… Pegasus 6 out," the colonel abruptly ended the transmission.

Kaleb dropped the hand mike and looked back at Hunt and Yao. "Well….this is just fucking great….. Hunt, plot me a nav course to our objective at the Intelligence and Science headquarters building. Yao, gather up and reconsolidate any weapons and ammo you can find and get the guys formed up, fire team wedge. Martinez…get me a sniper team on top of that blown out building over there and tell me what they can see."

"Roger Sergeant," Martinez and Yao responded at the same time, turning to go into action.

$$*\qquad*\qquad*\qquad*$$

Lance Corporal Burke and his spotter climbed over a fifteen foot-high pile of concrete block and rebar into the blown out second story of an adjacent building. Burke jumped up and grabbed the ceiling of the second story while his spotter held his sniper rifle. He pulled himself up onto the third floor of the structure, helping his spotter up as well. The sniper team moved over to a small window facing north towards the platoon's objective. Burke carefully set up the bipod on his MR-40A2 sniper rifle and set it on the window sill. He and his spotter scanned for possible targets as well as an avenue of approach to the Ares Intel headquarters that wasn't blocked by debris or fire.

"This is sniper team one, set up in position. I have over-watch out to one point five clicks, no enemy targets on scope; looks like there is an alleyway to our left that leads to a main road heading north. Probably would take us to the city center. There are plenty of blown out structures to provide cover along the route....wait one.... got something....looks like the silhouette of another downed Raptor, its resting on top of the roof of a three-story structure, some visible smoke or flames, ranged at eight-hundred and twenty-three meters to the northeast, how copy over?" Burke quietly transmitted over the platoon net.

"This is seven, roger good copy....could be some survivors up there...give us cover while we move into the alley then link back up with us once we're set, then we'll check out that crash site." Kaleb replied, acknowledging Burke's report. He was glad that Martinez had sent Burke to conduct the Recon. Corporal Headley was too indecisive and would have probably just babbled a confused report back to Kaleb over the radio.

Kaleb turned to the remainder of his platoon and gave the hand and arm signal to move out towards the alleyway. Corporal Hunt nodded from the point-man position and stepped off towards the platoon's objective. Kaleb couldn't help but think of how much of a suicide mission this seemed like. Twenty Marines alone in a foreign city with no air or armor support, out of contact with their company and battalion headquarters, walking aimlessly into a probable alien ambush. It still didn't seem quite real to Kaleb. A small part of him hoped he was still in a dream. He was just still waiting for someone to pinch him so he could wake up. He was surprised at how well his Marines were handling their current situation. Maybe they were just so scared they didn't have a chance to think about how dire their circumstances really were. Maybe the training was kicking in and the guys were just acting on reflexes. Either way, it gave Kaleb a small amount of comfort to know that his Marines were behind him, and if he died out here, at least he wouldn't die alone.

The Wolfpack platoon moved with precision and quickness as they tactically made their way up the alley and onto the main road leading north through the city. The crashed Raptor was now visible just a few city blocks to the northeast from their location. They bounded in and out between structures and rubble, cautiously closing in on the downed transport, still no sign of enemy forces. Kaleb gave the platoon a halt signal and peered up at the roof where the friendly Raptor was resting, now only a hundred meters away. He pulled up his assault rifle and peered through his tactical sight, zooming in to 3x magnification.

"Ok, looks like it's clear up top. Yao, your squad takes point, get in that building and make your way to the roof to check for survivors. Sergeant Chambers and I with the rest of 2nd will be right behind you. Martinez, give them some cover from the outside, cordon off the building as much as you can," Kaleb instructed.

"Roger seven, executing time now," Yao replied sharply, moving his Marines into action. Kaleb moved up with first squad to supervise the ascent up the stairs inside the building up to the roof. Sergeant Chambers, with his shattered arm and two remaining Marines, nodded at Kaleb as he moved past and followed his platoon Sergeant's lead. The Marines crossed a four-lane street littered with rubble and blown-out hydrogen-powered cars in order to get to the building, also having to step over several charred bodies of what appeared to be Ares colony civilians. Distant explosions continued intermittently in the background.

The familiar Mexican dialect of Corporal Martinez sounded over the platoon net. "Seven this is four, I have all egress routes covered, also have one sniper team with eyes on the roof....looks like we have at least two friendly dismounts around the crash site, over."

"Roger four...you're sure they're friendly?" Kaleb wanted to make sure as he made his way up the second floor stairs of the office building.

"Well, they definitely don't look like aliens through my scope at least Sergeant," Martinez assured.

"Ok, good copy, 1st squad is at the door to the roof time now, should be up top in a few seconds," Kaleb responded.

Corporal Hunt, on point for 1st squad, attempted to push open the metal door that exited to the roof. "Goddammit, thing is locked up tight," he cursed as he thrust his entire body weight up against it. Hunt turned to look back down the narrow staircase at the rest of 1st squad behind him. "Shotgun," he simply stated. One of the Privates from the squad immediately made his way up the stairs to Corporal Hunt and handed him his personal weapon, a 10-gauge tactical shotgun loaded with buckshot. Hunt swiped up the weapon with one arm and took several steps back. "Firing," he plainly said over the squad net, pointing the barrel of the shotgun directly at the mechanical lock in the door-jam. *Boom!* The report from the large-barrel weapon echoed throughout the stairwell. The mechanical locking device on the door blew into pieces upon the impact of nine separate .40 caliber slugs at close range. Hunt cycled a new round into the chamber and calmly turned, handing the weapon back to the Private. In a solid motion, he reared back and forcefully kicked open the exit door; it flew open with minimal resistance.

First squad ran up the stairs and out onto the roof level with weapons up, surrounding the downed Raptor from all sides. Kaleb followed suit and made his way up towards the craft. Two human figures walked out with their hands up from the backside of the ship.

"Don't shoot! We're freindlies, Flight Lieutenant Thompson and Chief Donnelly, USS Navy seventh fleet," a faint female voice pleaded out to the Marines.

Kaleb removed his helmet and squinted to view the two figures more closely. *I'll be damned, it's actually her,* he thought as noticed her unmistakable blonde hair and green eyes. He let out a faint smile and approached Jen and her crew chief. He noticed that she was clearly shaken from the crash.

"It's ok LT, it's me, Staff Sergeant Taylor, from 1ˢᵗ platoon, are you alright?"

"Kaleb! Oh my god it's really you! Thank god someone found us!" she couldn't help but blurt out as she ran over and hugged him.

"What the hell happened, how'd you end up like this, where's the platoon from Delta?" Kaleb asked urgently.

Jen Thompson wiped her face, which was covered in soot and grime, then spoke in a rattled tone, "Oh man…things are bad down here. We barely even made it into the upper atmosphere before one of those alien ships clipped my starboard control fin with a laser blast….I was able to hold the ship together long enough to make my drop with Delta Company on the eastern side of the city though. As we were lifting off after a successful drop of 2ⁿᵈ platoon's Marines…. well…that's when things totally went to hell. Swarms of those aliens closed in on the platoon along with cover from their small fighter drones. The whole platoon, forty Marines….dead…wiped out all of them only a few seconds after I lifted off…It was horrible…I tried to give them air support but there were just too many of them…. and those drones were all over me…couldn't shake them to save my life. That's when my main thruster overheated after a few direct hits from their lasers….had no choice but to put her down on this roof… my co-pilot…he didn't make it either…died in the crash…..it's just me and Chief Donnelly left now. I could've saved them….could've saved them all…I never should have made the drop…" Jen fought back tears of anger and despair as she explained her situation.

"It's not your fault LT, you did everything you could," Kaleb tried to reassure her, putting his hand on her shoulder. He looked over at the young, heavy set, blonde-haired crew chief standing next to her. "Chief, how bad is the Raptor? Is there any way to get it airborne again?"

The chief spoke up in an unusually high-pitched voice, "Well, Sergeant, it's possible to get it up and running again, but I can't get that control fin operational without help to set it back in place to re-fasten it. As far as the main thruster, I can probably re-route non-critical functions to lessen the power drain on the engine, hopefully preventing another overheat."

Kaleb nodded as he looked over the damaged ship. "Roger, how about comms? Or weapons? Do you have contact with any fleet assets?"

"Negative, the thruster overheat fried our communications interface, we've been in the dark ever since, weapon systems still appear to be functioning properly at least." the chief reported.

"Shit....go figure.....Ok chief, my platoon has a mission to complete, but this thing could be our only way off this planet so tell me how many men and how much time do you need to fix it?" Kaleb said in an obviously annoyed tone.

Chief Donnelly scratched his head and thought for a second. "With the limited tools I have onboard, I don't know, three, maybe four hours at best....and I'll need at least two of your Marines to stay behind to help with the control fin, as well as keep us secure in case any of those aliens come looking for us. The Lieutenant and I have very limited small arms combat training."

"Three to four hours? Damn....." Kaleb said as he ran his fingers through his hair. "Ok, well, that's all we've got to work with right now, we'll have to go with it." He turned to Corporal Martinez who was standing a few feet to his left, "Martinez, leave Lance Corporal Burke here with his spotter to help repair the Raptor and keep this site secure. The rest of us will move into the capital center and try to locate our HVT. Make sure Burke stays in radio contact throughout. I want to know first thing once this Raptor is fully repaired."

Corporal Martinez nodded in acknowledgement. "Understood, on it," he then turned and ran over to Burke to relay the order.

Kaleb put his helmet back on and keyed the platoon internal net. "Wofpack listen up, we're leaving a sniper team behind to guard this crash site and repair the ship. In the meantime we are going to continue on to our objective and secure our HVT. Sergeant Yao, your squad is on point; let's move into the capital center time now," he addressed the platoon as they pulled 360-degree security around the downed ship. Sergeant Yao got up from his security position and gave a series of hand signals, maneuvering his squad back down the stairwell of the building.

Lieutenant Thompson came up to Kaleb as he was about to move out off of the roof. She had begun to regain her composure. "Don't worry we'll get this thing fixed as fast as possible and I'll be able to pull you guys out of here, just promise not to get yourselves killed out there."

Kaleb looked back and nodded at her, "Just stay in contact with Burke's platoon radio and we'll be fine. See you in a few hours."

20

Ares, Capital City of Whetmore, alien occupation zone

As the platoon neared their objective, the Ares Intelligence and Science headquarters building, the Marines began to hear the faint echo of assault rifle fire ahead. Kaleb gave a halt signal to the platoon and the Marines took up defensive positions.

"Yao, you hear that? That's center-fire small arms. You think it could be one of our units?" Kaleb transmitted from his position in the middle of the platoon formation to Sergeant Yao in the front over the platoon net.

"Roger, sounds like they could use some help. We're supposed to be about seven-hundred meters from our objective but we can't see shit ahead of us from all these bombed out buildings. It sounds like the gunfire is coming from that direction" Yao answered.

Kaleb responded, "Martinez, get your snipers in spread out positions on high ground to give us cover on approach to our objective. We're going to move forward and try to make contact with possible friendly units ahead….Hunt, take us north, bounding over-watch."

Corporal Hunt took the platoon forward into a sea of rubble and debris for the next two-hundred meters. Finally, they came to an opening where the streets and building opened up into a large, open, capital square. They could still hear sporadic gunfire off to their left flank as Hunt took cover behind a large concrete jersey barrier. He peered over the top to see their objective.

"Seven this is point, looks like we made it to the capital center… see what looks like a few government buildings, a lot of open areas and courtyards leading up to them….holy-shit….uh…seven you're gonna want to get up here quick." Coporal Hunt reported from the front of the platoon.

Kaleb moved quickly up to the barrier Hunt was behind that sat of the edge of an open courtyard leading up to the congressional building. "What do you got up here?" Kaleb asked anxiously. Hunt didn't say anything; he just slowly pointed to three large figures walking on the steps of the Intel headquarters building just over four-hundred meters away. Kaleb's eyes widened as he focused on the strange bi-pedal creatures. He pulled up his assault rifle and looked through his 3x zoom tactical scope at one of the aliens. The near seven-foot tall reptilian-like humanoid had shiny black armor covering most of its brown-colored, smooth skin. Its right appendage appeared to be a large-barreled weapon instead of an arm. Its left arm was long, down to its knees with three fingers and large claws on each. Its big, rounded head and bulbous, almond-shaped, yellow eyes with black-slit pupils were uncovered, with no visible helmet device. It did appear to have some sort of breathing apparatus attached to its pointed mouth with a small tube leading out of it than ran to the backside of its armor.

Kaleb's heart pounded at his first ever sighting of an extraterrestrial being. A hostile, technologically advanced one at that.

"What the hell should we do?" Hunt asked, astonished.

"We do what I said we would, light those motherfuckers up… sniper teams…this is Wolfpack 7…. I have three enemy dismounts ranged at four-hundred meters at a bearing of three-five-zero from my location. Upon positive ID you are cleared hot," Kaleb transmitted over the platoon net with confidence.

Corporal Martinez had spread himself and Headley out on the tops of two different buildings on the edge of the large courtyard. The three alien soldiers suddenly opened fire to their left flank with the laser weapons on their right appendages. Automatic rifle fire countered the alien attack; the same unknown gunfire the platoon had heard earlier was now just a few hundred meters to their left. Martinez focused in on the muzzle flashes from the alien lasers with his scope.

"Targets acquired, engaging," Martinez replied, sounding un-rattled by the sight of the strange alien life form in his scope.

Boom..boom…..boom…boom, four deafening shots rang out in quick succession from above Kaleb and the platoon from the MR-40A2 sniper rifles. The rounds struck the three alien targets by complete surprise on their chest-plate armor, knocking two of them on the ground, one other stumbling to stay on his feet from the impact. The aliens slowly pulled themselves back up on their feet, only stunned by the impact of the 9.45mm rounds impacting on their armor. They turned their attention away from gunfire on the left flank and towards Kaleb's position. They began to sprint towards the Wolfpack platoon, firing the laser weapons at will.

"Fuck! Hit them again Martinez! Quick!!" Kaleb yelled over the net as he took cover. The laser beams impacted above Kaleb's head and crashed into the building behind them.

"Return fire goddammit! Get cover and return fire!" Kaleb yelled at his platoon, picking up his assault rifle and spraying on full auto towards the advancing aliens. The rest of the platoon followed suit and began to fire back at the aliens, their small, 6.8mm armor piercing rounds simply ricocheted off of the alien armor as they continued to close in on the platoon. Corporal Martinez took aim through his scope at one of the alien's exposed heads, now just one-hundred and fifty meters away. He squeezed the trigger as the crosshairs landed between the alien's large eyes. The alien's head suddenly exploded upon the impact of the tungsten, armor piercing round upon its skull. Dark black blood sprayed out everywhere as the creature fell lifelessly to the ground. The two aliens remaining instantly zeroed in on Martinez and his spotter's location on top of the building just behind Kaleb and the rest of the platoon. Corporal Martinez realized that his position had been compromised and instantaneously turned to his spotter.

"Go! Get the fuck out-!" Martinez screamed in desperation.

The aliens quickly fired two successive beams from their high-energy lasers, obliterating the concrete floor that Martinez was standing on. He and his spotter tumbled down three stories and were summarily crushed to death by the impact and the large chunks of concrete that landed on top of them.

"Fall back!! Fall back to cover now!!" Kaleb screamed as Martinez and Colby fell to their death behind him. Suddenly, out of nowhere, a rocket-propelled grenade detonated on the ground right between the two attacking aliens, blowing them to pieces just fifty meters away from Kaleb. He hit the deck as dust and pieces of alien flesh landed around him from the blast.

"Holy shit, what the hell was that?!" Hunt yelled. He stood up to see that the attacking aliens had been utterly destroyed by some outside force.

"I don't know!....Where'd it come from!" Kaleb exclaimed; standing up as well. He looked around to see what the source of the rocket attack was as the smoke and dust cleared. A voice with a strange accent suddenly rang out from behind a wall thirty meters on the platoon's left flank.

"Hold ye fire, we're human! We're comin' out," said a man with an outlandish colonial Ares accent. Eight men ran out from behind the wall and over to the platoon's position behind the jersey barriers.

Kaleb didn't recognize the strange greenish/gray camo armor or weapons they carried. *Now they are definitely not USS military*, he thought as he studied the approaching figures.

The man in the lead kneeled down next to Kaleb, and took of his tactical helmet, revealing a filthy, scarred face. Next he removed his right glove and leaned in to offer a handshake.

"Chock Leader Gavin, Ares Alliance Army….never thought I'd be so glad to see you guys here," the obviously rattled soldier enthusiastically shook Kaleb's hand with a grin. Before Kaleb could respond, Gavin anxiously continued, "You gotta shoot em in the head see? Or at least blow them to hell with a rocket, or grenade…. tough bastards…that armor will stop anything….you guys the rescue team? You got any reinforcements comin' in or what? I tell ya we're ready to get off this fuckin' rock…"

Kaleb could tell by his mannerisms that the Ares Chock Leader had been on the ground in combat for quite awhile. His face was covered in black soot and dust, hands were shaking, and eyes twitched back and forth rapidly. Kaleb returned the handshake and nodded. "Staff Sergeant Taylor, USS Marine 1st Recon Battalion. Thanks for saving our asses man. We've never seen anything like this before."

Gavin nodded nervously, "Yeah, you bet….we been fightin' these sons of bitches for three days now non-stop. They been blowin' our city to shreds, no one knows why the fuck they're here or where they came from. Crazy locals been callin' em the 'Uggae,' means 'Gods of Death' in an ancient language or some shit. I could care less. I don't give a shit what the damn things are called, I just want them off my fuckin' planet. Know what I mean? Me and my squad is all that's left of a five-hundred-man battalion that was trying to defend the capital center. We just been hidin' last few hours, hopin' for a rescue ship or something. Then you guys showed up."

"Well we aren't a rescue team that's for sure. Your guess is as good as mine as to how we get the hell out of here. I've got a mission to infiltrate that Intel and Science headquarters over there and rescue your Deputy Director of Intelligence. Apparently that asshole knows something pretty damn important which is why I'm supposed to deliver him to my command in piece…Now that we know we can kill these things, can you help us get in there and find him?" Kaleb asked.

Gavin shook his head quickly back and forth, "Oh no, no, no…. they got some kind of frickin laser turrets set up outside the entrance of that place. They took control of it a few hours ago, if that Deputy Director was in there, he's probably dead now. They sent you in here with only eighteen guys to do all that?"

"Well, just like you we're all that's left of a whole battalion. Our assaulting force got blown to hell by those alien starships up in orbit. We still have our orders though. One way or another we're going to have to try to get in there and finish the mission. I got no chance of extraction anytime soon, at least not for several hours. You can either help us and die fighting, or crawl around in this rubble hiding the whole time, till more of those things come after us." Kaleb gave an ultimatum.

Gavin looked at Kaleb like he was insane for a few seconds. "You're a crazy mother fucka aren't ya? Ok…okay….fuck it…I can roll with that. Guess we all gotta die sometime don't we?" Kaleb nodded at Gavin in agreement.

"So you and your squad will help us then?" Kaleb asked.

Gavin nodded, "Yeah….so long as you promise to get us a ride out of here once we're done, if we survive that long at least."

"Ok, no problem, so what else can you tell us about these 'Uggae' things and that Intel headquarters?" Kaleb inquired impatiently as Yao and Hunt circled in to listen to the exchange.

Chock leader Gavin squinted over at the intelligence headquarters building, five-hundred meters away just below the afternoon sun. "Ok, listen…." He drew a diagram with his finger in the sand below the kneeling Marines. You got the building here and these two laser turret things they just set up outside the main entrance. Now we gotta hurry cause they'll probably be wonderin' where these three assholes are at that we just killed…but anyway… if you can draw fire from these automated turrets you might have a chance to slip a team in the basement entrance on the side here. These turrets got like a three-hundred meter targeting radius…so you get within that and your fucked ok….so you draw fire with one squad and then hit em with something heavy from the flank… you got any antitank rockets or anything, we just used our last one back there savin' you guys."

Sergeant Yao nodded, "Yeah we salvaged two Centurions from the Raptor crash."

Gavin continued, "Good, cause your gonna need that shit ok… draw their fire, then hit them with those rockets and you might have a chance to slip that team in through the basement….Now I don't know what will be waitin for you guys on the inside, but there could be as many at twenty to forty of those aliens in there, I think they are lookin' for something….no fuckin' telling man….oh and another thing…we think they're telepathic…they can get inside your head and shit….seen them cause a couple of our own soldiers to turn on us in the middle of a firefight…crazy shit man….that's why they don't wear helmets or nuthin… so they can transmit their thoughts quicker. You gotta hit 'em in the head because nothing I know of penetrates that armor they got on."

Kaleb looked through a set of binoculars at the two odd-shaped alien laser turrets that were set up in front of the main entrance. They were pointed towers, about fifteen feet high with a black diamond-shaped object on top. As he studied the strange alien weapons he noticed four more tall figures exiting the main entrance of the Intel headquarters.

"Shit, we got four more of those enemy dismounts headed our way," Kaleb said.

Corporal Headley came over the net from his concealed sniper position four-hundred and fifty meters to Kaleb's right flank, "Staff Sergeant Taylor we've got enemy dismounts on scope, I'm gonna go for headshots." Headley and his spotter, PFC Landry, was all the remained of 4th squad with Martinez dead and Burke left behind at the crash site. He zeroed in his crosshairs and fired two bursts of sniper rifle fire at the alien soldiers, scoring headshots on both, knocking their lifeless bodies to the ground. The two laser turrets lit up with a bright yellow light and fired directly towards Headley's muzzle flash. He and Landry took cover under a top-floor staircase in the four-story building where he had set up their sniper position and braced for the impact of the laser blast. The building shuddered as the concentrated beam of light struck a main support column inside the structure. The floor vibrated heavily below the sniper team's feet as the already heavily damaged building began to collapse around them.

"Come on let's get out of here now! This thing is coming down fast!" Headley yelled over the sound of crumbling steel and concrete. The two Marines sprinted over to a large, shattered window. An eight-foot wide gap separated their current building with the edge of the roof to another, smaller building below the window sill. "We gotta jump man! Just do it or we're dead!" Headley screamed at Landry. The young Marine nodded and obeyed the order from his Corporal, stepping onto the windowsill and taking a giant leap across the alleyway that lay four stories below. His feet planted hard on the adjacent building's roof and he rolled over one time to dissipate the impact energy from the rough landing. Headley took up the same position on the window sill and closed his eyes. Still gripping his sniper rifle in his hands; he pushed off as hard as he could with his legs in order to leap across. As his feet left the structure, the building behind him completely collapsed in on itself. Headley tumbled across the roof of the adjacent building as he landed, spraining his ankles in the process, he had made it safely to more solid ground. Landry scrambled over to him and helped him back on his feet. Headley dusted himself off and leaned down to pick up his sniper rifle that he dropped during his landing.

"I'm good, come on, we gotta set up a new position and give Sergeant Taylor cover," Headley told his spotted as he grimaced in pain. He limped over to the outer parapet wall on the flat roof of the new building that faced the capital center courtyard and pulled out the bipod on his rifle, resting on top of the three-foot high wall. He peered through the scope and began scanning the area below for new targets.

Chock leader Gavin grabbed Kaleb's shoulder, "Sergeant, if we're gonna do this let's do it now before they zero in on us! My squad will bound forward into the courtyard and draw their laser fire. You guys get to that basement door quick, go! We won't have much time once they spot us!" Gavin suddenly jumped up and grabbed his seven soldiers. They fearlessly vaulted the jersey barriers in front of them and ran out into to open courtyard, running for a small spot of cover behind a copse of trees fifty meters ahead. The laser turrets turned their focus away from the sniper team and on the advancing Ares Alliance soldiers.

Kaleb yelled over the net, "Wolfpack on me! Move! Move!" He got up and ran towards the left side of the Intelligence and Science headquarters. The remainder of the platoon immediately jumped up and followed behind him in a dead sprint. The fourteen Marines ran across the courtyard towards a group of large, stone statues just one-hundred meters from the basement entrance to the headquarters building. The laser turrets fired several salvos directly at Chock leader Gavin's men huddled behind some trees on the front side of the building. The group of trees quickly gave way from the impact of the laser beams and splintered into a thousand pieces. Chock leader

Gavin and his men tried to take cover but not before losing three soldiers to the sudden blast. Kaleb saw Gavin's men pinned down across the courtyard and turned to Sergeant Yao.

"Yao, the Centurions! Now!" he screamed over the sound of laser fire and explosions. Sergeant Yao nodded and hand motioned for his two heavy weapons Marines to fire their shoulder-launched, guided missiles. The two Privates got up on a knee from their prone positions behind the stone statues and acquired their targets. In a bright orange flash, the two anti-tank missiles launched towards the laser turrets. The warheads shot up into the air almost eight-hundred feet before arcing down upon their targets from above. The flight time of the missiles to their target was less than three seconds. They simultaneously detonated on top of the two turrets as fire and smoke engulfed the alien weapons platforms in an earsplitting blast. The ground shook below the Marines' feet as they felt the shockwave pass through them. The two alien turrets buckled and crashed to the ground in a second, brilliant yellow-orange explosion.

"Hell yeah! We got 'em Sergeant!" one of Sergeant Yao's Marines' blurted out in excitement. The success was short-lived however as Kaleb looked through his tactical scope to Gavin's position behind the blown out trees.

The two remaining alien soldiers were right on top of the Ares Alliance squad. Kaleb watched in horror as the larger, stronger beings tore Gavin's men to shreds, limb by limb. Chock leader Gavin let out a final cry of anger as he fired his assault rifle on full auto into the alien's chest. The 'Uggae' soldier picked him up by his neck with its left hand and lifted him off of the ground. It pressed the barrel of its laser weapon directly into Gavin's chest-plate armor and fired. Gavin's body went limp as the alien effortlessly tossed the now lifeless vessel to the side.

Kaleb turned back to his Marines and yelled directly. "Get some goddamn fire on that enemy now!"

In unison, the fourteen Marines pulled out from behind the cover of the stone statues and opened fire with their assault rifles on the two aliens that had just killed Gavin's men. The imposing creatures turned and darted in and out of cover with acute quickness; so quick that Kaleb and his Marines were unable to get in a clear headshot.

"Goddammit Headley, are you still up there?!! Give us some sniper support!! Two dismounts closing in on our position, eighty meters west of the three statues!" Kaleb sent across the platoon net.

From the roof of the three-story office building, four-hundred meters away, Headley scanned the courtyard with his scope and caught glimpse of one of the aliens darting out from behind a concrete wall. "Roger Sergeant….I'm on 'em…..wait one…." Headley responded.

Out of nowhere, the lead alien leaped over the top of a blown out hydrogen fuel cell car just thirty meters in front of the Wolfpack platoon's position.

"Oh shit!" Corporal Hunt cried out. He instinctively cooked off a high explosive grenade and tossed it at the fast approaching alien. Assault rifle rounds ricocheted off of its armor as it ran towards the Marines. Hunt's grenade abruptly detonated below the alien's feet and surrounded it with smoke and dust. The large creature let out a high pitched cry as its right leg became separated from its body due to the blast. It fell to the ground and began to blindly fire its laser towards the Marines in cover behind the stone statues. Sergeant Yao placed his sight reticule on the cranium of the alien life form and fired a five-second long burst. Its skull caved in completely and a pool of black blood quickly formed below its body.

"That's one, now where the hell is the other one?" Kaleb asked over the net. "Dammit Headley do you have a bead on anything yet…..?" At that instant the second alien burst out from behind a row of bushes thirty meters to the rear of the platoon. Kaleb turned around to fire as fast as he could but it seemed like everything was going in slow motion. The alien had leveled his laser barrel on the center of the platoon and it began to glow bright yellow as it prepared to fire. Kaleb began to pull the trigger of his rifle, shooting from the hip. Before his first round popped off, a large tungsten round from Lance Corporal Headley's MR-40A2 rifle pierced through the aliens' left eye, dropping it to the deck, a clean kill. The shot echoed throughout the capital center courtyard and seconds later everything went eerily quiet.

Kaleb looked over at the dead alien, blood and brain matter surrounded its body. "Nice shot Headley, could you have waited any longer?" Kaleb transmitted over the net with dark sarcasm.

"Roger Sergeant, I've got your position covered," Headley immediately responded, breathing heavily.

Kaleb turned to Sergeant Yao who kneeled next to him behind one of the stone statues. "Ok, now is our chance to get in that building and find the HVT before it's too late…." Yao nodded and twirled his finger in the air to signal for his Marines to get ready to move out.

Kaleb keyed the platoon net, "Headley, hold your position and make sure none of those things follow us into the Intel headquarters. We'll keep radio contact with you on five minutes intervals, let us know what is going on outside."

"Roger Sergeant," Headley replied.

Kaleb stood up and gave the hand signal for the platoon to move. The platoon quickly covered the short distance through the courtyard to the basement door and took up defensive positions around the set of stairs leading down to it.

Sergeant Yao examined the heavy metal door, "Demo charges?" he asked Kaleb.

Kaleb shook his head and found a green button covered in dust and soot on the wall to the right of the door. Surprisingly, the Ares intelligence building had been left largely intact by the attacking alien forces. Kaleb rubbed his hand over the small button and pressed in on it. A pressure release instantly sounded and the heavy metal door swung open revealing the interior of the building.

Kaleb glanced at Yao, "This way's a little easier."

Corporal Hunt was the first to enter the basement with his rifle at the high-ready. It was pitch black inside, causing his heads-up display to engage low light image enhancement.

"Nothing on motion sensor," Hunt quietly reported as he traversed the walls of the first large room they entered. "Looks like a utility room or something, lots of machinery.....Got another center fed door, stacking." Hunt and the rest of his Alpha team stacked on the new door, two Marines on each side. Kaleb and Sergeant Yao moved in with the rest of the Marines behind Hunt.

"You want me to flash and clear?" Hunt whispered to Kaleb.

He held up his hand in a signal to hold off, "Hold on.....you hear that? Sounds like...shit, I don't know what it sounds like....but something's definitely in there," Kaleb said as he moved up to the closed door and put his head against it.

Hunt looked at Kaleb in confusion "So...then what are we doing?"

"Yeah....wait one," Kaleb placed his right hand on the door latch and slowly pulled it towards him. He quietly cracked the door open and looked into the large chamber on the other side. A small office fire slightly lit up the room. Kaleb could see shadows and movement on the far side of the space about sixty feet away. Suddenly a pungent smell hit his senses; the unmistakable odors of rotting flesh. The sound of jaws ripping into tissue and the smacking of lips became louder to Kaleb as he fully opened the access door. Kaleb noticed a four-foot high wall that ran across half the width of the room that separated several office cubicles. He motioned back for Hunt and his team to follow him into the chamber. The five

Marines squatted down and slowly moved up to the short partition wall. Kaleb cautiously pulled his head slightly above the wall in order to see the other half of the room. His eyes widened at what he saw. In the far right corner was a pile of six to seven human bodies, burnt and charred apparently from laser blasts. Squatting down next to the pile was two of the alien, 'Uggae,' apparently sharing a meal out of the appendages of one of the dead bodies. They ravenously bit into the arms and legs of the human remains, oblivious to Kaleb and his men.

Kaleb sank back down to the floor below the wall gave a desperate look to Hunt, he gulped and then whispered, "….Ok, put on your silencers and aim for the head."

He then raised up two fingers to hand signal two enemy dismounts ahead to the rest of Alpha team. The Marines nodded in acknowledgment of Kaleb's command and gently pulled out their silencers, screwing them on the tip of their assault rifle barrels. Hunt gave thumbs up to Kaleb once everyone had finished installing them. Kaleb nodded and then counted to three with his fingers. On the third count, the five Marines rose up in sequence and took aim at the backside of the aliens' large skulls. Ten quick *clicks* from their rifles and the two aliens dropped to the deck, suffering multiple headshot wounds. Sergeant Yao and the rest of the platoon immediately filed into the chamber to see what had happened. They found Kaleb and Hunt standing over top of the two dead alien soldiers. Sergeant Yao nervously walked up to Kaleb, not taking his eyes off the gruesome scene of the half-eaten human bodies.

"What kind of sick shit is this?" Yao softly asked, taking a closer look at the dead aliens.

Kaleb squatted down and looked at one of the aliens. Its dark black armor and laser weapon system looked totally foreign, made of a material unknown to him. Human blood was splattered over its mouth and chest. "I don't know man, never thought I'd see anything like this before," Kaleb stated in a strangely calm voice as he continued to examine the strange alien creature's body.

Hunt looked down at Kaleb, "You think our Deputy Director Rhenquist is in this pile?"

Kaleb glimpsed at the mess of bodies, "Maybe….but they said he was held up in some sort of high-tech emergency command post further underground. Maybe the aliens didn't find him yet…" Kaleb cued up the building's floor plan on his data pad. "Well, based on the floor plan I downloaded during the mission brief that command post should be down this next hallway, they'll be an opening on the right leading to an independent stair column that goes five levels underground. We at least have to check it out…..besides nobody's coming to extract us anytime soon, might as well finish the mission." Kaleb said, looking up at Hunt and Sergeant Yao.

"Shit…fucking fleet's probably blown to pieces up there by now anyway, there ain't no extraction team coming for us," One of Sergeant Yao's Marines protested while he pulled rear security.

"Hey lock that shit up goddammit, we're getting out of here one way or another." Yao protested.

Kaleb motioned with his rifle to Hunt towards the next center fed door leading to a hallway, ignoring the blatant protest from the 1st squad Marine. "The hallway we need should be on the other side of that door. Then we'll take the stairs all the way down to the command center level….let's move."

"Here we go again," Robbie Hunt let out a sigh and reluctantly took up the point position on the door.

21

"Sound collisional alarm!" the helmsman of the Cairo yelled across the bridge. The massive Jupiter-class battleship was on a collision course straight into what was believed to be the alien flagship. The USS fleet had managed to hold on in the closer range engagement longer than Admiral Beck had expected. The small, maneuverable USS fighters could bypass the alien laser attacks but did not have enough ordnance to do any significant damage to their vessels. They at least caused a distraction and bought the fleet some time though. The close range combat had brought the Cairo right on top of the alien flagship, the titanium hull of the battleship suddenly scraped across the top of the equally immense alien craft. Admiral Beck fell to his knees onto the deck of the Cairo's from the impact.

"Full vertical thrusters! Get us off of them before we breach our hull!!" Beck yelled at the helmsman. The Cairo angled its thrusters towards the top of the alien ship it was resting on and blasted off with full strength. The battleships' heavy turrets faced down towards the enemy ship and fired round after round of high-explosive warheads into its hull. Admiral Beck knew his time was short. He knew he only had eight ships left out of an original fleet of sixty-five. They had managed to bring down a few more of the alien starships but the battle had been grossly one-sided up to this point. The alien armor and weaponry was simply just too advanced. Two smaller alien ships closed in and set their sights on the Cairo as it attempted to distance itself from the alien flagship.

"Sir, two enemy ships closing in behind us! They are in firing position!" the scanners chief blurted out amidst the fires and explosions coming from inside the interior to the battleship.

Beck stood back up, "Evasive maneuvers! Take us straight down towards the surface of Ares!"

"But sir! We're already in low orbit, with our engines damaged we won't not be able to pull out of the planet's gravity well!" the helmsman replied back.

"Dammit son! Just do it!" Beck ordered firmly. *Come on you piece of junk, hold together for me,* Beck whispered to himself.

Unexpectedly, a substantial volley of EMA projectiles impacted on the two pursuing alien ships. Eight direct hits from the tungsten rounds split the smaller alien vessels into pieces. The ships' erupted into gleaming orange flashes and explosions. The shockwave from the EMA impacts could be felt passing through the Cairo's hull as Admiral Beck ran over to the scanners section on the bridge.

"Who the hell was that chief?!" the Admiral asked in shock.

"I have no idea sir, our ships are all in too close for EMA range," the chief answered, confused.

A loud, confident voice with a British accent abruptly sounded over the battle-net. "This is Admiral Fairchild with 2nd Fleet, We have your six and it is clear, over."

"I'll be goddamned, Fairchild made it from New Sydney!....... We might have a chance to take these bastards down," Beck said with renewed enthusiasm. Twenty-six starships from 2nd fleet exited Faust drive speed a few thousand miles outside the low orbit engagement and opened fire on the remaining alien ships.

The hellish bombardment caught the alien fleet by surprise as they attempted to evade the onslaught of EMA projectiles and nuclear-tipped missiles.

*   *   *   *

Chief Donnelly stood in the rear cargo hold of the downed Raptor. He reached up into a control panel access point above his head and proceeded to re-route a set of wires inside the engine compartment. Lance Corporal Burke patrolled back and forth impatiently outside on the roof as the Naval flight technician slowly went about his work.

"Ok ma'am, try it now," Donnelly yelled up to Lieutenant Thompson, who was sitting in the cockpit, flipping several switches up and down.

"Roger, attempting to engage main thruster," she answered back. Thompson gripped a lever on a control surface above her head and pushed it forward. A low-pitched wine sounded as the Raptor's systems attempted to restart. The cockpit lit up as control surfaces came back to life.

"I-I think it's working, systems are coming back online!" she said with a sense of renewed hope. The wine of the main systems booting up then fizzled out slowly, the cockpits systems and indicator lights dimmed and went out completely. "Dammit, we're losing it chief, startup overload warning light is back on....yeah I've got nothing, no power," Jen reported back to Donnelly with disappointment.

Donnelly cracked a smile, "Yeah, but she's breathing a little bit now LT. I can feel it. I think I know what's causing the startup overload. Just need a little more time to get to it and bypass the problem. Then hopefully we'll have something."

"Alright chief, glad to hear some good news for once, I'll get on the radio and let Sergeant Taylor know we're getting close to being airborne," Jen responded.

*   *   *   *

Corporal Hunt kicked-open the metal door that opened up to a long, dark, ten-foot wide tunnel through solid rock with metal grate flooring and railing on each side. The platoon cautiously moved forward up the corridor in search of the stairwell that supposedly led to the emergency command center. After traveling up the darkened tunnel for about twenty meters Hunt gave a halt signal. He looked up at the ceiling through his low-light image enhancement in disgust.

"Jesus....what the hell is this shit?"

About thirty feet in front of Hunt was a line of twenty to thirty mutilated human corpses strung up by their feet, simply dangling down from the top of the tunnel. Blood and entrails dripped down onto the floor in a horrific display of pure carnage. Kaleb moved up to Hunt to take a closer look, somewhat startled by the sight of the bodies.

"Put it out of your heads and keep moving, we've got to stay focused on getting down to that command center," Kaleb stated over the platoon net. He walked up behind Hunt and put his hand on his right shoulder. Robbie Hunt gave a slight jump, startled by the sudden contact.

"Come on man, let's go, nothing we can do for them now," he reassured his friend. Hunt nodded as he looked back at Kaleb, took a deep breath and continued forward through the tunnel. The Marines took care to skirt around the bodies dripping blood from above them as they moved forward once again.

"Ok...got the stairwell up here on my right. I've still got nothing on my motion sensors. You still wanna head down?" Hunt relayed over the net back to Kaleb who was leaning up against the metal railing now twenty feet behind him.

"Well fuck, that's what I said didn't I? Let's get down there, quick." Kaleb responded in an agitated tone.

"Ok, sorry, just wanted to make sure....It doesn't exactly look very inviting down there," Hunt replied quietly over the net. *Just trying not to get eaten by aliens that's all*, he sarcastically whispered to himself as he took the first step down the metal stair column.

The fourteen Marines made their way down the long stairwell, coming to a small entry room at the bottom, still not meeting with any additional enemy contact. The small room was lined with concrete and had a three inch thick solid metal door on the far side of the stair column. There was a small 8"x8" glass window on the upper half of the door. The Marines took up positions in the small stairwell entry room. Kaleb walked up to the door and peered into the tiny window. What he saw appeared to be what remained of the emergency command center; a large open room carved into the solid rock that existed under the headquarters building. There were overturned desks, papers, dead bodies, and a few damaged tactical display monitors strewn about the open chamber.

His heart started pounding when he saw what appeared to be the Deputy Director in the clutches of one of the alien beings. Only this alien looked different from the 'soldiers' they had encountered earlier. It wore a long black robe and had two organic arms instead of a laser rifle on the right one. The robe was lined with what looked like golden plates of some sort that emitted a strange glow. It was holding up the Deputy Director with its left arm, its three claws digging into the man's neck. It was staring straight into his eyes, its face just a few inches from the Director's. Six more alien 'soldiers' then came into view of the small window. They circled around the one in the robe and bowed their heads down.

Kaleb turned back to Sergeant Yao. "Shit...they've got the Director in there and are about to kill him, quick, rig this door with a breach charge, we gotta get in there now!"

"Smith! Get up here and rig this door with a breach now! Hurry up!" Yao shot out the order to Kaleb's former spotter.

"Come on Smith, we don't have much time, rig that shit…" Kaleb said as his former spotter set charges on the corners of the heavy door.

"Everybody get ready, when we blow the door all hell is going to break loose. I think there's at least seven enemy dismounts in there holding our HVT hostage, go in quick and hard, and *do not* shoot the Deputy Director, aim for the their heads" Kaleb said quietly as his platoon huddled up around him.

"Ready Staff Sergeant," PFC Kevin Smith reported a few seconds later.

Kaleb nodded, "Ok, stack up…..on three, ready, one, two, three!"

Smith punched his detonator switch, sending the mangled door hurling into the command center chamber with a piercing blast. The fourteen Marines filed in instinctively with their weapons up, acquiring their targets on their heads up displays. Bursts of assault rifle fire rang out and echoed throughout the large, open room. The third man inside, Kaleb plowed through the door opening and immediately picked out the robed alien as his target. He let the crosshairs on his head's up display lay over top of the alien's head and pulled his trigger, firing a three-round burst. The armor piercing rounds easily cut through the soft skin and skull of the alien being, causing it to release the Deputy Director from its clutches.

Sergeant Yao and Corporal Hunt dropped two more of the alien soldiers instantaneously with accurately placed rounds. The remaining four took cover behind a desk and countertop. Deputy Director Rhenquist fell to the ground and covered his head in a fetal position, screaming out in terror as gunfire filled the room. The aliens then began to move from their cover, quickly returning accurate laser fire which brightly lit up the dark room. PFC Smith, along with two other of Yao's Marines were cut down as the bright yellow laser beams ripped through their ABAS suits. One of the aliens suddenly leaped out from the behind the metal counter and landed on top of Corporal Hunt from twenty feet away, pinning him to the deck with his large, clawed feet. The creature reared its right appendage back in an effort to smash the Corporal's head in. From ten feet away, Kaleb sprinted towards the alien, firing his rifle on full auto. He lowered his shoulder and plowed into the imposing seven-foot tall alien soldier, knocking it off balance. Hunt, still on his back, grabbed his assault rifle and emptied a magazine into the enemy's exposed neck and head, leaving it unrecognizable. The three remaining aliens moved aggressively toward Sergeant Yao and two of his Marines who were pinned down behind a fallen concrete column. They fired their lasers into the column, disintegrating it into concrete shrapnel. A jagged piece of rebar flew across the room and pierced through the neck of another of Yao's Marines. The heavily-built Sergeant Chambers, without the use of his wounded right arm, charged towards the aliens, firing his rifle left-handed from the hip in an effort to get them off of Yao's squad. He was able to drop one of the aliens but was then utterly disintegrated into dust by a direct hit from another alien's laser fire. He gave Sergeant Yao a split second of a distraction however, which allowed him to pop up from behind the downed column and quickly take down the second to last alien in a three round burst to the head.

"There's one left! Take him down!!" Kaleb yelled as he and Hunt got back to their feet.

The nimble alien soldier ferociously jumped across the room and amazingly sprung itself off of a side wall straight towards the remainder of Sergeant Yao's squad. It tore through two Marines with its three inch long claws while simultaneously blasting away with its integrated laser rifle. Sergeant Yao turned as fast as he could towards the menacing being and engaged with his rifle only five feet away from the alien. It violently slapped Yao's assault rifle out of his hands and picked him up by his left leg, holding him upside-down. Kaleb and Hunt ran to try to get a clear shot at the alien but Yao was blocking their line of fire. As the alien moved its laser rifle barrel towards Yao's chest, the squad leader unsnapped a high explosive grenade from his assault belt and shoved it down the wide barrel of the alien weapon. As it went to fire, its right appendage suddenly detonated in a ball of high explosive, fire, and shrapnel. The blast sent Yao flying twenty feet across the command center and knocked Kaleb and Hunt off of their feet. The alien creature let out an extremely high pitched yelp as its entire arm was separated from its torso by the explosion. Its dark black blood spewed out of its shoulder joint as it picked itself up and charged towards Kaleb, who was still trying to get back up off the deck. Out of the corner of his eye, Kaleb saw the alien quickly approaching form across the room. He gripped his assault rifle and managed to pull himself up on one knee. Leveling his weapon sight on the attacking alien's head, Kaleb squeezed the trigger. *Click. Oh shit! Out of ammo!* He thought in despair for a split second before the one-armed alien rammed into him with astounding force, knocking him once again to the ground. Kaleb's helmet slammed back down on the metal floor as the alien pinned him to the deck with its massive, clawed feet. He reached up and pulled out his field knife from its sheath in a futile attempt to defend himself from the ravaging creature. The alien swung its remaining arm down towards Kaleb's face, its claws fully extended in preparation for a killing blow. Kaleb ducked out of the way just in time and its large, three-fingered hand connected with the metal floor a few inches from the side of his head. Kaleb, with all his remaining energy, thrust his field knife up into the alien's elbow joint, causing the creature to rear back in pain.

"Hunt! Get him off of me dammit!!!" Kaleb screamed as the alien shifted positions and pressed its right foot into Kaleb's neck, applying more and more pressure.

Robbie Hunt finally regained his senses after being knocked out for a few seconds from the grenade blast set off by Sergeant Yao. His vision cleared and he saw Kaleb across the room in a life and death struggle with the severely wounded alien. Placing the crosshairs on his head's up display over the head of the creature, Hunt fired a three round burst directly into the side of the alien's upper neck and skull, killing it instantly. Weighing nearly four-hundred pounds, the 'Uggae,' clad in its full battle armor, fell forward directly on top of Kaleb, who once again became pinned to the floor.

"Ah, fuck, get this thing off of me! I can't breathe!" Kaleb struggled to yell at Hunt. The Corporal ran over to where Kaleb was and grabbed the dead alien by its side, attempting to roll the body off of his platoon Sergeant.

"You're gonna have to help me push Taylor! I'm not Mr. Olympia here or anything," Hunt said, straining to lift the lifeless alien. "Ok, on three, one…two….three!" the two Marines pushed simultaneously and finally were able to roll it off to the side. Kaleb pulled himself back up to his feet, the alien's dark, black blood was splattered all over his ABAS suit. He looked up at Hunt and let out a deep sigh of relief.

"Thanks," Kaleb said as he wiped the alien's blood from his helmet visor. "Ok, quick, we have to check the bodies to see if any of our guys are still alive, then I've got to hurry up and find this Deputy Director before it's too late." Kaleb ordered.

Hunt nodded and surveyed the emergency command post interior. Human and alien bodies were sprawled out all over the floor as well as a few hundred shell casings from the firefight. He began to check each downed Marine to see if anyone else from the platoon had survived the close-quarters engagement. He came up upon Sergeant Yao who was lying on his back, he wasn't moving. The Corporal took off Yao's helmet. The 1st squad leader coughed and grimaced in pain, unable to speak.

"Come on you dumb son of a bitch, you're not ready to die yet!" Hunt exclaimed as he fumbled through his first-aid kit, searching for his morphine syringe and IV pouch.

With the alien threat in the command center neutralized, Kaleb immediately ran over to the Deputy Director who was still lying in the fetal position next to the now deceased, black-robed alien. Kaleb turned Deputy Director Rhenquist over, revealing severe wounds to his abdomen and neck. Rhenquist wheezed and let out a few faint coughs as he looked up at Kaleb.

"Hey! …Are you Deputy Director Rhenquist?" Kaleb asked impatiently. "I'm Sergeant Taylor, USS Marines, we're trying to save this colony and we need your help, fast!"

"Listen, you're supposed to know something crucial that can let us beat these things now what the hell is it?!" Kaleb said hastily. The Director nodded slowly as he tried to sit up.

Rhenquist cleared his throat as Kaleb helped him up and he spoke in a weakened voice, wheezing heavily in between phrases. "There isn't much time…you must listen….you must…destroy the alien device…Project Contrivance…..the device found on Gardner IV…..we brought it here…inadvertently activated it somehow…. they will not leave as long as it exists….they thought it was here with me…. ….they….they tried to extract the location from my mind….they can read your every thought and intuition….and I could see theirs…..their purpose…they come from….from a parallel universe….using Contrivance as an inter-dimensional gateway….. we angered them when we moved it here…..they will not stop until they retrieve it…..that is why they….. scoured our planet, searching for it….they use it to travel across dimensions…exploit and control weaker beings…if you can…..destroy Contrivance… they will no longer be able to travel and exist in…in our….in our…. dimension…. of space/time….it is…. the…. only way-"

Kaleb abruptly interrupted the delusional Director. "All this dimension crap is great Director but I need to know the location of the fucking thing first before we can blow it up."

The Director nodded, "It….it is in a hidden research facility…a hardened underground base fifteen.... miles south from here... hidden under the guise of a....food processing plant.....let me give... let me give you... the coordinates...I'll put them into your... data.. pad...." Kaleb quickly handed his data pad to the Director and he slowly typed in the grid location with shaky, blood-stained fingers.

Kaleb become extremely irritated, "Fifteen miles away?...Well that's just great. Let me just teleport myself there and set a few demo charges on it. The city is crawling with those aliens; we'll never make it on foot."

Rhenquist shook his head as he handed the data pad back to Kaleb. "You'll never.... make it there in time on the ground....you have to radio your fleet....only a precision...deep-underground.... nuclear strike...will be enough.... to destroy the facility holding Contrivance..... completely....take the grid...hurry...before your fleet is destroyed....the city... is...lost....leave ....me here...go," The Deputy Director let out his last breath of life as blood trickled out of the corner of his mouth. His body went limp and his eyes rolled back into his head. Kaleb carefully laid him back down onto the deck and covered his face with his suit jacket.

Kaleb put away the data pad and turned to look over at Hunt. "We've gotta get topside now and relay this grid to Colonel West! Is he going to make it? What about the rest of the guys?" Sergeant Yao coughed violently and began to breathe under his own power as Hunt responded.

"Yeah he took some bad shrapnel to his chest but it looks like his armor mostly held up. But you and I are going to have to carry him..." Hunt gulped and spoke in desperation, "I think everyone else is dead."

Kaleb nodded, "Ok...we'll come back for them, but first we've got to find the long range comms box, it was on one of Yao's guys. Without that we'll never get a message through to the Colonel." The two of them frantically searched the remains of 1st squad, searching for the platoon's long range communications device. The small gray metal box lay in a pile of human and alien entrails, covered in red and black blood. Kaleb quickly swiped it up and ran over to help Corporal Hunt pick up Sergeant Yao.

"Headley, this is Sergeant Taylor, how copy over?"

Lance Corporal Headly was in the middle of changing the ten-round magazine to his sniper rifle, smoke rose up from the barrel due to the heat from rapid firing. Static crackled over the platoon net, then Headley's voice came on, "Roger Sergeant! I'm in a little bit of a situation up here"….*boom*!…the sound of his MR-40A2 sending a round downrange was heard over the net.

"What the hell is going on up there Headley!" Kaleb answered as he and Hunt struggled to carry Yao up the stairwell. The wounded squad leader cried out in pain as he was pulled up over the steps.

"Uh, Sergeant…I've got those alien things closing in all around the courtyard, they started moving in about five minutes ago….. been able to take down a couple….don't think they spotted me yet but you better hurry up and get out of there…..they got some kind of assault vehicles rolling in fast to your position…you guys must have done something down there that really pissed them off," Headley replied, sounding distracted as he fired his weapon from his perch on the roof of the office building.

"Headley, you have to try to hold them off…we're coming up to the surface so we can get comms with Regiment," Kaleb said hopelessly.

"Ro…roger Sarn't, I'll do my best…"Headley's transmission ended with static.

Kaleb and Hunt slowly struggled up the stairwell to the tunnel leading back into the basement offices. They passed through the tunnel corridor and closed in on the exit to the courtyard with Sergeant Yao yelling out in agony the entire way as he continued to lose more and more blood.

"There's the basement door! Let's move!" Kaleb yelled as he and Hunt picked up the pace crossing through the room with the piled up human bodies. As they neared the open basement door to the outside they could hear Headley's sniper fire from his position about five-hundred meters away. They dropped Yao to the ground behind a tree and Kaleb frantically set up the long range comms box.

"Should get a signal from here right?" Kaleb anxiously asked Hunt as he set up the device. Robbie Hunt hopelessly shrugged his shoulders. At this point he was too physically and mentally exhausted to think.

Three bars lit up green indicating a good signal on the comms box. Kaleb immediately keyed the hand mike. "Pegasus 6! Pegasus 6!..This is Wolfpack 7, I have urgent radio traffic over!....."

Two large, jet black, wedge-shaped alien vehicles came into view across the courtyard, hovering just a few feet off of the ground. They opened up with heavy laser fire on the far side of city center towards the Intel Headquarters. .

"Pegasus 6 this is Wolfpack 7, I have urgent traffic, please respond over!" Kaleb continued his radio call in desperation.

"...(static)....ger Wolf..ck 7....this is Peg..s 6 send it" Colonel West came in broken.

"Sir, I have a grid from the Deputy Director of Ares Intel, break...it is for a deep underground facility that is holding some top secret device called 'Contrivance' that the aliens are using to attack us.....he says it is imperative to destroy the facility and the device immediately with an orbital strike.....how copy over?!"

"Roger Wolfpack, send me the goddamn grid already," West replied, already knowing in advance from General Austin about Project Contrivance and the need to destroy it.

"Roger, grid as follows: Alpha Golf, Hotel Sierra, two-three-six-five—seven-four-four-two.....I say again Alpha, Golf, Hotel, Sierra, two-three-six-five—seven-four-four-two, over"

"Roger, good copy Wolfpack 7…be advised, you need to find a way to get your asses out of the blast radius of the nuclear strike that will be occurring on that grid. I'm ordering the withdrawal of all USS ground forces from the city. I've got no air assets available to send to your locale for extraction at this time so start pounding ground at least ten clicks to the north to get to a safe zone ASAP, the orbital strike will be commencing in less than ten mikes. Pegasus 6 out."

Hunt slumped down and lowered his head, overhearing the Colonel's transmission. "That's great, so basically we're fucked, no way can we move ten clicks in time, especially carrying Yao the whole way." Several lasers fired from the approaching alien vehicles impacted on the outside of the Intelligence headquarters building in an earsplitting crash.

"Come on! Let's get to cover before this courtyard gets blown to hell!" Kaleb yelled as he and Hunt picked up Sergeant Yao again and dove into a nearby crevice created by two fallen steel columns. Suddenly, a familiar voice trumpeted over Kaleb's helmet radio.

"Any Wolfpack element, this is Flight Lieutenant Thompson, I have one Raptor on station with weapons hot, need grid location over," Jen transmitted over the platoon frequency as she lifted her newly repaired Raptor off of the roof it had crashed on just a few hours ago.

Kaleb's eyes widened as he looked at Hunt with a sense of hope. "LT, its Sergeant Taylor! We need extraction now! They are going to level the whole city from orbit, our grid is as follows: Alpha, Golf, Hotel, Sierra two-three –six-seven, eight-niner-niner-two, over!"

Thompson replied instantly on the platoon net, "Roger, good copy, ETA three mikes." Kaleb keyed the net again as over fifty alien soldier dismounts and several wedge-shaped hover-vehicles began to close in from across the courtyard towards their location.

"We've got a hot LZ down here, need close air support ASAP!

Marking our location with IR strobe, over!" Kaleb and Hunt opened fire on the fast approaching aliens, now only one- hundred meters away. Corporal Headley rained down sniper fire from his position across the courtyard on the roof, taking down three more alien soldiers.

"Shit!" Hunt yelled as a laser impacted on a concrete column in front of them, blowing it into pieces. The three Marines in the crevice ducked down as best they could to avoid the shrapnel landing around them. Alien dismounts began to close within twenty meters of the three stranded Marines. Kaleb and Hunt fired at close range, knocking several of the aliens to the ground but wave after wave continued after them. Kaleb hurled a high explosive grenade at the center of the alien onslaught. He covered his head and dove back down into the crevice. The grenade detonated in between three advancing aliens, tearing their bodies into several pieces.

"Man we might as well give up dude…it was nice knowing you guys….it's been fun I guess…never thought I'd be killed by aliens," Hunt declared his end as he continued to fire his rifle aimlessly.

Kaleb protested, "No one else from this platoon is dying today dammit!"

An engine thruster noise suddenly erupted from above their position, followed by the fast, deafening, *thump, thump, thump, thump, thump,* noise of a 30mm chain gun firing on targets below. The large shell casings fell down from the Raptor hovering fifty feet above and bounced on the ground just a few inches in front of Kaleb. The armor piercing rounds pelted the advancing alien dismounts, shredding their armor and flesh. Bright flashes followed by contrails fired out from under the wing stabilizers of the Raptor as it launched salvo after salvo of from its air-to-ground missile pods. The alien armored vehicles attempted to return fire with their heavy lasers but overshot Lieutenant Thompson's ship as she applied full thruster, banked hard right, and leveled back out to continue firing. The courtyard was engulfed in fire and explosions, causing the alien ground forces to scatter and seek cover. Thompson whipped the Raptor back around and swiftly brought it down the only small open area that wasn't littered with debris, about fifty meters from Kaleb's location.

"Let's go get onboard quick! I can't sit here forever!" Thompson transmitted to Kaleb over the platoon net as her Raptor touched down.

"We're moving! Come on let's go! Run!" Kaleb yelled at Hunt. They crawled out of the crevice overtop of a steel beam and pulled Sergeant Yao out by his shoulders. Kaleb grabbed Sergeant Yao and threw him over his back in a fireman's carry. Corporal Hunt ran out in front with his rifle up in order to clear the way to the transport.

Lance Corporal Burke, from inside the cargo bay, lowered the rear ramp of the Raptor and took aim with his sniper rifle as a group of alien soldiers bounded their way forward in an effort to intercept Kaleb, Hunt and Yao. Burke opened fired taking two of them down in his first four shots. He turned to his left and motioned with his arm for the three advancing Marines to hurry up and get on.

"Hurry up! I can't hold them off forever!" Burke screamed. He got down off the ramp and grabbed Yao off of Kaleb's back. Burke and Hunt carried the wounded squad leader up the ramp and into the cargo area, Kaleb collapsed to his knees after the weight was taken off his shoulders, exhausted from the sprint across the courtyard to the Raptor. Hunt ran back down the ramp and grabbed Kaleb under his arms, picking him back up off his knees and pulling him up into the Raptor.

"We're good ma'am! Let's get out of here!" Hunt transmitted through the platoon net up to Thompson in the cockpit. She immediately fired the lift-off thrusters and rotated the Raptor on its axis back towards the advancing aliens on the ground. She pulled the trigger on the control stick sending another barrage of 30mm rounds downrange into the last-ditch alien counterattack. Burke picked his sniper rifle back up and strapped himself into a safety hook on the deck of the Raptor so he could fire down out of the still opened rear cargo ramp. He picked out several targets in the courtyard a hundred feet below and opened fire.

Kaleb sat up against the bulkhead of the Raptor and held on tightly as Thompson conducted evasive maneuvers to avoid getting hit by laser fire from the aliens on the ground. He caught his breath and transmitted over the net, "Headley! Where are you?! Mark your location! We're not leaving you behind!"

Headley fired his rifle and then responded from his position on the rooftop. "Roger Sergeant, green smoke, rooftop, five-hundred meters to your four o'clock, over!" The Corporal responded. He detached the green smoke grenade off of his assault vest that was worn over-top of his ABAS, pulled the pin and tossed in a few feet behind him on the rooftop. It let out a popping sound and a bright green stream of smoke shot out from the top of it, quickly rising up into the air.

"I've got the smoke, moving in, it's going to be a tight landing. Burke, try to keep them off of me while I put her down," Jen Thompson ordered to the sniper still strapped in on the rear loading ramp.

"Roger ma'am, I've got you covered," Burke calmly replied as he changed magazines. Yellow bolts of laser fire shot past the Raptor as it flew across the large, open courtyard to Headley's position. Thompson approached the roof of the building at high speed. She then pulled back on the stick, applying downward thrust; abruptly bringing the Raptor from over one-hundred-twenty miles per hour down to a static hover in less than two seconds. Kaleb and Hunt held on for dear life as the maneuver nearly tossed them out of the rear cargo area. Thompson brought the Raptor over the top of Headley and sat at a hover just two feet off of the rooftop in front of him and his spotter.

"Got you covered! Get on!" Burke screamed at Headley. He and Landry ran out from behind the parapet wall and leaped onto the rear loading ramp. Headley grimaced in pain as he trudged through the pain shooting up from his two sprained ankles. Burke quickly un-strapped himself and dove back into the cargo area. Robbie Hunt slammed the large red switch on the starboard bulkhead, closing the loading ramp, sealing the Marines inside the Raptor.

"You're good LT, take us the hell out of here." Kaleb reported up to the cockpit as the ramp locked and sealed.

✳   ✳   ✳   ✳

Admiral Beck looked at the damage report on the Cairo's display monitor. They had lost all engine power and were beginning to fall into the Ares gravity well. Soon they would plummet in an uncontrollable descent towards the planet's surface. He pondered the order to abandon ship for a few seconds before his thoughts were interrupted by a loudspeaker transmission over the battle-net.

"Admiral Beck, this is Fairchild….we're not going to hold out much longer….but I've just received an urgent priority one message from a Colonel West in command of our ground forces on Ares. He's requesting an immediate precision, deep penetrating nuclear strike on a codename objective 'Contrivance,' with a grid coordinate on the surface of Ares a few miles south of the Whetmore capital center. He said you'd understand and comply upon receipt of the message."

Beck raised his head in hope, "My god the sons of bitches got the location…..This could be our last hope Admiral, Have your fleet hit that grid with everything they've got, now!" Beck ordered over the net.

"But sir? That could level the entire city…." Fairchild protested over the battle-net.

Beck stood his ground, "The city is already decimated Admiral and the distress beacon, hopefully our fleet is still out here somewhere…. oh man…wow….are you seeing what I'm seeing?" Thompson said quietly as the Raptor cockpit rotated back around, facing the surface of Ares.

*   *   *   *

The fusion reaction warheads housed in the deep-penetrating missiles erupted in a massive explosion of heat, pressure, and radiation, causing the hardened research base holding Project Contrivance to collapse in on itself. The alien device was summarily disintegrated into pieces from the multiple atomic blasts from above and then consequently melted down by the extreme temperatures created from the detonation. Thousand degree heat, colossal overpressure, and vast radiation dust clouds enveloped the entire southern half of the capital city of Whetmore. The large contingent of alien ground forces that had occupied the city were engulfed in the radioactive storm.

An exceptionally bright beam of light shot out from below the wreckage of the underground research facility and into space in the second that it was destroyed from the nuclear blast. It passed next to the human and alien fleets in orbit, emitting a strong electromagnetic pulse. At the end of the bright beam of light, a small black hole began to form in space a few hundred miles past what remained of the alien fleet. As the black hole expanded with ultra-dense matter, the alien fleet retreated towards it. The enormous gravitational pull created by the black hole began to pull Admiral Beck's ships towards it in an uncontrollable fashion.

"Sir! What the hell is happening?" The helmsman of the Cairo yelled desperately. The hull of the battleship shuddered violently as it neared the black hole.

"Full thrusters! Get us out of that gravity well now!!" Beck screamed. The Cairo's Faust drive roared as it struggled to pull away.

One by one, the alien starships entered the small black hole, suddenly vanishing from Ares orbit. A second later, after the last alien ship disappeared, the radiant beam of white light vanished without a trace, returning the native darkness to space. The small black hole subsequently closed in on itself and dissipated. The violent shuddering of the Cairo's hull ceased and the battleship began to pull away as the gravity well dissolved.

"Sir, we're steadying out, no longer picking up the gravitational anomaly, ship is returning to normal orbit," the helmsman reported, relieved.

Beck looked up at his tactical display monitors on the bridge in bewilderment. "Scanners chief, am I seeing this correctly? I've got no enemy ships on scope up here."

"Aye sir, readings confirmed, all alien ships seem to have vanished from space. All I'm picked up are friendlies from 2nd fleet," the scanners chief replied.

Beck wiped the sweat beads off his forehead, "My god it actually worked, they're gone…I can't believe it….Comms! Send an urgent interstellar message to Talos station: The enemy appears to be in full retreat…we have regained control of the planet," he ordered, still in a state of disbelief.

*   *   *   *

One hour later, low Ares orbit

Kaleb Taylor looked through the side view port of the Raptor down at the large radiation cloud that continued to spread over the surface of Ares. He was happy to be several hundred miles in orbit above the fast-spreading radioactive fallout. Everything was quiet onboard the

Raptor. Sound didn't travel in the vacuum of space. It was somewhat comforting given the hell they had just been through. The rest of the Marines in the cargo hold were also silent. Still in disbelief or shell shock from the intense combat they had just been through. Kaleb fought the urge to nod off to sleep but eventually succumbed to his own exhaustion. He began to dream about their drifting Raptor being rescued by a friendly ship and all of the Marines in his platoon being back alive, celebrating their victory together.

Back in the cockpit, a faint communication signal sounded over the speaker. "Unidentified transport, this is the USSN cruiser Vladivostok, we have your distress signal and are inbound at this time, over." A slightly damaged Naval cruiser came into Lieutenant Thompson's view through the cockpit.

"Roger Vladivostok, glad to hear it, we're standing by for rescue," Thompson replied enthusiastically. She unbuckled herself from the pilot seat and slid through a narrow compartment that gave her access to the rear cargo hold of the ship. She stuck her head through a small opening and looked at the seven exhausted Marines inside. "Hey guys…finally got some good news, got a friendly cruiser inbound to pick us up, it's over, we won."

Kaleb woke up out of his dream at the sound of Thompson's voice, realizing he was still inside the cargo hold of the Raptor. Hunt, Burke and Kaleb nodded in acknowledgment of the good news but did not have any cause to celebrate.

"Sarn't….does that mean we can we go home now?" Corporal Headley said quietly, looking up at Kaleb from across the cargo bay after wiping his sweat covered, bald head.

"Yeah Headley, we're going home, it's over," Kaleb responded as he looked and Hunt and gave a nod. The faint rumble of the USSN cruiser moving in over top of the transport could be heard in the background. Kaleb looked over at Jen Thompson and smiled, "Thanks LT, we couldn't have made it without your help."

Thompson smiled back at Kaleb, "You can buy me a drink when we get back to Talos station," she stated with sarcasm. "I've got to get back up front and direct the cruiser in. It'll just be a few more minutes till they are here."

Kaleb let out a sigh; taking off his helmet; he leaned his head back against the bulkhead and closed his eyes again. *Maybe they had in fact won the day,* he thought. He opened his eyes back up and looked around the interior of the Raptor transport. Thirty-five Marines from his platoon were missing. It surely didn't seem like much of a victory to him.

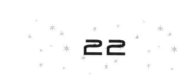

22

One month later, Talos Station, United Star Systems military headquarters

Kaleb Taylor stood at attention in the main mustering hall in his full dress uniform. To his immediate left were Yao, Hunt, Headley, Burke, and Lieutenant Thompson. Behind them stood what remained of the 26th Marine Regiment standing in tight formation. A giant United Star Systems flag was draped down behind the stage as a backdrop with Naval and Marine flags to its left and right. Fleet Admiral Beck and General Austin entered the hall followed by a line of high-ranking staff officers. Beck did a left face and stood directly in front of Kaleb. Kaleb saluted the Admiral and shook his hand firmly. Colonel West, the 26th Regiment commander, spoke into a microphone from a podium on stage.

"Men and women of the United Star Systems military…we are in formation here today to honor the proud individuals who fought valiantly to defend all of humanity in the recent battle of Ares. The men and women you see standing before you exemplify what it means to be a member of the United Star Systems military. Were it not for their courage and sacrifice in the face of an overwhelming enemy force, none of us would likely be standing here today. Let us also never forget those men and women who made the ultimate sacrifice on that fateful day....they will forever live on in future generations of USS Navy and Marines.....The service members we are honoring today hail from the 1st platoon, Alpha Company, 1st Recon Battalion. On behalf of a grateful interstellar community, these Marines and Naval Servicewoman are awarded the United Star Systems' highest military honor; the Interstellar Medal of Valor." Admiral Beck moved in to pin the gold-plated medal above the left chest pocket of Kaleb's uniform as Colonel West continued on.

"Outnumbered and outgunned, the Marines of the Wolfpack platoon fought their way into the capital center of Ares to liberate a key official of the Ares government. This key official held the secret to defeating the alien invading force and without his rescue. All hope would have been lost for our forces."

Beck smiled as he slapped Kaleb on the shoulder, "Damn son, you just can't seem to stay out of trouble can you? I knew you'd come back and see me. Congratulations on the battlefield promotion."

"You...remember me sir?" Kaleb asked, surprised.

"Of course, how could forget the young kid with an attitude problem that managed to survive the worst slaver attack in history, then vows to become a Recon Marine to get even. You've been through hell two times over without a scratch son, that's says something special about you; so hell no I didn't forget who you are," Beck replied.

"Roger sir, thank you. But all the medals and promotions in the world won't bring back the guys I lost from my platoon," Kaleb responded.

Beck nodded in agreement and paused for a moment. "As long as you never forget them they'll always be with you son, just like your family is," the Admiral said as he moved down the line to pin another medal on Yao's chest, who attended the ceremony in a wheelchair.

Colonel West carried on, "The awards are presented to: Lieutenant Kaleb Taylor, Flight Lieutenant Jen Thompson, Staff Sergeant Huynh Yao, Sergeant Robbie Hunt, Sergeant Wade Headley, and Sergeant Jason Burke."

Kaleb looked up at the United Star Systems flag and pictured his family in his mind. His thoughts drifted back and forth as Colonel West continued his long, drawn-out victory speech. It didn't mean anything to Kaleb. The arm-chair staff officers could bask in the glory of the battle all they wanted. He just wanted his friends and family back. The faces of the ones he'd lost, his father, mother, and sisters passed on in his mind. He knew they were looking down on him from heaven, hopefully proud of what he'd become.

Then came the images of his Marines: PFC Smith and Colby, Corporal Martinez, Sergeant Chambers, Lieutenant Freeborn, and so on; these were names he would never forget, the true hero's that weren't present to receive their awards. Kaleb hoped that their sacrifices were not made in vain. It would now be his duty as a Marine to carry on their legacy as the new Wolfpack platoon leader. After dragging on for twenty more minutes, Colonel West finally concluded his victory speech and Kaleb snapped out of his daydream.

"Regiment! Attention! Fallout!" West proudly yelled, signaling an end to the awards ceremony. The Marines saluted, took a step back and did an about face.

Kaleb walked over to Hunt. "Well, what the hell do we do now?"

Hunt smirked, "Well…Lieutenant…sir…now that you're in command of the platoon I guess you should send us out on shore leave….at least that's what I as your humble NCO recommend."

"Hah, yeah…I guess we never did finish our last shore leave back in Cancun did we? I figure the USS government owes us a few days off," Kaleb answered with a faint laugh.

"Sounds good, I'll re-book the hotel…but you see that good-looking pilot standing over there all by her lonesome?" Hunt smiled and pointed at Flight Lieutenant Jen Thompson, standing a few feet away in the mustering hall. "You better go and lock that down before you think about doing anything else…*sir*."

Kaleb glanced over at her and laughed at Hunt's statement. "Don't worry about me. I've got it taken care of. Be back in a second." He turned and walked over to her with a smile on his face.

"Hey LT, if I'm not mistaken, I was supposed to buy you a drink, does that offer still stand?" he asked.

She looked down on the ground and laughed. To Kaleb's surprise she moved in and wrapped her arms around him, looking back up at his face. "Always joking around still I see," she said quietly, closing her eyes as she moved and kissed him on the lips.

"I guess that means yes," Kaleb replied lightheartedly.

Jen nodded, "Of course….come on, let's get out of here. I know a good bar on the lower level of the station."

Kaleb looked back at Robbie Hunt with a smile and gave him a nod as he walked out of the mustering hall towards the elevator.

EPILOGUE

IO Director Michael Romanoff sat alone in his 72nd floor office at his headquarters in London. On his desk sat a small chunk of a heavy, dark-black object. The only piece remaining of what was known as the alien "Contrivance" that had caused such massive destruction. As soon as he heard word of the victory on Ares he had sent in agents to exploit ground zero of the destroyed underground research facility that was holding Project Contrivance. So far all they could recover out of the rubble was a small section of the base plate of the device. He studied it as he leaned back in his large office chair, smoking a cigarette. Three video screens were lowered down in front of him showing footage of the alien forces that attacked Ares and diagrams of their strange diamond and kite-shaped starships. He swore to himself to find out everything he could about what remained of the alien artifact, it was the only way to prevent another disaster like what happened on Ares. *There could be many more of these 'Contrivances' out there*, he thought. This was just the tip of the iceberg; and it would be his job to uncover this new mystery that existed within the galaxy.

His top analysts at IO concluded that once Contrivance had been destroyed, the aliens, now coined by the citizens of Ares as the "Uggae" or "Gods of Death," had purposefully opened up the black hole portal in order to return to their dimension of space/time. There were several reasons theorized behind this. The main theory for their sudden disappearance was because their ground forces had been wiped out in the nuclear bombardment of the city and the Contrivance was destroyed. After these events, it was hypothesized that they lost their purpose and objective for being in the human dimension and decided to cut their losses and retreat. Romanoff took his analysts' opinions with a grain of salt however. These alien beings, the "Uggae," were no doubt technologically superior to humans and most likely spiritually and philosophically greater as well. Romanoff believed it to be pure arrogance for a simple human mind to even attempt to understand the purpose or objective of an advanced alien species that was able to unlock the secrets of inter-dimensional travel.

In the meantime, it comforted Romanoff to know that once again, human-controlled space was now united under one banner. The Conflict for Unification was over, and the United Star Systems government and military had proved its value, securing its position as the protector of all human colonies. Now it was time to rebuild their decimated fleet and prepare for the next threat to humankind. Whether it be intergalactic or inter-dimensional in nature, wherever the threat came from, it would have to be stopped. As he sat in his office, his lead scientists and technicians were in the process of reverse-engineering alien technology salvaged from the battlefield on Whetmore. Hopefully they could use this technology to build better defenses in case of another attack form the ruthless Uggae. He would also most certainly use it as a tool to increase his Intelligence Office's sphere of influence and power within the galaxy.

Romanoff tapped his desk with his fingers, his mind immersed in deep thought. *One thing was for certain, humanity was not alone anymore in the universe, and it had damn well better be prepared to defend itself in the future.*